THE OTHER
DAUGHTER

THE OTHER DAUGHTER

SHALINI BOLAND

bookouture

Published by Bookouture in 2019

An imprint of StoryFire Ltd.

Carmelite House
50 Victoria Embankment
London EC4Y 0DZ

www.bookouture.com

ISBN: 978-1-78681-722-8
eBook ISBN: 978-1-78681-721-1

For my brave and beautiful daughter
who I love more than life xxx

CHAPTER ONE

THEN

She's inside a nightmare. She's inside hell. And nothing will ever be the same again.

The gears grind as Catriona puts her clunky old Ford Fiesta into second and turns right into slow-moving three-lane traffic. November rain lashes the windscreen and the wipers move frantically, barely making a difference, just sweeping with a dull squeak as water puddles down the glass. She can't even remember getting into the car. She just knew she couldn't stay in the house. Not afterwards.

A van honks to her left. She glances across to see an angry man mouthing something and making rude hand gestures. Catriona realises she's drifted into the wrong lane, so she jerks the wheel in the opposite direction, overshooting and causing more horns to blare. 'What does it matter anyway?' she mutters to herself. 'Who cares.' Her nose is running so she wipes her forefinger across her top lip, glancing in the rear-view mirror as she does so. She realises that her hands are still caked in mud. So now she has both mud *and* snot smeared across her face. Normally this would concern her. Not today. Not now. Not ever again. Still, she wipes her face again, with the sleeve of her sweatshirt this time.

More vehicles flash and beep her. She's trembling. She needs to get off the road. Up ahead are signposts into the shopping-centre car park. She'll turn in there. Park for a moment. She doesn't want to think about what she'll do after that.

There's a queue of traffic to get in, but eventually Catriona reaches the entrance of the multi-storey, drives in and pulls into a narrow parking space that faces a grey breeze-block wall. She kills the engine. The wipers come to a stop in the centre of the windscreen. It's quieter in here, away from the drumming rain and the roar of traffic. A sob almost escapes her lips, but she can't let it out. She doesn't deserve the luxury of crying.

She stiffly exits the car, closing the door after her. She doesn't bother locking it. She doesn't know what she's doing, where she's going. She just follows the pedestrian signs to 'Exit and Shops' then pushes open the heavy swing doors that lead into the bright, white, clean shopping centre. A change in air pressure, the echoing sound of music around her.

Her body doesn't feel as though it's under her control, and she's freezing all over despite the heat pumping through the mall. There's a coffee kiosk up ahead with tables and chairs ranged around it, interspersed with tall palms and frond-like plants. It's almost full – people coming and going, getting their caffeine fixes. But there are also a few women chatting leisurely and sipping their lattes. A water feature trickles and bubbles down one side of the café, and on the other side is a children's play area. The sound of running water makes Catriona need the loo. She glances around for a bathroom, spots a sign and heads towards it.

Inside a cubicle, she relieves herself and then washes her hands under a scalding tap. She tries to get some of the mud off. The stuff is caked beneath her fingernails, and after a few half-hearted attempt to rinse it away, she gives up. The mirror reveals an ashen face, red-rimmed eyes and cheeks smeared with brown dirt. It's a face that is at once recognisable and yet wholly unfamiliar. She washes off the streaks of mud, uses a paper towel to wipe it dry, and leaves the bathroom.

Back under the strip-light glare of the shopping centre, she heads to the coffee kiosk, the scent of cinnamon and freshly brewed coffee mingling with the smell of recycled mall air. Normally Catriona would specify what coffee she would like – a skinny mocha something or other with a flavoured syrup and all that crap – but after standing in line for what seems like forever, her mind has gone blank.

'Coffee please,' she croaks.

'Any particular one? Americano? Flat white?' the girls asks.

'Uh, just a white coffee,' Catriona replies. She waits at the other end of the counter while another girl prepares it. Again, she's aware of some kind of upbeat music being piped over the speakers, but it's muffled like it's underwater. Is that because the speaker system is faulty? Or could there be something wrong with her hearing? Either way, it doesn't matter.

A mug is placed before her and she's vaguely aware of the girl saying something friendly. Catriona doesn't respond. She takes her coffee to a spare table in front of the play area, which consists of a small ball pit, a red-and-brown plastic playhouse and some climbing apparatus with wide tubes to crawl through and slide down. There are no children playing there and it has an oddly sad and neglected air. Catriona sits down and sips her drink. Stares at the familiar play area until her vision blurs. Of all the places to come, why has she come *here*? After today, this should be the last place on earth she would want to be.

There's a bustle and clatter behind her as two women pushing designer prams arrive. They spend a couple of minutes loudly deciding where to sit, finally selecting a table by the water feature, hidden behind a couple of potted palm trees to Catriona's right. They remove their outer layers – gloves, coats, scarves et cetera – draping them over the pram handles.

Catriona catches her breath as she notices a little toddler, previously hidden from view, behind one of the prams. The sweet little girl can't be much more than two and a half years old. She's chestnut-haired and round-cheeked with sparkling eyes and barely contained energy fizzing out of her little body.

A slender dark-haired woman – presumably her mother – bends down and unzips her daughter's white Puffa coat. The girl wriggles out of it. She's dressed in branded pink leggings, a turquoise ballet skirt and a multicoloured top studded with tiny glittery hearts. On her feet she wears pink Uggs lined with sheepskin. Her outfit probably cost more than everything in Catriona's wardrobe put together. The little girl runs over to the playhouse, opens the door and disappears inside, banging the door shut after her.

Over at their table, one of the mothers checks inside both prams and takes a seat while the other woman heads to the kiosk. The little girl peeks out of the playhouse window. She catches Catriona's eye. Catriona smiles and gives the little girl a wave. The little girl waves back, *bless her*.

Catriona's own heart suddenly begins to beat faster. So loud that it thumps in her ears, drowning out the mall music and the echoing chatter of the other customers. She takes a moment to breathe, but the thumping in her body won't quiet down. Without thinking, she stands and walks back to the kiosk. Queues behind the mother who's now selecting an assortment of pastries to go with their drinks. Catriona's gaze sweeps across the cakes displayed behind the glass. They're all too big, too grown-up and far too messy for a child to eat. She gives an inward smile as she spies just what she's looking for in a large glass jar on top of the counter – a cookie in the shape of a rabbit, its long ears and small nose iced in pale pink. Perfect.

Catriona waits until the mother has finished ordering, and then she purchases the cookie along with a small chocolate bar to perk herself up – she's starting to feel a little light-headed, realising she hasn't eaten since breakfast. The girl behind the counter places the cookie on a small white plate on top of a napkin. This time,

Catriona smiles at the girl and thanks her. She winds her way slowly back to her seat where her coffee is cooling on the table. She wants to act straight away but restrains herself. Instead, she sits back down, eats her chocolate and sips at her drink without tasting it, absent-mindedly picking dried mud from beneath split fingernails. Her heartbeat is still far louder than everything else around her. Its insistent thrumming helping to focus her mind on what she's about to do.

Her face is warm now, her hands tingling, her head light and swimmy. But it's almost a *good* feeling. It blocks out all the other stuff, dampens it down so it can't be felt properly. Maybe it can all stay hidden way down there. Maybe she can squash it so small that it gets lost forever. Grains of dark grit floating endlessly down in a bottomless ocean.

The little girl waves at her again, emerging from the plastic house with a shy smile. Catriona glances over at the mothers, who are now deep in conversation, talking fast while shovelling pastries into their mouths and sucking down their frothy coffees. They're seated too far away from the play area. If she were that little girl's mother, she'd be sitting at the edge of the café with a direct view of her daughter. Not angled away and oblivious.

And yet, Catriona knows what it's like to snatch a few minutes for yourself – that blissful illusion of freedom. When you're out of the house talking to another grown-up person, let loose in the real world away from cleaning, cooking, toilet-training. Those moments when you remember who you were before becoming a mother. How luxurious it feels. How freeing. She shakes her head. *Stupid woman*. She's probably been looking forward to this morning. Wishing for it. Meeting up with her friend. Hoping the babies stay asleep and her daughter remains occupied in the play area. But it just goes to show… you should be careful what you wish for.

The little girl is now exploring the rest of the play area – throwing the balls around the ball pit and crawling under the plastic tubes. Catriona's heart is lodged in her gullet as she lurches to her feet, scraping the chair back too loudly. She glances back at the women, but they haven't noticed her. Their heads are together as they chatter away. Laughing, and then serious again. The rise and fall of their voices merging with the mall sounds. Catriona makes her way around to the far side of the play area, the side nearest to the exit. She pulls up the hood of her sweatshirt, keeping her face angled low.

A voice in the background of her brain is yelling at her to stop this. To go back home and deal with it all. But a louder voice screams that this is the only way to stem the tidal wave of pain that's threatening to drown her. It has to be fate that this beautiful little child is here right now. A dark-haired girl. A daughter.

'Hello,' she says softly to the child as she emerges from beneath one of the colourful tubes.

The girl smiles shyly.

'Do you like bunny rabbits?' Catriona holds out the biscuit and makes it do a funny little dance.

The girl giggles. A sound that makes Catriona want to sink to the ground and sob. Instead, she arranges her face into the warmest, most inviting smile she can create. 'Would you like this one? Look – it's got pink ears.'

The girl looks around, as though seeking approval from her mother. But the women are both hidden from view and neither of them are paying attention to the toddler.

'Your mum said it was fine. She said you could come and see a *real* bunny rabbit. Would that be fun? You can stroke it and hold it, if you like.'

'I got a toy bunny.'

'Have you? Well mine is real – it's white and fluffy and hops around the room. Here, have this biscuit bunny first, if you like.' Catriona hands her the cookie.

The girl takes it, looks it up and down, then nibbles a corner.

'Is it good?'

She nods twice and takes a bigger bite.

'Want to come and see the real bunny now?' Catriona holds out a hand, her pulse racing, the skin on her face suddenly hot while she waits for the child's response.

'What's its name?'

'Oh. Er, Mr Fluffy.'

'That's funny.' The girl giggles and takes her hand. At once Catriona feels her shoulders relax. She turns and walks quickly, merging easily with the crush of other shoppers, the girl skipping along at her side, munching away on the rabbit cookie. Catriona pushes open the exit door and then makes her way back to her car.

'Where's the bunny?' the girl asks.

'We're going to see it now. It's just a short drive away, okay? How's that bunny biscuit? Is it yummy?'

'I like the pink bits.'

'The icing?'

She nods.

Catriona opens the back door to the car. 'Up you hop.'

'Rabbits hop,' the little girl says.

Catriona gives a little laugh. 'Yes! Yes they do.' Suddenly she knows everything is going to be okay. Coming here to the shopping mall was destined. The little girl is adorable.

She's *her* little girl now. This was meant to be.

CHAPTER TWO

NOW

I zip up my coat and shove my hands into my pockets. The afternoon is sunny and bright, but this part of the playground is always such a wind tunnel, spanning the length of the long, low red-brick building that houses all the classrooms. I stamp my feet to warm them. The school bell rang at least five minutes ago, but Jess and Charlie's classes always seem to be the last ones out.

I jump at a tap on my shoulder. Thinking it must be a friend, I turn to find myself staring into a stranger's eyes. An elegant blonde woman in her thirties, wearing a green Boden coat and a worried, apologetic expression. 'Hi,' I say. 'Everything okay?'

'Hello, sorry, I'm panicking a bit. It's my children's first day here. The bell went ages ago, but I can't seem to see them. Just wondering if I'm waiting in the right spot?'

'What year are they in?' I ask.

'Amy's in year five and Kieran's year two.'

'Oh, same as my two. You're fine. This is the right spot. We used to have to pick them up from different playgrounds, but it was such a mad dash that now they've combined pick-ups for the first and middle schools. Our year groups are always late coming out though. I'm Rachel, by the way. Rachel Farnborough.' I stick out my hand and shake her leather-gloved one.

'Oh, thanks. That's a relief.' The woman smiles. 'I'm Kate Morris. Terrified newbie – in case you didn't get that.'

'Nice to meet you, Kate. And there's nothing to be terrified about. We're a pretty friendly bunch here at Wareham Park. So, what school were yours at before?'

'We've just moved here from London.'

'Wow, bit different to round here!' I grin, feeling suddenly proud of the peace and quiet of our pretty Dorset town. I've only lived here for seven years, but it really does feel like home. Wareham is a gorgeous place, set on the River Frome, with pretty shops and eateries surrounded by lush green English countryside. I love London too, but the capital is as far removed from Wareham as you can get.

'Just a bit,' Kate replies. 'But that's why we moved here. We've had a few family holidays in Wareham over the years and fell in love with the place. Plus, life was getting too hectic in London and we aren't keen on the senior schools where we lived. Amy is in year five, so we would have had to start thinking about all that again. The system's different in London, and the Dorset one works better for us.'

'So you didn't want to wait and start them after Christmas? It's only three weeks till the end of term.'

She pushes a stray lock of hair out of her eyes. 'We considered it, but thought it was best to dive right in, now we're here.'

'Makes sense. Who's your daughter's teacher?'

'Amy's in Miss Darlington's class.'

'That means she's in the same class as my daughter, Jessica.'

'Is she a good teacher, do you know?'

'Strict, but, yes, very good. Talking of which…' I catch sight of the diminutive Miss Darlington marching briskly across the playground, followed by a straggle of unkempt looking children – ties skew-whiff, shirts untucked, coats trailing across the concrete. And coming up behind, I see my son's year group in the same usual state of disarray. 'There they are.'

Kate's shoulders relax and she waves frantically to a blonde girl who's talking to Jess. The girl gives her a single dismissive wave and turns back to my daughter. 'Thank goodness,' Kate says. 'Looks like Amy might have made a friend. She was so nervous this morning.'

'That's my daughter she's talking to.' I feel a spark of pride that Jess seems to have taken the new girl under her wing.

'Mum!' A fair-haired boy races across the playground, crashing into Kate's open arms.

'Kieran! How was your day?'

'Awesome. I like it here, Mum. The playground's massive. We've got a lizard in our class and we get to take turns bringing it home.'

I catch Kate's eye over the top of Kieran's head and give her a thumbs up. She grins back and wipes her brow in exaggerated relief. I'm pleased for her. She seems nice and it must be intimidating and nerve-wracking to move to a brand-new area and a brand-new school. Luckily, my two started here right from the get-go, so we've never had to experience the upheaval of changing schools.

'Tell you what,' I say, 'why don't you all come to ours for tea one day after school?'

'Really? That would be so lovely!'

'Let me know what day's good for you. I can't do this Friday, but any other day is fine. I'll get you up to speed on who's who around here.'

My six-year-old, Charlie, finally appears. 'Hi, Mum, I'm so hungry, did you bring any snacks?'

I reach into my bag for a couple of satsumas, but Kate beats me to it, digging out a multipack of chocolate bars from her bag. 'Can I give him one of these?' she asks me.

'Oh. Thanks. If you're sure.'

She doles out the chocolate to all four children, much to the delight of my two. Then we swap mobile phone numbers and start walking out towards the gates, the thick evergreen trees that run the length of the school field bowing and sighing in the wind.

'Look at all our kids chatting away,' Kate says. 'I can't believe they seem so happy. I was dreading the pick-up, convinced one or the other would have had a bad day and would want to go back to London.'

'It's nice how they're all getting on so well.'

'Now I just have to hope that my other daughter gets on okay.' Kate's expression darkens.

'You've got three?'

'Yes – Bella's my eldest.'

'Which school does she go to?'

'St Margaret's Middle School.'

'How come she's going to a different school?'

'It's a long, annoying saga. But they didn't have spaces to fit all three at the same school. St Margaret's is closer to where we live so it would have been great to have them all go there, but the waiting list is huge.'

'That *is* annoying. I hope she had a good day today.'

'She had a routine hospital appointment, so she won't start until tomorrow. But I think she's quite anxious about it. She didn't have a great time at her old school, which is part of the reason why we moved here. Speaking of which…'

I follow her gaze to see a girl with long, dark hair leaning against a white Fiat 500 She's looking down at her mobile phone, talking to someone, but she doesn't seem very happy.

'Bella,' Kate calls out. 'I thought I told you to wait in the car!'

The girl glances up with a scowl.

The second I see her face, the rest of the world begins to shift out of focus. The rational part of my brain tells me that it's impossible. But the rest of my brain is in shock. 'Holly,' I murmur.

'Mum!' The girl stares at Kate accusingly. 'You were ages! You said you'd only be a few minutes. I didn't know when you were coming back, and you didn't answer your phone!'

Kate checks her mobile. 'Oh, it's on silent for some reason. Sorry, darling. Your brother and sister were late coming out.'

The girl is tall and willowy with dark wavy hair and a heart-shaped face. Her lips are full, and she has a snub nose sprinkled with freckles. But it's her eyes that have unsettled me the most. They're a vivid green. Just like Holly's.

This girl is the spitting image of my missing daughter. Older yes, but the resemblance is striking.

For a moment I stand, paralysed, unable to catch my breath. Flashbacks to my lost daughter laughing as I tickled her, or glowering at me with her emerald eyes before launching into one of her dreaded terrible-two tantrums. Me staring down at her as she slept, stroking the hair away from her heart-shaped face and kissing the freckles on her nose.

Right now though, this tween girl is looking at me as though I'm some crazy stranger. Which I suppose I am, really.

'Are you okay, Rachel?' Kate is speaking to me, but I can't find my voice to reply. I nod, still staring at her eldest daughter. I swallow.

'Mum!' Jess shakes my arm. 'Mum, you're being embarrassing.'

I drag my eyes away from Bella and give Jess a distracted smile. 'Sorry, what?'

'Come on, Mum, let's go. I've got to do my homework and then me and Amy are going to Facetime.' She smiles at her new friend and rolls her eyes in my direction.

'Okay, yes, coming.' My heart is pounding and my ears are ringing as I attempt to process my thoughts and emotions, but I'm trying to behave normally so that Kate doesn't think I'm an utter lunatic. 'So, Kate, we'll sort out that play date for the kids, okay? I'll text you.'

She gives me a puzzled look and nods.

Somehow, we say our goodbyes, and I stutter something vague about remembering something I have to do, trying to explain away my odd behaviour. They get into Kate's little Fiat and I start walking home with my two, the icy wind buffeting us as we go. The children talk about the various issues they've had throughout the day. I'm usually attentive and chatty, but right now I can barely decipher a single word they're saying, let alone respond.

All I can think about is Kate's eldest daughter.

Nine years ago, my almost three-year-old daughter, Holly, was abducted from a shopping centre on the outskirts of London. The police never found her, and they never caught the person who did it. All they had to go on was a piece of useless security footage – someone in a hooded sweatshirt leading my baby away from the play area while I was sitting with a friend having coffee in the mall, oblivious until it was too late. My younger daughter, Jess, was thirteen months old at the time, and she was with me in her pram, asleep. I was only a few feet away from Holly, but I was too busy chatting to my friend to keep a constant watch.

There isn't a day that goes by where I don't blame myself. I was negligent. I know that, even if all my friends at the time told me it wasn't my fault, that it could easily happen to anyone. That we can't watch them every second of every day. But that's the thing – it wasn't just 'a few seconds'. There was at least a minute where I was gossiping with Christina without paying any attention to my daughter. Instead, I got caught up chatting to my friend about our respective marital problems. I was relieved that Holly was occupied. Happy to have some time to talk about grown-up stuff. I knew Holly loved that little Wendy house. That it would keep her entertained for ages. I never understood the consequences of my inattention. The devastation that would follow.

For months after she disappeared, I read the papers and scoured the chat rooms for people's theories of what happened. I suppose I was hoping that I might stumble across the person who did it. I absorbed all of it – even though some of the comments made me physically sick. I read what people were saying about me. All those judgemental mothers in their cosy little vipers' nest forums talking about how I never deserved to have children. That I was an unfit mother whose other child should be taken away by social services. Some of them even implied that I was behind the abduction, that I had sold my own child to a paedophile ring. It made me realise how thoroughly nasty people can be. But part of me didn't blame them.

And now… today… seeing Kate's daughter, Bella. I've never had such a violent physical reaction in my life. I've never been in a situation like this before, where the sight of a child makes my heart stop. Of course, I've had moments over the years where I thought I glimpsed Holly, knowing in my heart of hearts that it wasn't really her. But this is different. This is a blow-to-the-stomach different.

As the shock subsides, I begin really questioning whether or not Kate's daughter Bella could actually be my missing daughter Holly. She's roughly the same age as Holly would be now, and she looks like her too – same dark hair and heart-shaped face. Same green eyes. But it can't possibly be… *can it?*

'Mum, why have you stopped walking?' Jess tugs at my hand. 'You're being weird again. I hope Amy didn't notice. I like her. She might be my new best friend.'

'Sorry, darling. A lot on my mind.'

'Is it work?'

I can't help smiling at my daughter's concern. 'No, no. Nothing for you to worry about.' My two don't even know about Holly. Jess was a baby when it happened, and I didn't want to bring that kind of distress into their lives. Maybe I was wrong to keep such a big thing from them, but I did what I thought was right at the time. Perhaps I'll tell them when they're a little older. Or perhaps new circumstances will mean that I'll have to tell them sooner. But what do I mean by *that*?

I start walking again, gradually dismissing my thoughts about Kate's daughter as ridiculous. It would be far too much of a coincidence, and Kate doesn't seem the type to snatch a child. Not at all.

But what if she is? How would you even tell?

I quicken my pace, to the relief of my kids, and try to put the whole thing out of my head. But now that I've opened the floodgates, all these memories of my lost daughter keep coming back, crowding my brain until there's no room for anything else. Asking that insistent question over and over again.

What if? What if? What if?

CHAPTER THREE

As soon as we turn into our narrow side street, I spot Matt's van parked outside our little whitewashed terraced cottage, two wheels up on the pavement to allow traffic to pass. Not that it's a busy road – normally we only get residents and visitors coming down here. I usually love it when Matt gets home early – he works long hours in his job as an electrician – but today I'm distracted and could really do with some alone time to get my head together and think about Bella Morris. And about Kate, and who she is. What she's like. She seemed like a perfectly lovely woman. The kind of person who could become a good friend. But looks can be deceiving.

'Dad's home!' Jess cries and starts running down the street.

Charlie lets go of my hand and follows behind. 'Daddy!'

His excitement is infectious, and I can't help smiling. 'Stay on the pavement!'

They hammer on our sage-green front door and ring the bell excitedly. Seconds later, the door opens and Matt peers out, his blonde hair flopping over his eyes. The kids hurl themselves at their father. I never get as enthusiastic a reception as that, but I don't mind. They see more of me than of him.

Matt is their dad, but he's not actually Jess's biological father. Her 'real' dad, Andrew, and I split up after Holly was taken. Our relationship by then was shaky at best, and the horror and stress of losing our eldest child finished us off for good. He was a borderline alcoholic. Not physically abusive, but not a kind drunk either. He alternately blamed me for what happened, and comforted me when his words wounded, eventually giving up completely and leaving me for good.

Andy doesn't keep in contact with us any longer, and lives in Spain. He had a high-flying job in finance and was always jetting off around the world to various destinations, but mostly to Spain. He has a whole new family and I suspect he met his new Spanish wife while he was still married to me. We were always financially well off, but he lost his job. Now Jess and I don't receive anything from him in the way of maintenance and I don't ask him for any. I don't even know if he ended up getting help with his alcohol issues. Maybe he lost everything. Maybe not. Either way, I would never ask him for a penny. Not after he left us both.

Thankfully, Jess doesn't remember him. She's only ever known Matt as her dad, and he treats her like his own, even though she knows he isn't her biological father. My only niggle is that Jess and I still have Andy's surname – Farnborough. I suppose I could have changed it back to my maiden name, but I didn't want to have a different name to my daughter, and I haven't plucked up the courage to contact Andy and ask his permission to change her name. It's the reason I won't marry Matt – I don't want Jess to be the only one with a different surname. We would all be Bernshaws while she remained a Farnborough. Although, like Matt keeps saying, there's nothing stopping me marrying him and keeping mine and Jess's names the same.

Charlie is Matt's biological child and is his doppelganger – both of them blue-eyed, blonde-haired Norse giants. Our six-year-old son is the tallest in his year – taller than a lot of the boys in the year above, too. I call them my two Vikings. Jess, on the other hand, looks like me. We're both slim with dark hair and brown eyes. Unbidden, an image of Bella Morris inserts itself into my mind, those green eyes staring, scowling, accusing.

'You coming in?' Matt calls. 'Or are you just going to stand there on the pavement all day?' He grins and raises an eyebrow.

'Sorry, miles away.' I hurry down the street and into my boyfriend's arms, where I let myself linger a while, feeling safe and loved. The kids have already squeezed through the narrow hallway and beyond into the kitchen to see what delights they can find in the fridge and cupboards. Which reminds me, I need to go shopping.

'Mmm, that feels good.' Matt gives me an extra squeeze before letting go.

I don't know why on earth I had the notion that I didn't want Matt to be home early. Even years after first meeting, he still has the power to make my stomach flip. 'How was your day?'

'Irritating,' he replies. I follow him into our pretty white-painted kitchen where he leans against the oak worktop, a frown darkening his blue eyes.

'How come?'

'Just people not showing up on time, so I can't get on with what I need to do. That's why I'm home early, and why I'll probably have to work late tomorrow.'

'That's annoying.'

'Tell me about it.'

'Don't eat those,' I say to the kids, who are about to open a packet of biscuits. 'You've already had chocolate. You'll ruin your tea. There are satsumas in the fruit bowl.'

The children wrinkle their noses and sidle out of the kitchen.

'Got any homework?' I call after them, feeling mean about asking them, as they've only just got in.

'Mathletics,' Jess replies. 'I'll do it now, get it out of the way.'

'No,' Charlie says, trying to slip out of the room.

I catch his arm before he can escape. 'What about your spellings? You've got a test tomorrow, haven't you?'

His shoulders drop.

'Go and practise them now, and Daddy will test you in a few minutes while I start cooking.'

Matt gives me a pained look, but I know he enjoys helping the kids. 'How was *your* day?' he asks.

I pause before giving him a light smile. 'Fine. You know; the usual.' I sit at the breakfast bar and pick at a dried-on milk stain left over from breakfast. 'One interesting thing – Dee wants to give me some extra shifts after Christmas.'

'Really? Are you going to take them?'

'I think so. As long as they don't clash with the school run.' Dee owns Row Your Boat – a busy café in South Street just up from the river. I've been waitressing there for the past five years, and Dee has become a good friend of mine. She and Matt have known each other since they were kids – even though Dee's a little older than us. But all the while I'm talking to Matt, I can't stop thinking about Bella. About Holly. About Kate, and if she might be the person who took my child. If she did take her then I should call the police. I'm desperate to race round to the station right now. But what if they don't take me seriously? They've never had any luck finding my daughter before. Back when she was first taken, the police said they had leads, but then everything fizzled out to nothing. I need to get definite proof before I go to them. I can't risk them dismissing my claims. And if they tip off Kate before getting enough evidence to arrest her, she could do a runner. Disappear with Holly again.

I can't believe I'm actually planning some elaborate strategy in my head. Am I crazy to be thinking that Bella is Holly? Maybe I should be thinking more about why my reaction to the likeness is so strong. Why I'm so convinced...

'You okay, Rach? You seem a bit... I dunno... distracted.'

'Yes, I'm fine. Just trying to work out how many more hours I should do for Dee.'

'Don't do it if it's going to stress you out. We can manage.'

'No, it's fine. I'm not stressing about it.'

'Okay, if you're sure.'

'Definitely. Now the kids are at school all day, there's no reason why I shouldn't do a few more hours.' I feel strange about not being able to confide in Matt. Normally we tell one another everything about our days – commiserating or congratulating, laughing or crying. But there's this one big secret he doesn't know about. And it's always weighed heavily on me.

We met not long after Andy and I split up and I moved to Wareham. Jess and I had just moved into a flat, but the wiring was faulty and kept tripping the electrics. I couldn't even put the kettle on without everything shorting out. After what I'd just been through, it was the last straw. I called my landlord and he sent an electrician to take a look – Matt.

I was in a terrible state when he arrived – barely holding back tears. It was less than a year after Holly went missing and, looking back, I think I was probably in the middle of a nervous breakdown. But when Matt showed up he was so kind. He fixed the wiring in no time, and afterwards, when I asked if I could make him a drink, he told me to sit down and relax and that *he* would make coffee for *me*.

As well as being drop-dead gorgeous, he was the sweetest man – asking if I was okay, and if there was anyone he could call for me. Jess was at nursery that day and so he and I were alone in the flat. He was staring at me with all this compassion and I thought I was going to start properly sobbing. Instead, I did something totally out of character – I leaned forward and kissed him.

It was shocking and passionate, like nothing I'd ever experienced before. We ended up sleeping together and then afterwards we both apologised like crazy. It turned out he had just been dumped by his long-term girlfriend and was feeling almost as vulnerable as me. Afterwards, we chatted for hours about everything and nothing. I told him about my break-up with Andy, but I didn't mention

Holly going missing. It was all still too raw and terrible, and I didn't want to taint the beautiful day we'd just spent together – a precious moment out of time. Before he left, he promised he would call me again. I hoped he was telling the truth, but honestly, I didn't believe he actually would.

True to his word, Matt called me the very next day, saying he couldn't get me out of his head. We started seeing one another and he was so lovely with Jess – patient and funny. She took to him straight away. Within a couple of months I discovered I was pregnant. I dreaded telling Matt, terrified that I would scare him off. But he was over the moon and asked me to marry him. I told him that I would love to marry him one day, but not yet. We had enough to deal with, and not a lot of money. I said just being together would be enough for me. He was a little disappointed but accepted my decision.

Somehow, I never got around to telling him about my other daughter, Holly. I don't know why. Maybe because I wanted to put it behind me. Not to forget her – never that. But simply to try to live a life that wasn't clouded in grief and uncertainty. I didn't want anyone's pity. I just wanted to remember my daughter in my own way, and to have some new-found happiness with my beautiful little family. Consequently, as far as any of my friends are concerned, I only have Jess and Charlie. None of them know about Holly. Sometimes I feel disloyal – not talking about her. Not having her photos on the wall. But I've learned to live with my new reality. It's like Holly and I existed in another lifetime. In a perfect, untouchable bubble.

But now… now grief and uncertainty are trying to claim me once again. The old feelings are resurfacing. And I have no idea what to do about it.

CHAPTER FOUR

I kept a look-out for Kate this morning on the school run, but I didn't spot either her or her white Fiat outside the gates. Then again, the kids and I were a little late getting in. And now I'm puffing my way down South Street, late for work, hot and sweaty despite the freezing December air. It's been one of those mornings when everyone got out of bed on the wrong side. Charlie spilt milk and cereal down his last clean shirt, Jess couldn't find one of her school shoes, and Matt was grumpy about the long day he had ahead of him. Meanwhile, I couldn't concentrate on anything and ended up snapping at everybody. I'll have to make it up to them this evening with some cupcakes from work.

Finally, I arrive at the café almost fifteen minutes late. But even the sight of its welcoming blue-and-white painted exterior doesn't cheer me up; my heart sinks further to see the place is already half full. Dee spots me straight away, her ash-blonde bob swinging as she weaves her way through the tables. Worse than having a go at me, she merely hands me a couple of plates piled high with her famous full English breakfasts. 'Table six,' she says briskly, turning away.

'I'm so sorry I'm—'

'No time for any of that.' She cuts me off. 'Tables one and three are still waiting to have their orders taken. I've already had two walk-outs this morning because they had to wait too long.'

My face flushes with shame. Dee Cavendish is such a hard worker. She built this business up from nothing. I hate letting her down. 'On it,' I reply, resolving to work like a machine in order to make amends. I deliver the plates to table six, grab an apron from the back, and get to work, taking orders and clearing tables. But even though I'm trying my hardest, my mind just isn't on the job. All I can think about is Bella. And each time her face comes to mind, a mixture of doubt and fear overwhelms me.

'Excuse me.'

I turn back to an elderly couple sitting by the window. The man is pointing at his bacon buttie. 'I didn't order this. I asked for eggs royale. And my wife wanted scrambled egg, not a full English.'

'I'm so sorry. Let me—'

'Hello! 'Scuse me!' Another customer is trying to get my attention. It's a young guy in dusty overalls seated with two other workmen. 'You've given us the wrong food.'

I realise I must have got the two orders mixed up, so I apologise profusely, my face heating up. Other customers are staring now. Dee glances across from the counter, taking in my mistake. She doesn't say anything, but she must be inwardly cursing me. I know how important customer service is these days. I just have to hope the couple don't go online to leave a negative review – they look the type, I think uncharitably.

Getting the orders mixed up isn't that big a deal; mistakes happen all the time. But I feel jittery and on edge, like I'm on the verge of losing control. Like I can't cope with any of this. In my haste to switch the food orders around, I'm not paying proper attention to what I'm doing, and the plate of eggs royale slips from my grasp as I cross the room. While trying to save it, I also manage to drop the plate of scrambled eggs and toast. I watch both plates fall as though in slow-motion. The two plates smash to pieces on the bleached floorboards, fragments of china and food bouncing and flying under tables and splattering on several of the customers' legs.

The whole café falls silent for the longest second. Then everything speeds up again. A few people cheer, and a couple throw me sympathetic glances. I don't dare look at Dee. Instead, I mutter apologies, drop down to the floor and start picking up shards of broken plate. I should really go and get a dustpan and brush, but I'm utterly mortified and shaken up. Not thinking straight at all. Thirty seconds later, Dee comes up to me with cleaning products and a broom. She apologises to the customers who were splattered and tells them their breakfasts are on the house.

'Go and have a sit down in the kitchen,' she whispers to me. 'I'm so sorry.'

She waves away my apology. 'Happens to the best of us. Go.'

I scuttle off to the kitchen, relieved at the chance to escape from all the stares. I'm such an idiot. I've allowed this business with Bella to interfere with my job. At this rate, Dee will be regretting offering me those extra shifts.

'Rachel.'

I jump at the sound of Dee's voice, and I pat my cheeks to try to get myself together. I turn around. 'I'm so sorry about my crapness today, Dee. You can take their free breakfasts out of my wages.'

'Don't be daft. It's just a few eggs. Is everything okay with you?' She sounds concerned, not angry, thank goodness.

'Uh, yes, everything's fine. It was just a hectic morning and my head isn't on straight. Getting the kids up and out was a nightmare, you know how it is.' As soon as I say that, I want to cut out my tongue. Dee was never able to have kids despite always wanting them, so it's a sensitive subject.

'You sure that's all it is?' She puts a comforting hand on my arm. 'If you want to have a chat later…'

'That's so lovely of you. But I'm fine, honestly. We should definitely go for a drink sometime though. It's been ages since we last went out.'

'Deal. We'll sort out an evening.'

'Thanks, Dee. Well, I better get back out there.'

'Tell you what, Chrissie's just arrived and it's calming down a bit now, so why don't you nip to the cash and carry for me instead. We're running low on stock. You can take the van.'

This is music to my ears. I'm desperate for a few moments to myself and I was dreading going back out and facing all those customers. Plus, I'll be able to get some proper thinking done while I drive. Dee hands me the keys and a list as I remove my apron and fetch my handbag from my locker.

'Can you try to be back before the lunchtime rush?'

I check my watch. It's already eleven o'clock. 'It shouldn't take me more than an hour. Thanks, Dee.'

She smiles, nods and gets back to the café. Normally she's the one to go and pick up supplies, so I appreciate the gesture. Although it's probably more likely that she wants me away from the café, where I was becoming a one-woman disaster zone.

I sneak out of the back door and slide into Dee's pale-blue VW Transporter, adjusting the seat and the mirror, as Dee is much shorter than me. She's had the exterior customised with the café's name and logo – Row Your Boat, with a rustic rowing boat beneath.

The cash and carry is only a ten-minute drive, but as soon as I hit the road, my mind flies back to Bella Morris and what I'm going to do about her. I really need to see her again, to make sure I didn't get it wrong. Maybe the next time I see her I won't have such a strong reaction. If I do… well then I can decide what to do about it. And I also need to find out how old Bella is. See if the dates match up. Although she probably would have been given a different birthday, so that might not help.

The other thing I need to make a priority is to really get to know Kate. Find out about her past and exactly where in London she used to live. I never asked if she's married or a single mum. If she's married, then could they both be in on it? That figure in the hoodie who took Holly – their gender wasn't obvious, so it could even have been her husband, if she has one, or her partner. I'm going crazy with all these unanswered questions. The ache in my stomach is growing stronger. The pull on my heart intensifying. After all these years, could I finally have found my missing baby?

My shift at the café finishes at two thirty, leaving me plenty of time to drive home and walk the twenty minutes to school. It would have been quicker to drive straight there, but the parking's a nightmare and I don't mind walking, despite the cold greyness of the afternoon. In any case, I wanted to pop home first and smarten myself up. Kate is so well put together that I feel dowdy by comparison, and if I want to get to know her better, I can't let anything stand in the way of that. I need to present myself in my best light. I opt for a pair of grey skinny jeans, a cream cable-knit jumper and my 'good' wool coat that cost way more than I should ever have spent on an item of clothing. I justified the purchase by telling myself it would be a nice classic item that I'd get years of wear from, but the truth is, I've hardly worn the thing. Trudging along the well-worn route to school, I almost feel like a yummy mummy in my perfectly casual outfit.

The rest of my shift at the café went much better than this morning's debacle – I'm still cringing at the embarrassment of it – but then it couldn't really have gone much worse. I managed to pick up all Dee's supplies from the cash and carry and made it back way before the lunchtime rush. After things quietened down again, Dee and I sat and worked out my new hours, and we also said we'd try to meet up for a drink next week. Chrissie, who was there this morning, might come too. I'm quite looking forward to it. It's been a while since I've socialised, other than snatched conversations outside school.

I arrive just as the caretaker is unlocking the gates. I usually chat to one or other of the mums or dads – most of them are lovely and we've all known one another since our kids were in pre-school. But today I purposely avoid eye contact with anyone, as I don't want to get embroiled in conversation in case I miss Kate. I needn't have worried. The moment I step into the playground, I hear my name being spoken and I turn to see her, her smile even friendlier than I remember. I smile back, relieved. I think I had convinced myself that she wouldn't want to chat to me again after yesterday. That maybe she'd think I was strange for staring at Bella. But perhaps that's simply me being paranoid. Maybe she didn't notice anything amiss after all. *Or maybe she noticed everything.*

'Kate, hi! How are you?' I flatten my smile, realising I need to tone it down a bit.

'Good, thanks. Amy couldn't stop talking about Jess last night.'

'Ah, that's great. Jess said she thought Amy was going to be her new best friend.'

'That's so sweet. Love your coat by the way.'

I feign nonchalance. 'Oh, thanks.'

As we talk, I find myself examining Kate's every inflection and expression. Every hand gesture and hair toss. Wondering if there's anything I'm not picking up on. But she seems genuine enough. I want to ask about Bella, but I can't seem too eager. I have to play it cool.

'So I was wondering if you'd all like to come back to mine tomorrow after school. The kids can hang out while we natter.'

Kate re-knots her floral scarf. 'We'd love to. Thanks, Rachel. I can't tell you how nice it is to be made to feel so welcome.' Unless I'm mistaken, I'm sure I heard a little crack in her voice. As if she's getting a bit emotional.

'It's my pleasure. I'll arrange a get-together with some of the other mums too, so you can meet some more people.'

'You're an angel.'

I'm not entirely sure I *will* introduce her to the other mums. Not yet, anyway. I need to keep Kate to myself until I've worked out who Bella really is. 'Bring Bella along tomorrow too – if you don't think she'll be bored.'

'Thanks, I will if that's okay. She'll be fine – she'll have her phone.'

'How old is she?' I try to sound casual, but I'm sure my cheeks are scarlet.

'Bella? She'll be twelve in February, but she's already displaying teenagery signs. Heaven help me!'

'Is she with you now?' I ask, my pulse quickening at the thought of seeing her again.

'No, she started at St Margaret's today, so I've got to shoot straight home after picking these two up.'

My heart drops with disappointment. But at least I'll get to spend tomorrow after school with her. Maybe I can engage her in conversation. Discover what she's like – her personality, her hobbies. See if she takes after me in any way. I know I'm getting way ahead of myself, but I can't help it. The school bell rings, yanking me out of my reverie. 'If you like,' I suggest, 'I can pick your two up with Jess and Charlie tomorrow, and walk home with them. That way you can go to St Margaret's to pick Holl— Bella up and come straight over to mine afterwards.'

She thinks for a second. 'Are you sure?'

'Yes, of course.'

'Okay, that would be great. Thanks.'

'You'll just need to let their teachers know. Send a note in tomorrow.'

'Brilliant. Thank you.'

I realise I'm probably coming across as too good to be true. She might start getting spooked by my over-friendliness. I need to rein it back a bit. I'm worried I'm losing my judgement, but I can't stop over-analysing everything. My brain is cloudy. I really do like Kate, but what if she turns out to be the person who ruined my life? Right now, though, I can barely concentrate on a word she's saying. I'm so nervous about seeing Bella again tomorrow that I'm not sure how I'm going to get through the next twenty-four hours.

CHAPTER FIVE

Driving out of the car park and merging into the long stream of traffic, Catriona tries to keep herself under control as the windscreen wipers do their frantic, noisy sweeping. If she can stay calm, and make herself believe that this is all okay, then she's sure everything will work out fine. She can't let herself think about anything else. She keeps telling herself that they've just been for a lovely afternoon outing to the mall, and now they're heading back home. All perfectly normal. Nothing odd about that.

Her little passenger fits perfectly in the car seat. It's as though it was bought especially for her. *See?* It really was meant to be. But as soon as she has that thought, there's a small whimper from the back seat.

'I want Mummy now.'

'We'll see Mummy soon.' Catriona prays she can cheer her up. 'Have you eaten all your cookie?'

'Yes. I want Mummy now. Mummy gets my juice.'

'Are you thirsty, sweetie?'

'Yes. I want juice.'

Sometimes Catriona keeps a bottle of water in the car. She throws a glance down at the passenger seat and into the door compartments, but there's nothing there apart from an umbrella and some old receipts. 'We won't be long. Just ten minutes, all right?' She glances in the rear-view mirror to see the girl's little face grow red, her eyes bright with tears.

'Shall I sing you a song?'

'I want Mummy!' the girl wails, working herself up.

Catriona feels like doing the same. But she has to stay calm. If she can just get them both home, get her little passenger a drink of water or juice and stop her tears, then she'll work out what to do from there. She'll just take this a moment at a time. If only the traffic wasn't so heavy. If only the rain wasn't so relentless and the sky so grey and dark.

'G-g-get Mummy! Now! I want Mummy! I want MUMMY!'

Catriona grips the steering wheel hard, tries to steady her breathing. It will be okay. It will all be okay. She starts to hum a tune to herself. She doesn't know what it is – a lullaby of some sort. To soothe the child and to soothe herself. But it can't be heard over the yelling and sobbing from the back seat. The little girl is straining against the seatbelt, pulling at the straps. Leaning forward and then flinging herself back in her seat.

Catriona's tuneless humming gradually turns into her own sobs. 'Oh no, oh no,' she wails over and over. 'What have I done? What am I going to do? Please help me. Someone help me.' If she's not careful she's going to crash the car and injure them both. She can't do that. She has to calm down. Indicating left, she noses the car off the dual carriageway and down a slip road. A little further on she finds a layby. She pulls in, takes a breath, opens her door and dives through the pelting rain to the back door. She slips in and pulls the door shut, her hair now wet from just a few seconds outside. She should have pulled her hood back up. Never mind.

'Hey, hey,' she croons to the child. 'What's all this noise? What are all these tears for? Are you still thirsty?'

The girl sobs and nods. 'Thirs-ty. Want Mu-ummy.'

'Tell you what… if you stop crying, we can go and get a nice long drink of juice, okay? But you need to be nice and quiet because I can't drive while you're sad. Do you know why?'

Her eyes widen a little and she shakes her head.

'Because when you're sad, I'm sad. And I'll be too sad to drive.'

'You're sad?'

Catriona nods. 'But shall I tell you what makes me happy?'

The girl's eyes widen.

'Singing a song always cheers me up. Do you like singing?'

The girl pouts and shakes her head.

'You don't like singing? But everyone likes singing!'

'No! Want Mummy!'

Catriona desperately needs to distract her. 'What's your favourite song ever?'

Her chin wobbles. 'Way in a Manger.'

' "Away in a Manger"? Oh yes, that's a good one. That's my favourite too!' Luckily Catriona knows the words, as it's one they've been practising for the pre-school Christmas concert. But she doesn't want to remember that. She can't think about the thing she's trying to forget. Instead, she opens her mouth and begins to sing softly and slowly. In that way that mothers do when they're trying to get their children to sleep.

The little girl puts her thumb in her mouth and plays with one of her own dark curls, rubbing it between the pads of her chubby fingers in a comforting motion. It's almost the exact same shade as Catriona's own hair – maybe just a touch lighter. Catriona wipes hot tears from the child's flushed face and strokes her hair while she sings. Gradually, the girl's body loses its tension. Her eyelids grow heavy and before too long she's fast asleep. She must have tired herself out with all that crying. Catriona sings another few rounds of the carol, making each line softer than the last, unwilling to stop in case the girl wakes up again. Finally, she chances it, holding her breath in anticipation of more tears. But the interior of the car is silent and still.

Catriona feels a little less fraught now the child is asleep. She allows herself a spark of hope as she climbs out into the rain and back into the driver's seat. A sense of calm descends. They'll go home, she'll put her to bed, and it will be as if none of today ever happened. She can go back to how it was before, and all will be well.

CHAPTER SIX

NOW

We sit next to one another in the lounge, sipping beers in front of the cosy wood burner while our chilli nachos warm in the oven. I made Matt's favourite tonight, thinking he was going to be working late, but he ended up coming home at the normal time, so he's in a great mood, his blue eyes soft and twinkling. He looks so handsome in his grey sweatshirt and joggers, his blonde hair still damp from the shower. I feel lucky every day that I have him in my life. The kids are already in bed, so we're having a few rare moments to relax.

'How was today?' Matt asks.

'Don't ask. Although I sorted out my new hours with Dee, which is something.'

'What happened?'

'I actually thought Dee was going to have to sack me instead.'

'*What?* Why?' Matt sits up straighter but relaxes again when he sees that I'm smiling. I tell him about the order mix-up and the dropped breakfasts, and he pulls me in for a hug. 'Poor you. At least Dee was nice about it,' he says. 'But it's not like you to muddle up orders and drop stuff. You're normally Miss Efficient. Is everything okay? Is there something going on I should know about?'

I blink and look down at my beer bottle. 'Going on? No, why are you asking that?'

'Come on, Rach, I'm not stupid. There's obviously something up. You've been acting strange these past couple of days.'

I don't reply straight away, wondering if now is the time to tell Matt about my past. If Bella turns out to be my child then it will all have to come out anyway.

'Rachel?'

I put my bottle on the table and shift back, turning to face him and twiddling a few strands of my hair.

'Okay, you're making me nervous now,' he says, wearing a worried smile. 'You're not pregnant, are you?'

I roll my eyes.

'Because it's fine if you are,' he adds hastily. 'I mean, not fine, it's great. Just… not sure where we'll fit everyone, but I'm sure we'll be able to work it out.'

'Don't worry; I'm not pregnant.'

'Oh.' His shoulders drop. 'Good. Because this house… I love it, but it's tiny, there's barely room for the four of us, let alone five, and thinking about the sleepless nights…' He breaks off. 'So, if you're not pregnant, then what is it?'

If I don't tell him now, while he's asking me, I'm not sure I ever will. I'm not sure I'm doing the right thing, but I find myself starting to explain. 'The thing is, Matt, there's something from my past. Something I never told you.'

'Okaaay.' He takes a sip of his beer and gives me an intense stare.

I swallow and rub the back of my neck, feeling the kinks and knots beneath the skin. So many conflicting thoughts swim through my head. It's not that I don't think Matt will handle it well – he'll be shocked and sympathetic – but he won't be able to help wondering why I kept such a big thing from him. Why I didn't trust him enough with it in the first place. But it wasn't about trust; it was about me not wanting to think about it or talk about it. Not wanting to unearth the pain. I'm not sure how to continue. The silence grows until Matt finally breaks it.

'Are you going to tell me what this is about?' His face is serious now, his blue eyes darker somehow.

'Remember how screwed-up I was, the day we first met?'

'I wouldn't say you were screwed-up. Upset, maybe.'

'Be honest; I was screwed-up.'

'Your ex had walked out on you. He'd left you alone with no money and a young child. It's no wonder you were upset.'

'The thing is, when I told you about my life, I missed out a bit. The *main* bit.' My voice doesn't sound as though it belongs to me. I can't believe I'm about to verbalise what happened to me all those years ago. I don't know if I can do this.

'You're scaring me, Rachel. What did you miss out?'

There's a whooshing sound in my ears. Why did I think this was a good idea? I run my fingertips back and forth along the gold velvet sofa, watching the colour change from light to dark, like a wheat field on a windy day.

'Can you just tell me what it is?' Matt presses.

'Okay, but can you hold my hand first?'

Matt takes one of my hands in both of his. 'You're freezing!' He starts rubbing my hand, breathing his warm breath onto my icy skin.

His touch gives me the courage to continue. As I speak, instead of looking at his expression, I gaze at his large, rough hands, so gentle and tender. 'Before I met you, something terrible happened.' I break off. Clear my throat. 'Before I met you, I had another daughter.'

Matt drops my hand.

I look up at him. His skin is pale. His mouth has fallen open. He shuts it abruptly and swallows. 'You had another daughter... you mean...'

'She was abducted from a shopping centre nine years ago. I never saw her again.'

'Jesus, Rachel.' Matt is rigid with shock, and then he gives himself a shake, pulls me in close and hugs me tightly. 'I can't believe what you're telling me.' He's still hugging me, but I can't quite relax into his arms. I'm stiff and unyielding, unable to move, so he relinquishes his hold, letting me go, so that we're sitting awkwardly beside one another.

'What happened, Rach? I mean, *how* did it happen?'

I can't look him in the eye, too afraid to see the pity there. I know I'm going to have to elaborate, but I'm afraid to relive it so I talk quickly without emotion, simply relaying the facts. 'Her name was Holly. She was almost three years old. I was at the mall with a friend – Christina. Holly was in the play area while Christina and I were chatting next to her with a coffee. Jess was in her pram by my side. We'd only been there five minutes or so. I was checking on Holly periodically, looking up to see if she was okay. But then, the next time I looked, I couldn't see her. I assumed she'd gone back inside the playhouse, but when I went over to have a proper look, she wasn't there. She wasn't anywhere.'

Matt looks like he's about to cry. The only time I've seen him so full of emotion was when Charlie was born. He manages to choke out a reply. 'This is… I can't believe it.'

'I know. I'm a horrible person. I lost my daughter.'

'That's not what I meant!' Matt takes my limp hands in his once again. 'I meant, that's a terrible thing you've been through. A horrific thing. The *worst*. In no way do I think you're a horrible person. And you shouldn't think that either.'

'You don't have to try to make me feel better about myself,' I say flatly, knowing that he's only trying to be sympathetic. But I don't want to accept his sympathy. I don't deserve it.

'I'm not trying to do that. I'm just trying to…' He runs a hand through his hair, gets to his feet, paces a little way and then sits back down. 'I don't know. What can I do? What can I say? Rach, I'm so sorry you went through that. Why didn't you tell me? I'm here for you whenever you want to talk about this. Whatever you need. I still can't believe it.'

I feel sorry for my boyfriend. I've dropped this bombshell on him and it's so much to take in. He's a sensitive person. A kind person. He'll be feeling so bad for me. But right now, I can't feel much at all. Just a strange heaviness. A feeling that mine and Matt's relationship won't be the same after this. I know he'll say he doesn't think I'm to blame, but surely a small part of him must be wondering what kind of mother I am to have let this happen to my child.

'Rachel, are you okay? What can I do?'

'Maybe turn the oven off. I can smell burning.'

'What? Oh, yeah, of course, but you know that's not what I meant. I meant what can I do to help? To make you feel better?' He shakes his head. 'I'll just go and… I'll turn the oven off then I'll come straight back.'

I'm getting stupid thoughts in my head now, like Matt's probably hungry and dying to eat the chilli nachos, but he knows it would be insensitive to bring up the subject of dinner at a time like this. Come to think of it, I'm hungry too. But how can either of us eat? I should have waited until after dinner to talk about this. I feel as if I'm losing my mind a little. Spinning out. It's because I've kept all this suppressed for so many years. And now… after seeing Bella, it's all racing to the surface once again.

Seconds later, Matt returns from the kitchen.

'Are you hungry?' I ask.

'What? No.'

'But you've been working all day.'

'Rachel, I'm worried about you.'

'I've lived with this for nine years. I'm okay. I mean, it's not something you ever really get over, but I'm managing.'

'Why didn't you tell me about this before?' He walks over to the French windows and stares out into the darkness. 'I mean, we've been together for years. Why now?'

'I don't know why I never told you. I never told anyone round here. It was just a really hard thing to talk about. When I came to

Wareham, it was nice that no one knew me as the woman whose daughter was abducted. I was just Rachel, Jess's mum. A single mum. Divorced. But nothing out of the ordinary. Not a subject for gossip. I thought it would be easier if I simply started my life afresh.'

He doesn't reply. I know I should have told him about this earlier. Either that, or I shouldn't have told him at all. He's obviously upset with me for keeping such a big secret. My head swims at the thought of my revelation driving a wedge between us. At the thought of him losing any trust in me. 'Matt, I'm so sorry I didn't tell you before.'

'I get that you wouldn't want everyone else knowing about it. But what about *me*? What about after Charlie was born. Don't you think it was…? I mean… don't you think you could have trusted me with your history?'

'It wasn't anything to do with not trusting you. It's just that I wasn't strong enough to talk about it. To relive it all. Just mentioning her name makes me feel shaky. Even now, I feel like my mind is imploding. Like if I let myself think about it all properly, I'll end up having another breakdown.'

He nods as though he understands, but I can see his mind working behind his eyes. The hurt expression on his face at the realisation that I kept such a big part of my life from him.

'I'm sorry.' I say the words again but even to my ears they sound hollow.

He shakes his head. 'You don't have to say sorry.' But his initial shock and sympathy has already given way to something else.

'So much for a relaxed evening of beer and nachos,' I say, attempting to lighten the atmosphere. But my heart isn't in it, and Matt doesn't even attempt a smile.

He turns away from the window to face me. 'Did the police have any idea who took her?'

'There was some footage of someone in a hooded top leading her away…' I try to shake the image from my mind.

'A man?'

'They couldn't tell. The CCTV quality was so bad.'

'I can't even imagine what you must have gone through.'

'It was a rough time. But starting over helped. Being away from where it happened.'

'Is this why you're so overprotective with Charlie and Jess? I mean, I know I'm always on at you to let them have more freedom. Now I feel bad.'

'I know the chances of it happening again are remote, but I don't like to lose sight of them – ever. It makes me feel physically sick.'

'Of course. Of course it must. I can't imagine…' Matt stoops to pick up his beer bottle from the coffee table. He drains it in a few long gulps and sets it back down. 'Could it have been someone you knew? I mean, they say that, don't they? That crimes are usually committed by people you know.'

'The police interviewed everyone – neighbours, friends, family.'

'What about Andy?'

'What about him?'

'You said you were going through a rough patch back then. Could it have been him who took her?' Matt's voice takes on an intense quality. He has one of those brains that never lets anything go. He always has to find the answer to anything – puzzles, quizzes, TV mysteries. I hope he doesn't want me to go over every single detail of what happened that day. I don't think I'm up to it. Not right now.

'It wasn't Andy,' I reply.

'But how can you know for sure? Maybe he did it so he could get custody of her without going through the courts.'

'The police checked him out. He had a watertight alibi. He was out of the country, working in Spain at the time.'

'Maybe he got someone else to do the actual abducting.'

'Matt, I can't do this now.'

He raises his hands in surrender. 'Of course you can't. I'm sorry. I don't know why I… I just want to try and make it right. Get her back for you. I don't know what to do.'

'There's nothing for you to do, Matt. All you need to do is be here with me. Accept that I had this nightmarish thing happen to me, but that I'm still here. Still alive. I have you and Jess and Charlie. And I just have to pray that if she's still… if she's still alive, she's happy.'

Matt nods, and I know what he's thinking, because it's what everyone thought when she first went missing. That the chances of Holly being alive are remote. And even if she is alive, the chances of her being happy are almost non-existent.

The smell of the chilli nachos is turning my stomach. My whole body feels like it doesn't belong in my skin. I wish I hadn't started talking about this. I knew it was a mistake.

'Rach, are you okay?' Matt comes back over to the sofa and sits next to me.

I shake my head and a hot tear splashes onto my cheek. He gathers me into his arms again and for now I'm happy to be comforted, letting my pain wash down my face and onto his sweatshirt, while he murmurs soothing words and strokes my hair.

CHAPTER SEVEN

'Don't run too far ahead!' I call down the road to Charlie and Kieran, who are behaving like a couple of overexcited puppies, bounding through puddles and getting their uniforms wet and muddy. By contrast, Jess and Amy are lagging behind, arms linked, heads down, entranced by their phone screens. They shunned my offer of an umbrella, preferring to use their hoods to shelter from the drizzle. As arranged, I've picked up Kate's two with mine, and Kate will be coming to our house once she's collected Bella from school.

Bella.

I'm nervous about meeting her again. What if I see her and don't get that same feeling? What if I realise I got it all wrong and she's not my daughter? But what if she *is*? My stomach roils and I put a hand to it as though that will somehow eliminate all the turbulent feelings inside. I tell myself to be calm and cool. Not to do or say anything that might jeopardise my friendship with Kate. If Bella really is my missing daughter, then I'll have to approach this whole situation carefully.

I didn't air my suspicions to Matt last night. It was enough that I told him my history. I don't want to mention Bella until I have proof. Or at least until I'm absolutely sure in my mind. Perhaps, after this afternoon, I'll know more. But I'll have to see her again in order to know for certain.

A car horn makes me jump. I look up to see Kate's white Fiat drive past, indicating into our road. The boys are already around the corner, out of sight; behind me the girls are oblivious – either that or they're not bothered, heads still bowed over their phones. Kate's car is out of view before I get the chance to look for Bella in the passenger seat. I quicken my pace.

Kate has parked outside our house behind my red VW Polo and is giving Kieran a hug. He squirms out of her grasp and boomerangs back to Charlie. Kate raises a hand in my direction. I wave back and lower my umbrella. I can't see Bella yet. Perhaps she's still in the car, but the windows are obscured by raindrops.

'Hello.' I'm slightly out of breath when I reach her. 'You found us okay, then?'

'Yes, although I did take a couple of wrong turns. My satnav got a bit confused.'

'Ha, my satnav gets confused sometimes, too. I think it's all the narrow country lanes around here.' I smile and glance into her car, my heart sinking when I see the passenger seat is empty. But then, I think, maybe Bella's got an after-school club and Kate will be picking her up a little later.

She follows me up to the house and I open the front door. The boys tumble past me into the hallway first, discarding coats and shoes and racing up the stairs. 'Come in.' Kate follows me inside, bringing a whiff of rose perfume with her. 'Is Bella not coming?'

Kate rolls her eyes. 'Well, I went to school to pick her up, but she came out and casually informed me she's going to a friend's house after school. I didn't want to say no, because of course I'm relieved she's making friends. But I wish she'd texted me earlier, so I hadn't wasted all that time trying to get parked. Never mind. This hopefully means she's going to settle in okay.' She shrugs off her coat. I take it from her, turning away, trying to hide my crushing disappointment. I attempt to make some space on the rack, managing instead to dislodge half the other coats, which slide to the floor.

'Go through. I'll be in in a sec.' I wave Kate into the kitchen as Jess and Amy finally come in through the front door, handing me their coats and sloping off upstairs. Despite my smiles, I feel like crying. I'm tempted to chuck all the coats on the floor and leave them there, but instead, I calmly hang them all, trying to pull myself together.

What's the point of today if Bella isn't even going to be here? Now I'm going to have to spend all afternoon making polite conversation with a woman who's potentially a child abductor. As I hang up the final coat, I realise that I'm being stupid. I should treat this as a fact-finding mission. This is my opportunity to quiz Kate about where she's from and what she's doing here in Dorset – see if I can glean any useful information. I need to be friendly and charming and not give her any cause to suspect what I know. My brain knows this is a good idea, but my heart is heavy with longing.

Last night in bed, I lay there imagining a perfect reunion with my daughter, a bright glow of recognition in her eyes. I pictured the scene in minute crystal-clear detail. How we'll talk about her deep-rooted feelings that she never really belonged to her family. How she always felt so different. We'll hug one another and weep for all the lost years. But then we'll resolve not to waste a minute more steeped in regret. Instead, we'll make up for lost time, and do all those mother–daughter things we never got to do together.

She'll meet her biological sister, Jess. And although she grew up with Amy as her sister, they were never that close… or maybe they were close, and the three of them will become inseparable. Kate will have to go to prison – there's no other option. Not after putting me through years of hell. But I'll be dignified about it. I won't rail and rant…

Back in the present, damp and dishevelled from the rain, I head into the kitchen and give Kate what I hope is a genuine smile. 'Can I make you a cuppa?'

'Tea would be lovely.'

'Have a seat.' I gesture to the white Ikea stools lined up against the breakfast bar. Our kitchen is regrettably too small for a table.

Kate perches her neat bottom on one of the stools and plops her handbag on the counter next to her. 'The kids have been so excited about today. They could barely sleep – although don't tell Amy I said that. She'd be mortified. They've been missing their friends, so it'll be nice to make new ones.'

'My two were the same last night. It's great how they've hit it off.' As I bustle about the kitchen making tea, I surreptitiously examine Kate Morris's features and attributes. 'I wish my hair stayed as straight as yours in the rain. Mine always turns to frizz.' I realise that her blonde hair is exactly like Amy and Kieran's, whereas Bella's hair is dark, lustrous and wavy.

Kate pulls a lock of her hair out from her head, wrinkling her nose. 'Isn't it funny how you always want what you haven't got. My hair is boringly straight, whereas yours has so much body. I'd kill for a bit of a wave in mine.'

I'm pretty sure she's just being polite. 'How do you take your tea?'

'A dash of milk, no sugar please.'

'So, does Bella take after her dad?'

'Hmm?'

'You know, with her dark hair?'

'Oh, you know what – no. We've all got blonde hair and blue eyes, but she's our little changeling. Although' – Kate pats her hair – 'my natural hair colour is more grey-brown these days.'

'So you used to be naturally blonde?'

'When I was a kid. But back to your question – Bella gets her colouring from Shaun's mum.'

'Shaun's your husband?'

'Yes. He's naturally fair-haired, but his mum is part Spanish. It's funny how the genes get distributed, isn't it?'

I nod, not trusting myself to speak for a moment. Trying instead to absorb everything she's telling me. Wondering how she can lie so easily – if indeed she *is* lying. I pick up our mugs of tea. 'Shall we go into the lounge? Be a love and grab that biscuit tin, would you?'

Kate does as I ask and follows me next door to the lounge.

'Wow, it's beautiful in here.'

Our lounge is situated next to the kitchen at the back of the house, and although it's tiny – like the rest of the house – it looks out through wooden French doors onto our pretty courtyard garden. Matt installed a wood burner and stripped the floors. We added squashy velvet sofas and a fluffy rug, so it has a lovely cosy feel. I'm used to it now, so I forget how cute it is in here. 'Thanks. Have a seat.' I put our mugs down on the wooden coffee table and add another log to the burner, getting soot on my hands and wiping it off on my jeans. Taking a seat opposite, I pull my feet up under me and cradle my tea, enjoying the warmth on my cold hands.

'How long have you lived in Wareham?' Kate asks. 'You don't have the local accent.'

'I was born in London, but we moved here seven years ago.' I don't tell her that it was just Jess and I who moved here. That could lead to more questions about my past, and I want to find out about her – not the other way around.

'Whereabouts in London?'

'Stoke Newington.'

'Oh! Not too far from us. We were in Crouch End.'

My heart rate goes up a notch. That's surely more than a coincidence. We were only twenty minutes away from one another. The shopping centre where Holly was snatched is midway between the two places. I offer Kate a biscuit, but she declines. I should probably call the kids down to offer them a snack and a drink, but I don't want to break off from our conversation. I need to quiz Kate further.

'So why did you move here?' I know she already gave me some generic answer about London being too busy, but it can't hurt to ask her again.

'Oh, uh, you know, usual reasons. London was getting too busy and Shaun and I wanted the children to experience life in the country. I guess I was worried about them being teenagers in such an urban environment. We figured Dorset's a safer place than London.'

'Although they say small towns can be worse than cities.'

'Don't tell me that now we've schlepped halfway across the country!'

'Don't worry, I think on the whole it's a good place for kids to grow up. Everyone knows everyone. The schools are great. And if there's any gangland violence or drug wars going on, I haven't noticed.'

Kate fakes mopping her brow. 'Well that's a relief.'

I sip my tea. 'You said you used to come on holiday here. It seems like quite a drastic change to move to a place after only a couple of visits.' I'm aware that my questioning is becoming a little intense, but I can't seem to stop myself. Ever since I clapped eyes on Bella, I've had this buzzing in my head telling me something's not right. Call it a mother's intuition or a gut feeling, but I feel as if I have no choice but to act on my instincts. I actually want to grab Kate's collar and shake the truth out of her. I put my tea down and shove my hands between my thighs to keep them trapped. If Kate really did snatch my daughter then it surely can't be a coincidence that she's here, now, in Wareham. She must have sought me out on purpose. But why? It makes no sense. If she took my child, surely she would want to get as far away from me as possible, so there's no danger of her being discovered. Unless she's playing some twisted game. Or this really is a crazy, huge coincidence, and Kate has no idea who I am.

She shifts in her seat. Is she feeling uncomfortable because she knows I'm onto her? Or is it because I'm going a little overboard with my questioning. 'I guess moving here *was* a little drastic, but it's good to shake things up a bit every once in a while, wouldn't you agree?'

I pick up my tea again and move my head from side to side non-committally. 'I'm afraid I'm not one for shaking things up.

I prefer a quiet life. I think Dorset living must have rubbed off on me.'

'Maybe it will rub off on us too, and we can finally feel settled. As long as our kids are happy, we'll be happy.'

I want to ask, *but are they really your kids?* Of course, I don't say anything of the kind. I keep all my fears and suspicions to myself. But having her here is affecting me more than I thought it would. I thought I'd be able to play a part and act normally. Instead I feel like screaming and accusing. It's as if I've got ants in my brain, crawling around and itching my scalp from the inside. Did this woman steal my daughter?

It's no good. I have to excuse myself before I say something I shouldn't. 'Just nipping to the loo. Won't be a minute.'

Kate nods.

I set my tea down too loudly on the coffee table and rush off to the bathroom, locking the door behind me. I put the seat down and perch on the edge, trying to get my breathing under control, trying to halt the trembling in my fingers. Am I being irrational? Maybe I'm mistaken. Maybe Bella isn't Holly. But what about her distinctive green eyes? Her hair colour? The shape of her face? All of it. And even Kate said she was their 'changeling' child. Was that comment meant as a taunt? As a dare, to goad me into saying what I'm thinking? Perhaps it's me who's got it all wrong, but my brain is so muddled right now. I honestly don't know what to think. And I have no clue what to do next.

CHAPTER EIGHT

After Kate and her children leave the house, I close the door and exhale, exhaustion pulling at my limbs. After my mini-panic attack in the loo earlier, I managed to pull myself together enough to re-join Kate in the lounge. I decided to try to treat the rest of her visit like any other normal cuppa-with-a-friend afternoon. Otherwise I was going to be in danger of scaring her off, and then my chances of seeing Bella again would dwindle to zero.

So I relaxed and we chatted about schools and kids and all kinds of normal, mundane things. We actually got on really well, sharing a similar sense of humour. The kids had a blast, hanging out in each other's rooms. I made them pasta and gave them ice cream for afters. It ended up being the perfect, paint-by-numbers play date. So much so that I almost forgot the reason I invited Kate over in the first place. *Almost.*

But now that she's gone, I've had an idea about something I should have done when I first saw Bella. I actually don't know why I didn't think of it earlier. I ignore the mess in the kitchen and dining room and head back into the lounge with my phone. As I sit on the sofa, there's a thundering of feet down the stairs and the lounge door swings open. It's Jess, clutching her phone, eyes bright.

'Mum, I'm just talking to Amy. Would it be okay if she comes for a sleepover at the weekend? Please say yes. Please, please, please, please.'

I frown, wondering whether it's a good idea or not. 'Let me think about it.'

'We won't make loads of noise, we'll just be in my room.'

'I said I'd think about it.'

Jess's face falls and she slopes back upstairs. Maybe I should say yes. But then Charlie will want to have Kieran over and it will be chaos, with no sleep for anyone. Although… I could also invite Kate and Shaun round for dinner. That way, I'll get to meet Shaun too, and I can do some more digging. I haul myself off the sofa and close the lounge door again. Matt will be home soon. I don't have much time to get back to what I was about to do before Jess interrupted me.

I open Facebook on my phone and tap Kate's name in. But of course there are hundreds of people called Kate Morris. I narrow my search down by place, starting with London and then trying Wareham. I feel a thrill of excitement when her photo finally pops up. Annoyingly, her profile is set to 'private', so I send a friend request, realising that it could be ages until she accepts – if indeed she even does accept. She might not want me to see her page, or maybe she's someone who hardly checks her social media.

My fears are unfounded – almost straight away my phone pings and a notification pops up that Kate Morris has accepted my friend request. Facebook asks me if I'd like to wave to her. No, I would not. Instead, I click on her profile and start scrolling through her photos, hoping she's the sort of person who puts up pictures of her kids. I needn't have worried.

There aren't too many recent ones, but as I page back a few years, there are plenty. My heart skips as I see picture after picture of Bella. And the more I stare at them, the more I'm convinced that I'm staring at photos of my daughter. Photos of Holly. Of when she was ten years old. Eight years old. Seven. Six. And in the pictures where she's with the rest of the Morrises, she sticks out like a sore thumb. Her warm skin tone and dark hair are nothing like her parents' and siblings' colouring. It's crazy that no one's said anything about it before – although maybe they have. And those green eyes – she's an absolute beauty.

I scroll back, trying to locate pictures of Bella as a baby. That will be the decider. If there are photos of her under the age of three taken with Kate, then maybe I'll have to conclude that this has all been a terrible mistake on my part. But I get the feeling I won't see those baby photos. I'm more and more convinced that this is my missing Holly berry. That's what I used to call her – my Holly berry. Something close to rage sparks in my chest. But it's the type of rage that has tears. I clench my fists and take a breath, scrolling on down through the photos. And wouldn't you know it – Kate joined Facebook six years ago, when Bella was six years old. Holly was taken from me when she was two years and eight months. So where are those baby pictures? They're not here. And I would be willing to bet they're not anywhere, other than in my own photo album.

I stare at my phone screen, at this beautiful six-year-old child – the child who looks uncannily like my missing daughter. The child I never saw grow up.

I want to hurl the phone across the room in anger. Instead, I clutch my mobile to my chest, hands folded over the top of it, pressing the image on the screen closer to my heart as though I could rewind time to make her mine again. As though the collection of pixels is my flesh-and-blood daughter.

'Rachel! Rach, I'm home!'

I lift my phone away from my chest, steal a last glance at my child and exit Facebook. 'Hi, Matt. In here!'

The door opens and my boyfriend walks in, a huge bouquet of flowers in his hand. I get to my feet and look at him quizzically. 'Hello, it's not an anniversary is it?'

'Hi. No. It's just, after what you told me yesterday, I wanted to get you something. I know flowers aren't anything much – not compared to what you've been through – but…' He tails off, his eyes full of sadness.

'Oh, Matt, that's just so thoughtful and lovely of you. Thank you!'

He lays them on the sofa and holds out his arms I step into them and kiss his warm lips, momentarily forgetting what I discovered on Facebook. We're interrupted by the children, who come clattering down the stairs, calling out to their dad.

'Hey, you two.' Matt lets me go and pulls them into a bear hug.

'Amy Morris came over after school today,' Jess says. 'She's so cool. She's moved here from London and now she's my best friend.'

'From London?'

'Yeah. Like me.'

'And me,' Charlie says.

'You weren't born in London,' Jess says.

'Yes I was! Wasn't I, Dad?'

'No, buddy. Jess is right. You were born in Dorset, like me.'

Charlie's face drops for a moment, but then he smiles again. 'So I'm the same as you, Dad?'

'That's right, Charlie boy.'

'Ha!' He sticks his tongue out at his sister, who rolls her eyes.

'Okay, guys,' Matt says. 'I need you to go up to your rooms for a bit while I talk to your mum.'

'Are those flowers from you, Dad?' Jess asks.

'They're a present for your mum,' Matt replies.

'Why?'

'Why not? Go on now, up to your rooms and then I'll call you back down later. Maybe we can play a board game before bed.'

'Monopoly?' Charlie asks.

'Not tonight, it takes too long.'

'Twister!' he cries.

'How about Pictionary?' Matt suggests.

'Yeah!' Charlie spins around and does a Superman pose.

'Okay,' Jess replies. 'I'm going to be on Mum's team though.'
I wink at her and she winks back.

Once the two of them have disappeared back upstairs, Matt
and I sit down. He gives me a concerned look. 'How are you
doing? I couldn't stop thinking about you all day today. Sorry I
couldn't call – we're working in a no-signal area at the moment.
So annoying.'

'I'm okay. It's more of a shock for you than for me. I've lived
with it for years – you only just found out about it.'

'You should have told me before. I mean, I think I get why you
didn't – it can't be an easy thing to talk about. But it's *me*. We tell
each other everything. Or at least I thought we did.'

Matt's right. We're not like those couples who lead separate
lives. Most people I know who are in relationships socialise
with their friends more than with their partners. Some of them
even choose to go on holiday with friends rather than with their
families. But Matt and I have always been a tight unit, preferring
one another's company to other people. So I understand this
must feel weird for him. Almost like a betrayal. I would probably
feel the same in his situation. I can tell he's hurt, but he's not
giving me too hard a time because of the awfulness of what I've
been through.

'I'm sorry. I know I should have told you ages ago. Honestly,
I don't know why I didn't.'

'It's okay.' But he shrugs, like it's not okay.

I don't know whether to hug him or not. If I'm too apologetic,
he might think I really am in the wrong. But if I'm not sorry
enough, he could get annoyed. I don't even know why I'm analys-
ing how to react. Surely I should just *react*. This whole situation
with Bella has screwed with my brain. I'm not thinking straight.
I don't feel quite like myself.

Matt clears his throat. 'How did you… I mean, how are you
even keeping it together, Rach? If it was Charlie or Jess who

was abducted, I think I'd lose it. I don't know how I'd ever be normal again.'

'You don't know how you'll be, until it happens to you. But anyway, I was in no way *keeping it together* back when you first met me. You know what I was like. I was a mess. Quite honestly, I was pretty astounded that you showed any interest in me. I wasn't exactly my best self.'

'I just thought you seemed a little bit lost. But I never imagined…' Matt exhales. 'I never guessed how much you must have been suffering.'

I nod and chew my lip, trying not to put myself into that time. Trying to keep from remembering how I felt back then.

Matt leans forward. 'Did you ever talk to anyone about what happened?'

'Not really.'

'Not even a friend?'

'I suppose I did, but I can't remember many specifics from that time. It was all just a horrible, blurry mess.'

'Surely the police must have recommended counselling or something.'

'I went to a couple of sessions. But I was so out of it that I don't think anything went in. I just nodded and said some stuff I thought she wanted to hear.'

'I think you should see someone now.'

'See someone? What, like a counsellor, you mean?'

'Yeah. Exactly.'

Of all the things I would have expected my boyfriend to come up with, this is the least likely suggestion. He's a straight-down-the-line guy. Therapy isn't something I would have imagined to be anywhere near his radar. I hope it isn't because he thinks I might be mentally unstable. What if he thinks I might be unfit to look after our children?

'I didn't know you were into all that therapy stuff.'

'I'm not *into* it.' He's a little embarrassed now. 'I just think it would help to talk to someone who's used to advising about those types of things.'

In my head, I respond with, *What? A child-abduction advisor?* But that would be a shitty thing to say. And anyway, I couldn't bring myself to say the words 'child abduction' out loud.

'What do you think?' he persists.

'I don't know.' In truth, I can't think of anything worse. Raking over all those old feelings, picking at scabs, making me relive it all. I don't want to do that.

'I could have a look online for you. Find a good one. Someone with five-star reviews who's helped other people. Will you at least give it a go?'

I really hope that keeping such a big secret from him hasn't made Matt lose trust in me. For the hundredth time I wish I'd never told him. Either that, or I wish I'd told him a long time ago.

I think about my latest discovery – that I believe I may have found my missing daughter. The appearance of Bella Morris is worth a million therapy sessions. But I can't tell Matt about Bella. I can't confide in him about my worries. Not yet. And it's not because I don't want to. I hate keeping secrets from him – there's nothing I'd like more than to share my doubts, to get his support and his opinion. But the problem is, I'm scared of what that opinion will be. Of what he might say. I couldn't bear it if he told me I was overreacting or being paranoid, or that I was simply mistaken. So I'll keep quiet for now. I at least need the illusion of his support.

'Okay,' I say instead. 'I'll go and see someone.'

'You will?' His eyes brighten. He looks surprised and so pleased.

'If you think it's a good idea, then of course I'll go.'

He strokes my cheek with his fingertips. 'I really think it will help.'

I know that it won't. But if it makes Matt happy, I'll do it.

CHAPTER NINE

THEN

Luckily there's a parking space right outside the front door to their ground-floor flat. Catriona eases her Fiesta into the small gap and turns off the engine. The thought of going inside makes her stomach turn. But she can't stay out here all day. Not with her little passenger asleep in the back seat. She squares her shoulders, unclips her seatbelt and steps out onto the slick pavement. At last the rain seems to be easing, even if the sky is still leaden, the late-afternoon air heavy with moisture.

Catriona opens the front door to her flat, its white plastic handle peeling and scratched. A wave of nausea sweeps through her body as she steps inside. Despite it all looking exactly the same – cream walls, laminate floor, the little hall table piled up with unopened mail and a half-finished mug of tea – the air smells different, the atmosphere dark and oppressive. She can't think like this. *Nothing is wrong*, she tells herself. *Nothing is wrong.* She strides straight through to the back bedroom, closes the sunshine-yellow curtains with a swoosh, and pulls back the covers on the toddler bed. Rushing back outside into the drizzle, she opens the back door of her car and peers in at the sleeping child. The similarity is remarkable. Or is that simply wishful thinking?

The little girl's top is covered in biscuit crumbs and both her boots lie on the floor of the car. She must have kicked them off earlier when she was upset. Catriona unclicks the car-seat straps, eases her hands beneath the child's warm body and gently lifts her out. The child mumbles in her sleep, presses herself into Catriona's chest and neck. Catriona dips her head to breathe in the scent of her hair, but she rears back a little when she smells an unfamiliar shampoo – berries or something, rather than the lavender one she uses. After a second of panic, she tells herself it's no problem. A bath and a hair wash later will fix everything.

For now, Catriona carries the sleeping child into the flat and through to the darkened back bedroom. She's glad they painted it yellow. It's a nice cheery colour for when she wakes up. And the multicoloured stencilled flowers on the walls are perfect. This all feels strange right now, but surely it will become normal soon enough. Once a few days or possibly weeks have passed, they'll hardly be able to recall these upsetting events. They'll all simply become a distantly remembered bad dream.

As she sets her down on the cool sheets, unwinding her little arms from around her neck, the girl opens her eyes. Catriona stiffens, willing her to go back to sleep. She really doesn't think she can cope if she starts crying again. It will be too much. She begins to stroke her hair, like she did earlier when they were back in the car. Her prayers are answered as the child closes her eyes once more, rolls over and pulls the covers up to her chin, settling back into her slumber.

Catriona perches on the edge of the bed and gazes at the sleeping child. A scream forms inside her gut, clawing to get out, but Catriona won't give it a voice. Instead, she turns to more practical things… She stands and heads into the kitchen, closing the blinds to block out the view of the garden and the church beyond. She slides open the cutlery drawer. The scissors are right there, next to the knives. Her fingers close around the black plastic handles. She lifts them out and tests them in the air, snipping them open and closed a few times. They should be sharp enough.

Back in the bedroom, she stares down with regret that she has to do this. But, honestly, she has no choice. Not if her plan is to have any hope of succeeding. Catriona sits on the side of the bed once again and inches the covers down from around the child's neck. Her hair is messy now, matted together in damp, sweaty clumps. Catriona gently lifts a hank of hair off her face, takes the scissors and cuts through the dark mane just below the chin. She's good at cutting hair, but it's quite tricky doing it like this. She'll have to roll her over in a minute to trim the other side. It will probably need evening out after she wakes. But it will do for now.

As the hair is snipped away, Catriona feels marginally better. Like this child is truly becoming her own. Next, she'll have to get rid of the clothes and wash away the stink of that berry shampoo. She wishes she could do it all now but decides that it would be worse to wake her up. She doesn't feel strong enough for the inevitable tears and questions. No, she'll let her sleep as long as she likes. Catriona can put up with the wrong clothes and smell for a few more hours.

After the last of the girl's long locks are cut away, Catriona stands and surveys her handiwork with a critical eye. *Good.* In the gloom, with the curtains drawn, while the child is curled up in bed with her face smooshed against the pillow, you would never know the difference. She won't think too hard about what will happen when she wakes up.

Catriona realises she still has mud caked in her fingernails. Her clothes are still a bit muddy too. She should go and have a shower before Darren gets home. But then she remembers… and with that vivid flash of memory, her body begins to tremble once more – a strange, unsettling shaking that she has no control over. And she realises there's no way she's going to be able to go back into that bathroom.

CHAPTER TEN

NOW

I lay the silverware on the dining-room table, giving each piece an extra polish as I set it down. The house is immaculate. All four of us have spent the day cleaning, tidying and making the place festive. Normally, I mention the word 'cleaning' and the kids disappear off to their rooms to tend to something that urgently needs their attention. But throw in a box of Christmas decorations and the promise of a sleepover with friends and they're suddenly clamouring to help.

Kate and Shaun are coming for dinner this evening, and we also invited Amy and Kieran for a sleepover. Unfortunately, despite including her in the invitation, Bella won't be coming, as she's going to a friend's house. I can't say I'm surprised. It would be deadly boring for her here with only adults or young kids for company. She's in that tween middle-ground age where she doesn't quite fit in either camp. Not that I would know how that feels as a parent, as Jess isn't quite there yet, and Holly… well, Holly isn't mine any more. But it's ironic that of all the members of the Morris family who are coming over this evening, the one I want to see the most is the one who won't be here.

I glance around the dining room, proud of how the small space looks – opulent yet cosy. The deep green of the Christmas tree blends beautifully with the dark-blue walls. The fairy lights twinkle, reflecting off the wine glasses, and the brass wall-lights glimmer and shine. The fireplace is laid, ready to be lit before they arrive, and Matt has sorted out a mellow music playlist.

Kate looked a little taken aback when I first invited them over. I suppose it might have seemed a bit full on, seeing as she only came to visit the other day. But I told her that we were going to be so busy over Christmas that this Saturday was the only free day we had until the middle of January. After her initial surprise at my invitation, she became overwhelmed and a little teary. She said that she had never expected to be made to feel so welcome. That she had received more kindness here in two weeks than in the years she'd spent in London. I gave her a brief hug and said it was my pleasure.

I do one last sweep of the dining room before declaring it perfect and returning to the kitchen, where the Moroccan casserole is bubbling on the stove. I'm making pizza for the children, which we've said they can eat in the lounge while watching a movie. Matt comes into the kitchen smelling fresh from his shower and starts helping himself to the nibbles I've laid out on the counter. I throw him a look.

'What? I'm starving. And it all smells so good.'

'You're ruining my arrangement.'

He gives me a cheeky grin and eats another olive. 'You're really going to town tonight. You must like this Kate woman a lot. But will *I* like them? What's her husband like? Have you met him?'

'No, not yet. His name's Shaun.'

'Hmm. I hope he isn't boring.'

'I doubt it. Kate's really nice so I'm sure she wouldn't have married someone dull.'

'You don't know that. They say opposites attract, don't they?' Matt takes a handful of cashew nuts, tosses one up in the air and catches it in his mouth.

'Matt!'

'What?'

'Leave the nuts alone.'

'Sorry.' He scoops up a few more and shovels them into his mouth.

'Matt!'

'That's the last time, I swear.'

I suck air in through my teeth.

'You're a bit tense, Rachel. Want a glass of wine?'

'Not yet – I'm trying to keep a clear head till I've finished cooking.'

'You sure this was such a good idea? It's a lot of effort for people we hardly know.'

'That's the point. We *want* to get to know them.'

'Do we though?'

'Yes. Why not? But anyway, it's more to do with the kids. Jess and Charlie have made friends with their kids, so it's good to make an effort. It's nice to meet new people.'

The doorbell rings and I swallow down my nerves. This is going to be a perfectly enjoyable evening. I only wish I'd thought more carefully about the questions I'm going to ask. About the kind of information I want to get. About how I'm going to do this without coming across like a crazy person. 'Can you get the door, while I check on the food?'

'Yeah. What's his name again?'

'Shaun. Shaun and Kate. Don't forget!' I call after him. I know he's just messing with me, but I need this to go well. We all have to bond, to become good friends so I can create another opportunity to see Bella. I'm banking on them inviting us to their place in return. That's probably the only way I'm going to get to see Bella again.

My heart thumps as I hear Matt welcoming our guests. He sends the children upstairs to Jess and Charlie's rooms and ushers the Morrises into the kitchen, which is exactly where I didn't want them – as it's where I'm cooking – but never mind. I turn away from the stove and plant a smile on my face.

Kate's blonde hair has been artfully arranged into an elegant up-do. She's wearing a gorgeous print wrap-dress and leather ankle boots that I'm now coveting. Shaun is wearing jeans and an expensive-looking designer shirt.

'Hi, Rachel!' Kate comes over to give me a hug.

'Hello! So lovely to see you.' We kiss on both cheeks.

'This is my husband, Shaun. Shaun, this is Rachel.'

'Nice to meet you.' Shaun is medium height, medium build, with fair hair and a subtle cockney accent. His blue eyes crinkle into a friendly smile. He seems like a nice guy. I'm pretty sure he and Matt will get on well.

'Hi, Shaun. Thanks so much for coming.'

'Thanks for inviting us. It's nice not to be nobby-no-mates any more. Here's some wine. Not sure what you prefer so we brought a red and a white.'

'We'll drink anything!' Matt takes the wine from Shaun and starts pouring drinks for everyone. He passes me a glass of red and I take a large slug.

Kate hands me a pretty bunch of pink roses and a box of chocolates.

'Thank you so much. These are beautiful! Matt, do you want to show Kate and Shaun into the lounge? I'll come through in a minute. I'm just going to put the children's pizzas in. Take those plates of nibbles with you.'

Matt nods.

Once they've left the kitchen, I take a steadying breath. I need to focus and not lose sight of why I invited them here. This is about one thing and one thing only.

I check on the food one more time, take another gulp of wine and make my way after them into the lounge. They all seem to be getting on well if the laughter is anything to go by. The four of us make comfortable small talk for fifteen minutes or so until the oven beeps, letting me know the pizza's ready. Matt takes Kate and Shaun through to the dining room, while I sort the children out in the lounge with their food and film. Once they're settled, I dish up the adults' casserole and carry it through to the dining room, where Matt is regaling the Morrises with anecdotes from when we were renovating our cottage.

'It wasn't funny at the time,' I add. 'Not when we were ankle-deep in black sludge and the electrics failed on Christmas Eve when Charlie was still a baby.'

'That sounds like a nightmare!' Kate looks truly horrified.

'It wasn't the best Christmas ever,' I reply, setting the plates down.

'But at least your place is gorgeous now,' she says.

'Small but perfectly formed,' Matt says. 'So where are you guys living?'

There's a short pause before Shaun answers. 'We're renting a place just outside town.'

'Settling in okay?' I ask.

'It's a bit of an adjustment,' Shaun replies, 'but we're getting there.'

'Can I do anything to help?' Kate asks me, making a move to get up.

'No, I'm fine. Stay where you are. I won't be a minute.' After a couple more trips to and from the kitchen, everyone has their food and we're all digging in. I'm next to Kate, opposite Shaun. Matt sits next to Shaun, opposite Kate.

'This is delicious.' Kate has already eaten almost half of what was in her bowl.

Shaun touches his fingers to his lips and makes a lip-smacking sound of appreciation. 'Bloody lovely.'

Matt gives me a subtle wink. I'm glad he's enjoying himself. This evening would be much harder if he hadn't clicked with our visitors.

'So…' Matt turns to Shaun, 'are you working down here? Or do you have to commute back to London?'

Shaun has his mouth full so he can't answer right away. Kate jumps in for him. 'Shaun's a builder. He does extensions and renovations, that kind of thing. Now we're in Dorset, he'll be starting from scratch, building up his contacts.'

'I thought London was booming,' Matt says. 'You won't be able to charge the same rates here, you know that, right?'

'Matt's an electrician,' I add.

'Yeah?' Shaun suddenly looks interested. 'Maybe you can hook me up with some other trades? I'm looking for new contacts.'

Matt nods. 'Happy to, mate.'

They turn to one another and start talking in more depth about the Dorset building industry. I turn to Kate. 'So, how's *your* job hunt going?' I know from our previous chats that Kate is looking for work, but she hasn't gone into any detail.

'Honestly, I have no idea what I'm looking for!' She flushes. 'I've never really had a proper job before. I was always too busy with the children. How do you balance the café with the kids?'

I tell her about my shifts and how I slot them in around childcare. She seems interested and almost impressed. Which is strange, because it's just a regular job.

'I really have no idea who would employ me,' she says. 'Could you let me know if you hear of anything going, preferably something that doesn't require any qualifications or experience?' She laughs.

'Don't sell yourself short.' I move my food around my bowl, not feeling at all hungry. I take a few large sips of my wine instead. 'You've raised a family – that takes a lot of hard work and dedication. And you've got *three* children. It's hard enough with two. Not sure how people with three children do it!' I force myself to say that, because, of course, I would give anything to have my three children.

'It's no hardship. I love my kids,' Kate replies with a dreamy expression. 'It's all I've ever wanted – to be a mother.'

'Did you always plan to have three?'

'I would have had more if I could. But I was really ill when I was pregnant with Kieran. Had to spend the last few months on total bedrest, which wasn't fun. Especially as I had Bella and Amy to look after. Shaun isn't exactly the domestic type.' She rolls her eyes indulgently. 'So we made the decision to stop at three.'

'So your first two pregnancies went okay, before Kieran?' The wine is taking the edge off my earlier nervousness.

'Bella was a breeze. But I had terrible morning sickness with Amy. And Kieran was fine apart from the last few months, like I said.'

I want Kate to elaborate on her pregnancy with Bella, but my brain is becoming slow and fuzzy. I don't know how to get her to talk about it without her growing suspicious.

'How about *your* pregnancies?' she asks.

'Mine were fine,' I reply, unwilling to elaborate. Because then I would have to exclude Holly's. 'No major dramas.'

'That's good.'

There's a bit of a lull in the conversation. Shaun and Matt have fallen quiet too.

'Thank you again for inviting us,' Kate says. 'You'll definitely have to come over to ours once we've unpacked a few more boxes. We've still only got five of everything – five dinner plates, five mugs, five knives, five forks. It's driving me nuts. The rest of the kitchen stuff ended up in the loft by mistake and Shaun promised he'd get it down for me.' Kate stares pointedly at her husband and smiles. 'Didn't you, Shaun?'

He raises his hands. 'Okay, okay, hint taken. I promise the kitchen boxes will come down tomorrow.'

'We've got witnesses.' She grins. 'I'd get the boxes myself, but I don't do heights.'

I catch Shaun's eye. 'Kate's been telling me about your children. I met Bella the other day. She's got such distinctive colouring – those green eyes are amazing.'

'Yeah, lots of people notice those eyes.'

'Do green eyes run in your family then? Because I noticed the rest of you have blue eyes.' I know my question is verging on inappropriate, so I qualify it with, 'I'm really interested in genetics and family traits.' I catch Matt raising his eyebrows for a second in the corner of my eye, as if to say, *News to me.*

'My mum's got dark hair,' Shaun says. 'But we think her eyes are some recessive gene that's popped up.'

'Interesting.' I pretend to think for a moment. 'So did you ever do any digging into your family history to find out?'

'No.' Shaun shakes his head and looks a bit bemused.

'I'd love to see some baby photos of Bella. I'll bet she was a cutie.' I turn to Kate. 'Do you have any?'

'What? Baby photos of Bella?' Kate frowns. 'Uh, no. Not on me. They're either in albums or on my old phone.'

I realise that was a weird question for me to ask and it didn't come out as casually as I was aiming for. In fact, it was probably verging on creepy. But I can't help myself. When I saw Bella my reaction was so visceral that I can't ignore it. There has to be some reason why she provoked such strong emotions in me. The only explanation I can think of is that it's some mother–daughter bond. Of course there's the chance that she *isn't* my daughter. That it's just a coincidence she happens to look so much like Holly. But how can I ignore the possibility that she *might* be. If there's even the tiniest probability that she's my missing child, then I have to find out for certain.

I'm pretty sure Matt is raising his eyebrows at me again, so I purposely don't look in his direction. Instead, I turn back to Shaun, unable to stop my line of questioning now I've started. 'It's funny, isn't it, how she has such different colouring when your other two have such fair hair and blue eyes?'

Shaun shrugs, starting to appear slightly uncomfortable. 'I suppose so.'

'Because Jess has dark hair and dark eyes like me. And Charlie has fair hair and blue eyes like his dad.'

I glance at Kate, who suddenly looks a little pale. I notice she's stopped eating and has started tearing strips off her paper napkin.

'Anyone for another top up?' Matt interrupts. I can feel his eyes trying to connect with mine, trying to silently ask what the hell I'm wittering on about. I can feel how forced my questions are becoming. But I can't seem to help myself. These people are here in my house, and there's a chance they're the people who ruined my life. I know this is the worst way to go about finding anything out, and it's not as though they're going to tell me the truth anyway. All I'm doing is making everyone uncomfortable and pushing the Morrises further away, when I should be endearing myself to them and keeping them close.

I notice everyone's bowls – apart from my own – are empty. I stand abruptly. 'Let me get you all some seconds.'

There's obvious relief around the table. The previous awkward topic of conversation is relegated to the past and Shaun turns back to Matt to resume their conversation about building, this time including Kate. I leave the room to get the casserole dish and more bread. I try to give myself a talking to about reining it in, but the wine is slowing down my thinking. I should have eaten some more food. In the kitchen, I tear off a piece of bread, shove it in my mouth and start chewing. But I'm pretty sure I've left it too late to soak up the three – or is it four? – glasses of wine I've already had. And I'm not sure I'm in any state to win the Morrises back around.

CHAPTER ELEVEN

I return to the dining room and dish out second helpings of the main course for everyone except me, as I've barely touched my first helping. The atmosphere in the room feels a little strained and I have this swooping feeling in my stomach and a rising heat in my cheeks. I wish I'd never invited the Morrises round. What was I thinking? Either they took Holly and their playing some horrible mind games with me, or they didn't take Holly and they think I'm a crazy person.

'I checked on the kids,' I say. 'They've demolished the pizza and ice creams – now they're laughing their heads off at the movie.'

'That's good,' Kate replies, nodding a little too much.

'What are you guys up to for Christmas?' Matt asks.

'Not too much.' Kate pushes her plate away. She's barely touched her second helping. 'I think we'll just be having a quiet one.'

'Same here,' Matt says. 'It'll just be the four of us. We'll go to my mum's on New Year's Day, but she's spending Christmas Day with my brother in Devon.'

'I'm actually not feeling too well,' Kate says, holding her stomach.

'Oh no, I hope it wasn't anything you ate!' I'm mortified by the thought I've given everyone food poisoning. But I can't think how – the meal was freshly cooked. 'Does everyone else feel okay?'

Matt and Shaun nod. And there's nothing wrong with my stomach, apart from an anxious swirl of emotions that's been there for days.

'I think I might need to go home.' Kate gets to her feet. Her lips are pressed tightly together. I try to catch her eye to give her a sympathetic smile, but her head is bowed, and it feels as though she's purposely avoiding eye contact.

'Of course,' Matt says. 'Let me get your coats.'

Kate really doesn't look well. The colour has completely drained from her face and she's holding onto the back of her chair as though for support. 'We'll take the children home too, I think.'

Shaun comes over to his wife and puts an arm around her. She murmurs something to him, but I can't make out what it is. They follow Matt out into the hall and Shaun goes into the lounge to get Amy and Kieran. There are howls of disappointment and all four kids come into the hall wearing indignant expressions.

'Mum, please can we stay!' Amy wheedles.

Kate is gingerly putting on her coat and opening the front door.

'No arguing,' Shaun says to his daughter.

Amy nods and bites her lip. There's no way Jess would have backed down so quickly. Both Amy and Kieran look downcast, while my two are utterly incandescent at the unfairness of it. But they're too unsure of Shaun and Kate to voice their disapproval, especially as Kate looks so stern – her eyes hard, her lips a hard line. No, my two will wait until the Morrises have left to show their disappointment.

It takes a few moments for Amy and Kieran to gather up their belongings, and then, less than one hour after they arrived, the Morrises are leaving.

'Sorry about this,' Shaun says as he follows his family out of the door.

'Hope Kate feels better soon,' Matt says.

I don't say anything. I just watch them go and flinch as the door bangs shut behind them.

'Right, kids,' Matt claps his hands, 'time for bed.'

'What?!' Jess puts her hands on her hips. 'First we were supposed to have a fun sleepover and now we have to go to bed early?'

'It's not early, its…' Matt checks his watch. 'Oh. Okay, it's only eight thirty. Well, you can chill out upstairs for a bit.'

'With my phone?'

'Yes, okay, just for a little bit.'

Jess doesn't need any further prompting. She takes the stairs two at a time.

'Why did they have to go?' Charlie frowns. 'We were watching the film and we hadn't even built our Lego castle yet.'

'Sorry, mate. Kieran's mum didn't feel well. Why don't you go and build the castle yourself, and I'll come and take a look at it when you're finished?'

'Okay,' he grumbles and slopes off upstairs.

I feel bad for them. 'Do you think she really was ill?' I ask Matt.

He turns to look at me. 'What do you mean? Why would you think she wasn't?'

'Well, it came on a bit suddenly, didn't it?'

'Food poisoning can hit quickly.'

'You think it was food poisoning?'

'Whatever. Food poisoning, stomach bug. Don't worry, it wasn't your cooking. We all ate it, remember? And I feel fine.'

'I … I think it was an excuse so she could leave.'

'Don't be daft. Why would she do that?'

'Because I was asking questions about Bella.'

'Who?'

'You know – their eldest daughter, Bella.'

'Come and sit down.' Matt takes my arm and tries to lead me out of the hall.

'I need to clear up the dinner things.'

'Leave all that. Just come in the lounge for a minute.'

I do as he asks and plonk myself onto the sofa. Matt turns off the TV and stacks all the empty plates and bowls on the coffee table. The room is a mess, but I don't care.

'What's going on, Rachel?' Matt sits opposite me.

I know I'm going to have to tell him my theory, but I also know that he's going to be sceptical.

'Rach… you were acting really weirdly in there with them. Talking about their daughter and genetics and all that stuff. What's going on? Is it…?' He tails off and gives me a long look.

I know what he wants to ask me, and he's right of course, but I feel paralysed.

He takes a deep breath. 'I don't want to ask this, but is it about what you told me the other day? About your daughter?'

I run my tongue over my teeth. I need to brush them. My mouth tastes sour.

'Rachel, will you talk to me?'

'Yes,' I murmur. 'Yes, all right?'

Matt sits back in his seat and pushes his hair off his forehead. 'So… is it because we talked about Holly? Is it all coming back to the surface again? Do you need some kind of help, I mean to talk to someone? I don't feel like I'm supporting you properly. I feel useless.'

I shake my head. 'Matt, I'm not cracking up or having a breakdown. Something's happened. Something that's going to be hard to believe. But I need you to trust me.'

'Okay. What? What is it?'

I feel sorry for Matt, for dragging him into all this. He didn't sign up for any of this when I met him. He thought I was just a single mum who'd had a rough time. He had no idea about the trauma. He had no idea that one day he'd be put in this situation. 'This is going to sound mad, but I need you to listen to me.'

'Just tell me, okay.'

'I think Kate might be the person who abducted my daughter.'

My boyfriend doesn't respond. Even his facial expression doesn't change.

'Matt? Did you hear what I said?'

'I heard. I'm just… I'm thinking about it.'

'Her eldest daughter, Bella… I saw her the other day and, oh my goodness, Matt, you should have seen her. She's the spitting image of my daughter. I mean, there can't be two people in the world who look so similar. Unless they were identical twins. And I didn't have twins.'

'Rachel, how old was Holly when she was taken?'

I'm ready for this question. 'I know what you're going to say – that she was much younger, that she would have changed over the years. But people don't change that much. You can still see them in their baby pictures, you can still tell it's that person.' I'm sounding too desperate, manic. I need to calm down. 'Wait here.' I stand and leave the room, jog up the stairs and into our bedroom. I yank open my T-shirt drawer and pull out the slim album that rests underneath my clothing. Squaring my shoulders, I head back downstairs, nipping into the kitchen to get my phone. It smells of burned cherries and I remember the cherry tart we were supposed to have for pudding. I turn off the oven and head back into the lounge.

Matt is sitting where I left him, staring at the wall. Eventually he looks my way and glances at the album in my hand. I sit next to him and open it up. There are only a few pages of photos. Most pictures of Holly are on my old phone that needs to be charged, but I have a few special ones that I printed and put in this album.

'This is my daughter.' I show Matt the precious photographs of my Holly berry before she was taken. Her dark hair and those vivid green eyes.

'Wow, she's beautiful, Rach.' Matt takes my hand and squeezes.

I try not to let his emotion affect me. If I cry, I won't be able to explain myself properly. While he looks through the album, I open Facebook to Kate's page and find the earliest photo of Bella, when she was around six years old. 'This is Kate's daughter, Bella.' I hand Matt my phone.

He stares at the image of Bella and holds it next to various photos of Holly.

I let him have a few moments to compare. 'Well?' I finally ask.

'They look similar,' he admits.

'More than similar!'

'I don't know. It's hard to tell.'

'But that's because you're just looking at photographs. Holly was my daughter. I knew her better than anyone. Are you telling me that you wouldn't recognise Charlie nine years from now?'

'I'd like to think I would, but honestly, I don't know. Look, I know it's not what you want to hear, and I hate saying this, but the chances of Bella being your missing daughter are tiny. Just because they look like one another, it doesn't mean they're the same person. I know you want to believe it—'

'It's not about wanting to believe it. It's about a mother's intuition. About knowing something deep down in your gut. I've gone years and years and I've never mistaken anyone for my daughter. This is different. And don't you think it's odd that after I was asking Kate and Shaun about their daughter's genes, Kate suddenly got sick and had to leave?'

'Okay, let's say it was Kate who took your daughter, why the hell would she come anywhere near you? Surely she'd stay as far away as possible.'

'I know. I thought that too, but who knows what goes on in people's heads? And there's something off about them. They were pretty cagey about why they moved here and where they live now.'

Matt places my phone and photo album on the arm of the sofa. His voice is low and soothing as he turns back to me. 'The way I see it, there are three possible options. One: Kate abducted Holly and has come here to befriend you as part of some twisted plan.'

I nod, glad he's willing to see the possibility.

'Two: Kate abducted Holly and in some giant coincidental twist of fate, she has ended up befriending you without knowing who you are. Or, option three: Bella really is Kate's daughter who just happens to look a lot like Holly.'

'Not just "a lot" – she's the spitting image.'

'Maybe she is the spitting image. But, Rachel, you have to see that it's just so unlikely.'

'I know, Matt. But unlikely things happen. I can't stop thinking about her. About the fact that she could be mine.' I know that logically Matt is probably right. But I still feel in my gut that she's my daughter. 'I got such a strange vibe off the Morrises, like they're hiding something. I really think I should contact the police.'

Matt's eyes widen in alarm. 'What? No, honestly, Rach, don't do that.'

'But they'd be able to look into it for me. They could do a DNA test and that would prove it one way or the other.'

'You can't go accusing Kate and Shaun of something like this. Not without proper proof. Think how devastated they'd be if they're innocent. And what about Bella? If she's not your daughter they'd all be put through a hell of a lot of trauma.'

'What about *my* trauma? What if she *is* my child?'

'Before you do anything, will you do something for me?'

'What?'

'Will you please start seeing someone about your grief over Holly – a counsellor or therapist.'

'I already said I would.'

'Good. But you need to go and speak to them before you do anything about Bella Morris. Promise me.'

Anything to get Matt believing me. 'Okay, I promise.'

'And you also need to tell the therapist what you just told me about thinking Bella might be your daughter.'

'So they can talk me out of it, you mean?'

'No. Well, not really. Just that they might be able to advise you better than I can. I'm no good at this stuff.'

'No one is,' I reply. 'Especially not me. I feel like I'm going crazy with the need to know.'

Matt pulls me into his arms and kisses the top of my head. 'I can't imagine what you've suffered, Rachel. You know I'll support you. We just need to be absolutely sure before we go accusing anyone.'

'Thanks, Matt.'

'I love you, Rach.'

'Love you too.'

I only hope that this situation doesn't test our love too much.

CHAPTER TWELVE

I stand on the wet pavement outside the brightly lit bathroom showroom, press the door buzzer and wait, hoping I don't see anyone I know. I keep my head bowed and pray for him to buzz me in sooner rather than later. I'm here to see Robin Blake, the counsellor that Matt found for me. His rooms are in the centre of town above this bathroom showroom, but it's early evening so at least town is relatively quiet – less chance of bumping into someone I know who might ask what I'm doing.

Robin doesn't normally see people on a Sunday, but it turns out he's actually someone Matt went to school with, and Matt made out that it was an emergency, so Robin made an exception. I told Matt he shouldn't have done that. That the poor man should at least be allowed to have his weekends to himself, but Matt shrugged, saying my well-being was his priority and that Robin didn't seem to mind.

It feels a little weird, coming to talk to my boyfriend's school friend. But Matt assured me that everything I say to Robin will be in the strictest confidence. Of course, I told Matt that I wouldn't be telling Robin anything I hadn't already told Matt. But who knows how my first session will go? I'm not exactly optimistic. The last thing I feel like doing is opening up to a complete stranger. I'm amazed I managed to hold it together so well when I revealed my secret to Matt. Right now, I'm afraid of completely breaking down with this counsellor. And if that happens, how will I be able to function? How will I be able to do my job and look after my family?

'Hello?' A soft, well-spoken male voice comes through the intercom.

'Hi. It's Rachel Farnborough to see Robin Blake.'

'Hi, Rachel. Come on up.'

The door buzzes and I push on it, feeling it click and give. I walk into a narrow entrance hall that smells fresh and clean. There's a slim console table to my right with an arrangement of Christmassy flowers. I touch one of the leaves. I think they're fake, but they're realistic enough for me to be unsure. Ahead of me lies a steep flight of beige-carpeted stairs. A door opens at the top. A tallish man with a beard steps onto the landing, gives me a wave and beckons me up.

Nervousness overwhelms me, and I wonder again why I agreed to do this. But Matt was adamant. He said he was making me go because he loved me and wanted to help me. But it feels like I've been railroaded into this.

'Hi, I'm Robin.' The bearded man smiles and holds out his hand. I reach the top of the stairs and shake it. His grip is cool and firm. 'You don't need to look so terrified. Honestly, all we're going to do is chat for a short while. That's it.'

I nod, still not feeling in any way at ease.

'Come through.' Robin shows me into a light, airy room with stripped wooden floors, rugs, lamps and Scandi furniture. There's no desk or therapist's couch like I imagined there would be. Instead, there are two sofas opposite one another, separated by a low square ottoman stool. On the stool is a tray with a jug of water and two glasses. Next to the tray is a box of tissues – so he's expecting tears.

Robin sits on the furthest couch and picks up a notebook and pen. He gestures to me to take a seat on the other. I place my handbag next to me.

'Take your coat off if you like. The heating's on.'

I realise it is quite warm, so I do as he suggests and slip off my parka, draping it over the back of the sofa.

'So, how's Matt doing?'

'He's fine. Working hard at the moment.'

'Nice guy. I always got on with him at school. It's a shame we lost touch.' Robin's hair is dark, and his eyes are blue. He's kind of handsome in a geeky way – not my type though. That's a good thing. It would be hard to talk freely to a stranger I found attractive. I'm not even sure why I'm having these thoughts. Maybe because it's distracting me from the other stuff. 'Anyway,' he continues, leaning back into the sofa, 'why don't you start by telling me why you're here?'

'I'm not sure how much Matt told you…'

Robin shrugs. 'He gave me a rough outline, but why don't we just pretend he said nothing. I'd prefer to hear about it in your own words.'

I clasp my hands on my lap and stare down at them, taking a breath. And then I launch into the same story I told Matt. About how my daughter went missing. Again, I tell it dispassionately, almost as though I'm reading it off a script. I can hear how cold and detached I sound, but I'm scared to really engage with my words because I don't want to get emotional in front of this stranger.

There's a short silence after I finish talking, as though the room is resettling and adjusting to the information.

'That must have been a traumatic experience, Rachel.' He holds his chin. 'When did it happen?'

'Nine years ago.'

'Have you spoken about it with anyone during that time? Family or friends?'

'No. I only just told Matt last week.'

'What about at the time when it happened? Did you have counselling then?'

'A couple of sessions, but I can't remember much about them if I'm honest.'

He nods thoughtfully. There are a lot of pauses between my answers and his questions. I guess he's waiting for me to elaborate, but I still feel on my guard, scared of saying the wrong thing. Scared of opening the floodgates my emotions are pushing against.

'Did friends and family offer support back then?'

'My husband at the time – Andy – he blamed me. We split up not long after and now he lives in Spain with a new family.'

'That must have been hard on you.'

'I suppose it was at the time, but looking back, I think it's a good thing we're not together any more. We weren't right for each other. I'm much happier with Matt.'

'That's good. Do you think much about Holly now?'

'Every day.'

'So you think about her every day, but you never talk about her?'

I consider his question for a few moments. 'I don't know. Maybe I just got used to keeping her as a secret. I was scared to open up because I was scared of breaking down, I suppose. And I was aware that Matt would start looking at me differently. He might not think I was a fit mother for our children, after what happened.'

'Do you really believe he would think that?'

I shrug. 'Honestly, I don't know. Do you mind if I…' I point to the jug of water.

'Help yourself.'

Pouring out the water allows me a few seconds respite from the conversation. I wasn't expecting it to get so intense so quickly. Robin is gently spoken but his questions have a way of cutting to the heart of things. I'm not entirely sure I'm strong enough to do this. I take a sip of the water and then another before replacing the glass on the tray and wiping my mouth with the knuckle of my forefinger.

'Okay?' he asks.

I nod. 'Don't get me wrong, Matt is the best – kind, caring, a great boyfriend and father. But surely a small part of him must think I was negligent. Letting my toddler out of my sight in a busy shopping centre.'

'You said she was playing in a Wendy house near you.'

'Yes, but I wasn't watching her the whole time.'

'Do you think all other parents watch their children one hundred per cent of the time?'

I exhale noisily. 'No, of course not. But I was more interested in talking to my friend than watching my daughter!'

Robin nods and pours himself a glass of water. 'What do other parents do when they take their children to play centres and parks with friends?'

I scowl, knowing exactly what he's attempting to do. 'What do you mean?'

'I mean, do they watch their children for every second that they're there? Or do they maybe read a book, or chat with friends while their children play?'

'I know you're trying to tell me it wasn't my fault, but unless one of your children has been abducted while you were busy enjoying yourself, I'm afraid you haven't got a clue!' I clench my fists then release them. 'Sorry, I didn't mean to be rude. It's just, you'll never be able to convince me that it wasn't my fault.'

'No need to apologise. I understand.' Robin sips his water. 'And you're right. I haven't had that experience, so I don't know how you feel. But… you're here talking to me. So maybe we can unpick those feelings a little and try to make some sense of them. That's all. See if we can give you a little peace of mind.'

I nod, feeling tears prick behind my eyes.

'And Rachel…'

'What?'

'The person who's at fault here is not you. It's the person who took your child. Don't forget that.'

We talk some more about letting go of feelings of guilt and Robin gives me some breathing and meditation exercises to help when I'm feeling overwhelmed or panicky. By the time our hour is up, I feel absolutely exhausted, like I've run a marathon or spent a weekend camping in a storm. But there's a part of me that also feels a little lighter. Like someone is sharing the burden and taking some of the heaviness from my shoulders. I can't say it was an enjoyable experience, but I think – I hope – it was worth it.

As I walk back to my car, beneath the rain-spattered hazy street lights, I wonder if I did the right thing, not telling Robin about Bella. That I really think she might be my daughter. I tell myself the reason I kept quiet about her is because there wasn't time – it never cropped up in the conversation. But I know that's not the real reason.

I worried that he would only tell me what Matt told me – that I'm mistaken. That the chances are miniscule. That I'm only seeing what I want to see. But a mother knows these things. The more I think about it, the more I truly believe that Bella is my missing daughter. I know it in my gut. Especially after yesterday evening with the Morrises. Kate texted me this morning to thank me for dinner and to apologise for them leaving early. But it wasn't a chatty, friendly text. It was formal and detached. I replied that I was so sorry she'd been unwell and I hoped we could reschedule when she was feeling better. Her reply took ages to come through and when it did it was the shortest text ever: *ty* – short for thank you. A sudden shot of anxiety hit me when I read it. She's pulling away from me. How will I get to see Bella now?

There's something very strange going on with the Morrises. Perhaps Kate is getting some twisted kick out of befriending me. Perhaps she's been taunting me with the daughter she stole and now I'm on the scent, she's backing off. A sudden, glaring anger drenches my body. How dare she! How dare she flaunt my child in my face. She's denied me the right to be a mother to my daughter. As the rage builds, my hands begin to shake. I think back to what my counsellor said – that it wasn't my fault Holly was taken, it was the person who took her. I can hardly believe that at long last I might be able to get some justice. To make my child's abductor pay.

I finally reach my car and take deep steadying breaths to stem the threatening tears. Who will believe me? Who will help me? A smidgeon of doubt creeps in once more. Has Kate *really* been raising my daughter all these precious years? But if it's true, how would she have got away with it? I can't let myself be deterred from discovering the truth.

Suddenly I have an idea of how I might be able to find out more.

CHAPTER THIRTEEN

THEN

The light outside has dulled; grey afternoon faded to a bone-chilling darkness that envelops the building and seeps through the windows. Catriona sits on the sofa, knees pulled up to her chest, feeling the varying weights of everything – the ache of what lies beyond the garden, the heavy shape of the child in the back bedroom. And the deep dread of what it will be like when Darren arrives home. Sweet, kind, doting Darren – her boyfriend, her rock, her home. The father of her child. But what will happen next?

Catriona rushes into the kitchen and throws up in the stainless-steel sink. There's nothing much left inside of her to get rid of, but her body is determined to expel every last drop. She gasps and heaves and then rinses her mouth directly from the tap. As she spits out clean water and wipes a hand across her clammy forehead, she hears the front door slam. Her stomach lurches and she retches once again, but nothing comes out this time. She straightens up and takes a breath. She must stay calm. She can't let her body and emotions betray her.

'Hey, Caty! It's me! Why's it so dark in here?' The hall light comes on, tentacles of light spreading into the kitchen, trying to reach her. 'That's better. Where are you both? Caty? Grace?' Darren finally pokes his head around the kitchen door. Catriona winces as he switches on the light and gives her his usual grin, his dark-brown curls sprinkled with plaster dust. She blinks and squints, hoping she doesn't look too much like the walking dead. 'Blimey, what were you doing in here in the dark?' He stands there in his dusty, plaster-covered work clothes. 'Shit…' Darren stares at her, his smile disintegrating into shock, his dark eyes filling with worry. 'You okay, Caty? You don't look well at all. What's wrong? You ill?'

'Uh, yeah… stomach bug,' she says automatically, putting a hand over her queasy belly, realising that the lie will only get her so far.

'Oh, poor baby. Why don't you go and have a lie down? Where's Grace? Is she okay?'

'She's… in bed.'

'Oh no. Has she got it too?'

Catriona feels the edges of her sanity peeling away. 'She's not great at the moment.'

'Really? Did you call the doctor?'

Catriona shakes her head, wondering how to detangle herself from the untruths that are starting to knot themselves around her. *Is this what life will be like now?* 'Don't worry. It's just a bug. She'll be okay after a sleep.'

Darren frowns, unconvinced. 'She hasn't got a temperature, has she? Let me grab the thermometer from the bathroom.'

This is why she loves Darren so much – he's always so thoughtful, so caring. But right now, she wishes he was a little less concerned. She wishes he would just ask what's for dinner and plonk himself in front of the telly with a beer.

'No, wait!' Catriona cries a little too loudly as he turns to leave the room.

Darren stops and turns back to stare at her, bemused.

'Sorry.' Catriona realises she overreacted. 'It's just, I've only just managed to settle her down. Don't worry. I took her temperature earlier. She's fine. It's better if you let her carry on sleeping.'

Darren looks Catriona up and down. His eyes narrow. 'You've got mud on your jeans... and on your sweatshirt. What've you been doing? Not gardening in this weather?'

She manages a small laugh, but to her ears it sounds forced and strangled. 'No, don't be silly. Gracie and me, we went to the shopping centre – don't worry, I didn't buy anything – and when I got home, some bloke in an Audi drove through a puddle and splashed us.' Catriona notes again how easily the lies are coming, like flecks of mud floating on a treacherous oil slick.

Darren shakes his head in sympathy. 'I was about to jump in the shower, but if you want to go first...'

'No. You go.' The thought of going into the bathroom sets her trembling again. She wraps her arms around her body.

'Oh, Caty, you're shivering. You're really not well. Go and get into bed and I'll bring you a cup of tea.'

Why does he have to be so nice? A tear slides down her cheek. She turns away and starts filling the kettle, so he doesn't see she's crying. 'You go and have your shower. I'll make us tea.' Quickly, she wipes away the tears with the back of her hand and inhales deeply to staunch the impending flow.

'Are you sure?' he asks, his voice heartbreakingly tender.

'Yeah, course.' This feels worse than she could have possibly imagined. How is she going to manage to keep herself together? To stay functional?

'Okay then, I won't be long.'

Catriona is still facing away from him, willing him to leave the room. Instead, he comes and puts his arms around her. Bends to kiss the side of her neck. She closes her eyes and savours the moment, before shaking herself out of it. 'You shouldn't get too close. I don't want you catching what me and Grace have got.'

'Good point. They won't be happy on site if I have to call in sick.' Darren's a freelance plasterer, currently working on some fancy new-builds across town. It's a decent contract that will keep him employed for at least the next couple of months. And they really need the money. Things have been slack this year and they've already burned through their meagre savings. As Darren finally leaves the kitchen, Catriona grips the worktop and breathes deeply, trying to slow her racing heartbeat and clear her vision. She prays he'll go straight into the bathroom without checking on Grace first.

No such luck.

'Caty!' He calls, agitated. 'Catriona!' Footsteps pound across the laminate and back into the kitchen.

She turns and gives him what she hopes is an enquiring look.

'Where's Grace? Who's that little girl in her bed?'

'What? What are you on about?'

'Come with me and look!' He takes Catriona's hand and leads her out of the kitchen, into the back bedroom. 'Am I going mad?' he mutters.

'Darren, you're scaring me. What are you talking about? Keep your voice down. You'll wake Grace.'

'That's the point,' he snaps. 'It's not Grace.'

The door to the bedroom is wide open, the hall light illuminating the small room enough to show the little girl's features. She's now curled on her side, facing towards them, eyes closed, undeniably a beautiful child. Undeniably *not* Grace.

'Who is that?' Darren hisses, pointing.

'What do you mean, *who is that?* It's Grace. It's our daughter.'

Darren ushers Catriona back out into the hall, his hazel eyes roaming her face, searching for some kind of explanation. But Catriona is resolute. 'Are you okay, Darren? Don't tell me you're coming down with this bug too.'

'Catriona! Stop it. You can't honestly tell me that you believe that's our daughter in there?' A pulse in his jaw twitches.

'Of course it is. Who else would it be?' She holds his gaze, trying to look as though she has no idea what he's talking about, convinced he must be able to hear the hammering of her heart.

As long as Catriona doesn't waver in her conviction, then everything will be okay. Darren will realise that he's mistaken. Because the alternative… well it doesn't even bear thinking about.

CHAPTER FOURTEEN

I sit at the breakfast bar sipping tea from my favourite mug – a piece of chunky blue-and-white pottery made locally. It belongs to a set of four that Matt gave me one Mother's Day a few years back. I'd wanted them for ages, but they'd been well out of my price range, so it was a gorgeous surprise when he bought them for me. Sadly, the other three mugs have long since broken. I wonder why it's always the beautiful, favourite things that end up breaking, rather than the crappy cheap mugs, which seem to live forever. Anyway, at least I have this one precious mug left. I'm sitting here grabbing a few moments of peace before the crazy morning rush to get to school and work.

Glancing at the wall clock, I see I only have a few minutes at most until Matt chivvies the children downstairs. Icy winter rain patters down the back window. What I wouldn't give to creep back upstairs with my tea and slide back under the warm covers. But there's no point torturing myself with those kinds of thoughts.

The door swings open and Matt walks in with his usual energy. 'Hey, you're up early.'

'Morning.' I tip my face up to kiss him, tasting toothpaste.

'So how did it go with Robin last night? You didn't really say much when you got in.'

'Yeah, it was okay.'

'*Okay?* Was he any good though?'

I find myself squirming under Matt's intense gaze. I really don't want to talk about this now.

'Mum, can you tell Charlie to stop using my toothbrush! It's gross!' Jess stomps down the stairs and into the kitchen, an outraged scowl on her face.

'Just give it a rinse under the tap. It'll be fine.'

'I need to disinfect it. Can I boil the kettle?'

'No, just give it a rinse.'

'But—'

'Do what your mum says then come straight back down for breakfast. Send Charlie down too.'

'Ugh. My brother's so annoying. I can't live like this!'

Matt stifles a grin as Jess flounces back upstairs. Normally we'd both be laughing fondly about her dramatics and teasing her until she saw the funny side, but I can't seem to summon my sense of humour today.

'So you were telling me about Robin…' Matt pours himself a coffee and a huge bowl of granola.

'Oh. Yeah.' I drain the rest of my tea. 'He seems like a nice guy.'

'Good, that's really good. I didn't really hang around with him much at school, but I always liked him. Did you tell him about Holly?'

I'm saved from having to answer as the children pound their way down the stairs and into the kitchen.

'Have we got Cheerios?' Charlie asks.

'Cornflakes or granola.' Matt holds up the cartons.

Both kids frown. 'Cornflakes,' they reply unenthusiastically.

I vacate my stool as Charlie and Jess hop up and make a start on their breakfasts, bickering about the name of some YouTuber's dog, if I'm hearing correctly. As I begin tidying the kitchen, Matt asks me about Holly again. I glare at him and shake my head.

'Who's Holly?' Jess asks.

'No one. Someone at work,' I snap.

'I thought you worked for Dee.'

'I do. But there are a few new people who've started there too.'

'Oh.' Jess pours milk on her cereal and all over the breakfast bar. 'Are they nice, the new people?'

'They seem nice.'

Matt mouths sorry at me over their heads, but I'm furious with him for talking about such a sensitive subject at this time of the morning while the kids are in the room. What was he thinking? I slam the breakfast things back in their cupboards and load up the dishwasher with last night's plates. Maybe I'm overreacting, but my emotions are all over the place at the moment.

Jess and Charlie have shovelled their cornflakes into their mouths in record time and are already sliding off the stools. 'Up you go and get your bags,' I say, trying not to let my internal anger spill out. 'Then I need you back down in five minutes.'

Once they're out of the room, Matt tries to come over and put his arms around me. I hold my hands up to ward him off and take a step back. He freezes, his lips pressing into a firm line. 'I said I was sorry.'

'Matt, this isn't the time to be talking about any of this. And I can't believe you mentioned her name while Charlie and Jess were in the room. This is hard enough as it is without you pressuring me to talk about it at breakfast.'

'But you didn't want to talk about it last night either.'

'That's because I was knackered from spilling my guts about the most traumatic event of my life to a total stranger.'

Matt's jaw tightens. 'Sorry for caring.'

I stifle a sigh. 'Please don't get angry, Matt. I will talk about it, but you have to give me some space.'

'Yeah, but you made this huge revelation, and now you don't even want me to mention it.'

'Shh, keep your voice down.' I look up at the ceiling, mindful of the children hearing our disagreement. 'I get that you want to know what happened, but will you please let me talk about this in my own time? I know it's been a bombshell for you and it's a lot for you to take in. But I'm losing my mind a bit here.'

'Fine.' Matt scowls. 'I'm just worried about you, that's all. And I don't…' He shifts his gaze away from me for a moment. 'I just don't want you to do anything… not stupid, but… *hasty*. Not without talking it through first.'

He's obviously talking about me wanting to report the Morrises to the police. 'I'm not doing anything stupid or hasty. I'm just catching my breath. Talking to Robin last night was full on.'

'Rachel…' Matt starts chewing his lip. I know that look. I know I won't like what he's about to say.

'What is it?'

'I know this is all very sensitive, but what if we told my mum?'

'No!' I cut him off immediately. Matt is wonderful, but he does have this annoying habit of telling his mother *everything*. And if she finds out what happened, she'll be round here, fussing over me like I'm some kind of invalid.

'But she always gives really great advice, and it will be good for you to—'

'Matt, I said no. I've only just confided in you and Robin. I can't cope with any more people knowing about it.' I also can't stand the thought of the two of them discussing me behind my back. I know it will be well-meaning, but even so.

'Okay, okay, I'm sorry.' He really does look contrite now.

'It's all right.' I cross the gap between us and wrap my arms around him, pressing my head against his chest.

'I love you, Rach. All I want is to take away your pain.'

I step back from him again, a thought occurring to me. 'Maybe *you* should have counselling too?'

'*Me?* Why would I need counselling?'

'Well, because, it's been a shock for you, hasn't it? You obviously want to talk about it, but I just can't at the moment. It's too emotional. It's enough that I've started speaking to Robin.'

Matt looks dubious. 'I'll think about it. And I'll really try not to pressure you any more. It's only because I'm worried about you.'

'I know. And don't think I'm not grateful. I'm lucky to have you.'

'Yeah, I'm such a catch.' He buffs his nails on his sweatshirt.

I mock punch him. 'I can just as soon change my mind, you know.'

Although things are back on an even keel for now, Matt won't be content with my silence. He'll try to work every last detail out of me. I don't blame him for it; it's just the way he is. Wanting to make everything better for everyone. But his intensity about the situation is driving me deeper into my shell. Making me even more reluctant to confide in him again. Part of the reason for that is because he doesn't believe that Bella is my missing daughter. But he also doesn't have any idea of what it's like to lose a child. He can't comprehend the anguish.

Suddenly I'm hit so hard by the pain I can hardly breathe. It's as though it's happening all over again. The realisation that my baby girl has gone. Fresh as if it was only moments ago. A tear drips. I watch as it falls as though in slow-motion onto the kitchen floor, making a tiny, barely perceptible splash. I turn abruptly and start clearing the kids' bowls away.

'Hey, you okay?' Matt asks warily.

'Yeah, fine, just tired, you know.'

He comes after me and runs his fingertips down my cheek. I wish he would give me some space so I can shake off this sadness before work, but I don't want to hurt his feelings again, so I let myself be soothed, despite the fact that inside I'm twisted up with grief, and still burdened with the desperate need to know about Bella.

After dropping the kids off at school, I park in one of the backstreets behind the café and turn off the car engine. I still have twenty minutes until I'm due at work. Normally I go in early – Dee's always grateful – but today I'm going to make the most of these spare minutes. I unclip my seatbelt and pull my phone from my handbag.

As the rain streams down outside, the windows quickly fog up, obscuring the road, and it feels as though I'm cocooned inside a misty storm cloud. I open Facebook and go straight to Kate's page. This time I ignore the photos and click back to her earliest post four years ago, working my way forward in time.

They're all the usual Facebook fare – funny things her kids have said and done, their achievements and milestones, family holidays, incidents that have annoyed her. There are a few memes about motherhood and some links to yoga sites. She's also shared links to some of her friends' businesses. Kate actually comes across pretty well on social media – not too much of a show-off or a moaner. I take my time, reading each post carefully, and taking special note of the comments.

When I reach her posts from two and a half years ago, it looks as though something traumatic must have happened in her life because a few people were asking Kate how she was doing and saying that if she needed anything she was to let them know. Maybe she had a bereavement? But there's no mention of anyone dying. Frustratingly, there's no mention of *anything* happening – just a few friends offering their support. There's also a post by Kate with a meme that says: *When you're up, your friends know who you are. When you're down, you know who your friends are.*

So something definitely went wrong in her life back then. I scroll forward through the posts, which since that time have become very sparse, until I reach one from a couple of months ago. And I read a comment that makes my blood freeze…

CHAPTER FIFTEEN

Frustratingly, I have no more time to examine Kate's Facebook post and look for further evidence of what I think it might mean. If I don't get out of the car right this minute, I'm going to be late for work. I can't be late again. Dee would not be happy. I slip my phone back into my bag, grab my brolly and leave the damp warmth of the car interior. As I negotiate puddles and pedestrians, I can't stop thinking that the comment could very well lead to the evidence I need to prove that Bella is my daughter.

I get chills when I think that Kate and Shaun were actually in our house. What was I thinking, inviting them over to dinner and into our lives? I wish I didn't have to work this morning so I could get back on social media and dig deeper. But I can't afford to lose my job, so I'll just have to wait. I've been without my daughter for nine years now, I guess a few more days is nothing in comparison. Yet the physical ache in my bones is saying otherwise, the deep yearning to have her back. My pain has been dialled down over the past few years, smothered below the surface. But with the appearance of Bella, it's flaring up again, burning through every cell in my body like a raging fire that won't be put out.

I reach the café, shake out my umbrella and push open the steamed-up door.

'Hi, Rachel.' My boss gives me a warm smile as she deposits an order of beans on toast and a pot of tea in front of Bernie, a regular customer who's in his eighties. He's seated at his usual table by the window. Dee usually serves tea in mugs, but Bernie always likes a cup and saucer.

'Morning, Dee.' I plaster on a smile for my boss. She doesn't need to see my inner turmoil.

'Hope you didn't get too soaked; it's absolutely vile out there.'

'Tell me about it. I almost drowned on my way in.'

She gives me a sympathetic look and then turns back to Bernie. 'Can I get you anything else?'

'No thanks, dear,' he replies. 'I'll just have a sprinkle of pepper.'

'I'll get it,' I say.

I bring over a salt and pepper set from an empty table next to me and place it next to his plate.

'I hope the river isn't going to flood,' Dee says. 'The Environment Agency say they're keeping an eye on it, but they've told us to put out the sandbags just in case. It's already creeping over the causeway.'

Bernie pours his tea with gnarled arthritic fingers. 'If they stopped building on the floodplains, this constant flooding malarkey wouldn't be happening.'

'You're right.' Dee starts wiping down the next table. 'But they're running out of places to build on. Where are all these new families supposed to live?'

'It's simple physics.' Bernie adds a few drops of milk to his cup and then heaps in a large teaspoon of sugar. 'If the excess water can't spill out onto the plains, it'll find another place to go.'

I remember the last time the river flooded. The water surged over its banks and into the car park. We were all holding our breath to see how far it would get. Luckily it didn't reach South Street, but we all pitched in helping the other businesses on the quay clear out their ground floors, just in case.

I make my way through to the back, where I dump my bag in the office and grab an apron. I'm hoping that keeping busy will distract me from this morning's discovery. But I can't stop thinking about that comment on Kate's Facebook page. It's making me feel quite nauseous. As I walk back through the kitchen, the rich scent of frying bacon turns my stomach. Out in the café once more, I start clearing tables and taking orders, being overly attentive and friendly to all the customers to compensate for my dark, anxious mood. My face feels as though it's a mask, my words like they're lines from a play.

After the lunchtime rush, the café quietens down a lot. More than usual in fact. Probably because the awful weather is keeping everyone indoors. The only customers left are a couple dawdling over their lunch, and a table of workmen having coffee and doughnuts. I clear and wipe down all the other tables and sweep the floor until it's spotless. There's half an hour until my shift is due to end and I then have to race over to the school to pick up Charlie and Jess. That leaves me no time to go back on Facebook to analyse that comment and see if there are any other similar ones.

'Dee…'

'Yes, go on, you can go,' she says drily.

I feel simultaneously relieved and guilty. 'Am I that transparent?'

'I don't know what's been up with you these past few days, but there's obviously something you're itching to go and do. So go on.'

'I love you, Dee.'

She rolls her eyes. 'You've worked bloody hard today and it's pretty dead in here now. I might even close up early, go home, run a bubble bath and finish my book.'

'Sounds like heaven. I've just got to run a quick errand before picking the kids up. Is there anything else you need me to do before I go?'

She flicks a wash cloth in my direction. 'No, scoot! Before I change my mind.'

'Thank you.' I blow her a kiss, grab my bag, coat and brolly and head back out into the downpour. I can't believe I managed to get through my shift in one piece. That was the hardest bit of play-acting I've ever had to do. My heart begins to race as I make my way back to the car, barely registering the lashing downpour soaking my jeans and the water running in rivulets down my neck. I use my umbrella as a shield as the rain flies at me sideways.

Finally I reach my Polo and wrestle with my handbag, keys and umbrella until I manage to get myself into the car. Despite the muffled clatter of rain against the windscreen and bonnet, it feels relatively quiet in here. Just the thump of my heart and the sound of my breathing.

I unzip my parka and dry my hands on my sweatshirt before getting my phone out of my bag. I still have around twenty minutes until I need to drive to school so I'd better make it count. When I tap the Facebook icon it opens on exactly the same page where I left it this morning. And there, below Kate's post, is the comment I saw earlier from a woman called Marie Damerham – presumably one of Kate's old friends. I read it again.

Hey, lovely, I hear Shaun gets out next week. Anything you need, let me know.

Shaun gets out.

Those are the words I've been mulling over all morning. The words that have made me sick to my stomach, worrying about what they mean. Did Shaun Morris go to prison? What else could Marie Damerham have meant? I mean, where else would someone go where you could say they 'got out'? A psychiatric unit? Possibly, but prison is what immediately springs to mind. And the fact that this Marie woman is offering her support sounds like it wasn't anywhere good.

If Shaun was in prison, what was he in for? How would I go about finding that out? It could be anything from tax fraud to violent assault.

Again, I think about the fact that he was in my house with our children. What if he has violent tendencies? What if he's a serial offender? He might be really unhinged. Perhaps he took my child all those years ago and is now playing some sick game. My mind keeps jumping from theory to theory… What if Shaun snatched my daughter before he met Kate and then gave Kate some story about being a single father? He could have married Kate, who then raised Holly as her own. So maybe Kate knows nothing about the abduction and it's all Shaun's doing.

I know I'm speculating wildly, and I shouldn't jump to conclusions, but it doesn't look good. I already suspected the Morrises of being child abductors. Knowing Shaun has been inside does nothing to alleviate those fears.

It's crazy that Kate would even leave that comment up on Facebook. If it was *my* page, I would have deleted it as soon as it appeared. Then again, Facebook does have this annoying habit of not showing you everything. Maybe Kate never even saw it. Maybe she has no idea it's there. After all, she didn't reply to it, and she seems to reply to most of her comments.

Thinking about it, it was pretty out of order for her friend to comment on it in the first place. If Shaun did go to prison, Kate didn't mention it anywhere on her page, so for one of her friends to post it up in black and white for all to see feels quite passive-aggressive. Either that, or just plain thoughtless.

I wonder how long Shaun was inside for. I scroll back through Kate's posts once more, and then the notion hits me. He must have been put away around the time Kate's friends were offering her help and sympathy – two and a half years ago. I keep scrolling back until I come to that part of her timeline and begin to re-read the posts with fresh eyes:

Thinking of you, lovely.
Anything I can do to help, give me a call. Happy to have the kiddiwinks if you need a break.
Sending hugs xoxo
Kate, we're all here for you.

Sounds like she had a pretty good support network. Although it's easy enough to type a few helpful lines on social media. Much harder to actually follow through and do something practical. I had the same thing after Holly was taken – people offering to help, but not actually doing anything practical. Don't get me wrong, it was nice to know people were thinking of me, and everyone has their own problems, but true crises really show you who your friends are. It must have been hellish for Kate to have her husband found guilty of a crime and carted off to prison. Not that I can stretch to any sympathy right now.

I open up Kate's friends list to find Shaun. Maybe his page will have more information about what went on. Kate has over a hundred friends, so I start paging down the list, but none of them is Shaun. Maybe he's not the social-media type. Or maybe he removed himself after he was sentenced. Perhaps he did something so bad that he was harassed online. I need to curb my mind jumping off on wild tangents, but it's hard not to try to connect the dots. After finding out about his prison stay, anything is possible where the Morrises are concerned.

I type his name into Facebook's search bar, but there are too many Shaun Morrises to wade through and after several minutes of trawling, I give up – none of them looks or sounds like the Shaun I'm searching for. I try Google next, typing in Shaun's name in the hope that a news story involving him might show up. Once again, there are plenty of Shaun Morrises – sportsmen, artists, musicians and more – but no one that sounds like the Shaun I'm looking for. I get to page ten of the search results and finally stop looking.

I sling my phone onto the passenger seat in frustration, wondering what my next move should be. I'm still too apprehensive to contact the police. They made such a cock-up of the initial abduction investigation that I've lost all trust in them. I don't want them to tip off the Morrises before I've found concrete evidence, in case they do a runner with Holly. No. I'll have to find out what happened some other way. But quite how I do that is another matter...

CHAPTER SIXTEEN

Another morning, another school run, but whereas I usually go about my life with an easy confidence, these days it all feels so different. I have this constant anxiety in my belly and a heavy-as-lead weight in my head. Sometimes I can go for a few minutes without remembering why I feel so odd, but then it all comes rushing back and I get this floundering sensation where I'm not sure whether I'm sad, angry or scared.

Absent-mindedly, I kiss the tops of my children's heads as we reach the playground gates. Charlie gallops in, full of his usual energy, but Jess is downcast, her head bowed, the drizzle making her hair wavier than usual. I want to run after her and give her a hug, but she wouldn't thank me for being so affectionate in front of all the other kids. There's definitely something up with Jess this morning. And she was moody last night as well. I'll have to speak to her tonight. Find out what's going on. It's not like her to be so withdrawn.

With my mind so full of Holly and the Morrises, I've been neglecting Jess and Charlie. I need to spend some good, quality time with them. At least it's the holidays soon so they'll be at home and we can plan some fun activities.

'Rachel, glad I caught you.'

I turn to see Heidi, one of my school-mum friends, her grey eyes and warm smile a welcome sight. 'Heidi! How are you? Feel like I haven't seen you for ages.'

She laughs. 'I'm fine. And I know what you mean. I've been trying to catch you for days. We keep missing one another.'

It's my fault we haven't spoken for a while. I was so obsessed with making friends with Kate that I haven't had time to catch up with my other friends. 'Everything okay with you and Ella?'

'Yes, fine. All a bit manic now that we're getting to the end of term. We've got the Christmas Fayre next week. I wanted to ask – are you able to man one of the stalls for an hour or two? It's after school on Wednesday.' Heidi runs the PTA for Wareham Park Middle School and although she doesn't work, she's always a bit frazzled, as it can be as demanding as a full-time job – especially near the end of term when there are all kinds of fundraising events to organise.

'Yes, sure, I can do a couple of hours. Text me the times you need me.'

'You're a lifesaver.' Heidi exhales. 'Thank you. I thought I had everything covered, but I had a few people drop out last week.'

'I'll ask Matt to help as well, if you need him.'

'Yes please. Amazing.' She puts a hand to her heart. 'You've just saved me a boatload of stress. Thanks, Rachel. Anyway, I've got to go and drop these forms in at the office now, but we'll catch up soon, yes?'

'Definitely.'

I watch her march off towards the school office and then I turn and start heading back to the car, feeling slightly more uplifted. It's amazing how a simple quick conversation with a familiar friend has helped to ground me a little. Set me back into my environment. I've been feeling so unanchored since seeing Bella that I'd almost forgotten how comfortable my life had become. How easy and relaxed. I hope I can go back to that feeling. If I can only get to the bottom of this Bella business and find out who she really is.

A sudden burst of laughter catches my attention. From the corner of my eye, I see a flash of blonde hair, and I know it's Kate before I even check. She's standing over by the far wall, chatting with a group of mums from Charlie and Kieran's class. I know them all well, but I'm reluctant to join them. Nervous I suppose, after what happened on Saturday night. It wasn't quite a falling out, just uncomfortable and awkward. After what I learned about Shaun I also wonder if maybe Kate might be a little dangerous too.

For a split second, Kate turns her head and catches my eye. I can't very well ignore her, so I smile and give a little wave. To my astonishment, she drops eye contact and turns her back on me – a deliberate snub. I'm so astonished I almost give a bark of laughter. 'Cheeky cow,' I murmur to myself and carry on walking down the path and out of the main gates.

Well, at least I know where I stand with her now. I guess I won't be expecting any reciprocal play dates or dinners. I shake my head at the nerve of her, but maybe it's for the best. Ever since I discovered that her husband probably went to prison, I feel uneasy about the couple. In fact, I'd even go as far as to say that the thought of talking to the Morrises turns my stomach.

But for the sake of finding out about Bella, I should have kept things friendly between us. It's my own fault for pushing things too hard. I would never normally have been so intense. But this is *my daughter*. The stakes are high. I guess I'm not as skilled at hiding my feelings as I thought. And the wine certainly didn't help. Too late now. What's done is done. I'll just have to adjust my strategy and find out about Bella some other way.

Later that day, I park a few streets away from St Margaret's Middle School, praying this busy residential street isn't where the Morrises live. That would be just my luck – to accidentally park outside their house and bump into Kate, especially after her pointed snub this morning. I know they live walking distance to Bella's school, but they didn't mention whereabouts, so I have no idea if I'm in the vicinity. Luckily, it's raining again, so I have the hood of my parka up and my umbrella held low over my head. It's almost school pick-up time, so the traffic is heavy and aggressive. Tempers fraying at the lack of nearby parking spaces and the prospect of being late and getting wet.

I walk purposefully towards the unfamiliar school, looking for all the world like just another parent. I called Matt from the café earlier this morning and asked him to pick up Jess and Charlie from school today, telling him that I just remembered I had a dental check-up. As luck would have it, he didn't kick up a fuss, and said it shouldn't be a problem. Even so, I feel bad lying to him. It's not something I'd normally do. But he wouldn't understand if I told him the real reason I'm not doing the school run.

It's bad timing, because I really wanted to pick up Jess today. I'd planned to try to get her to open up about why she's been so down the past couple of days. But it'll just have to wait until I get home. Maybe I'll text Matt to have a word.

Wareham Park finishes a little earlier than St Margaret's, so my kids should be out by now. I slip my phone out of my pocket and text one-handed, almost dropping it a couple of times:

Hey, did u pick the kids up okay?

Yes, we're home. No disasters yet.

Great. Can u check if Jess is okay? She's been a bit down.

No problem. I'll cheer her up. How's the dentist?

On my way there now.

Okay. See you later xx

Guilt kicks in once more. But Matt absolutely wouldn't understand what I'm doing. I'm sure he'd think I was being stalkerish.

On the face of it, I probably am. But it's not *like* that. It's just that I've still only seen Bella the one time and I need to make sure I wasn't imagining the resemblance. I've seen photos of her on Facebook, but that's no substitute for seeing someone in real life. And, if I'm honest with myself, I'm craving another glimpse. How can it be that I'm the one whose daughter was taken, and yet I'm having to behave like a criminal just to see her?

I reach the school entranceway and follow the other parents into the visitors' car park and through a set of double gates. These school grounds aren't as pretty as Wareham Park. St Margaret's seems to be all bricks and concrete. There's hardly any greenery at all, which is a shame. I suddenly realise that it's a mistake to come right into the school grounds, as there are an awful lot of doorways and gates, any of which Bella could come out of. It would be so easy to miss her. I'd be better off standing outside the main gates. That way I should be able to get a look at every child who leaves the school.

The bell shrills long and loud, making me jump. Quickly, I make my way back out of the playground, through the car park and out onto the narrow pavement. I wait for a gap in traffic and cross to the opposite side of the road, watching the gates intently and waiting. I'm not prepared for the sheer volume of people streaming out of the grounds. Plus, everyone is so bundled up against the weather, I can barely see their faces, let alone hair and eye colour.

I tell myself to calm down. That I'll know her when I see her. There's a row of dogs tied up on the railings outside school and a congregation of parents and children gather in a cluster to pet or untie them. It's blocking my view of the gates and making me even more anxious. I glance around, wondering if there's a place to stand that might afford me a better view, but wherever I am, it will be impossible to keep an eye on every individual child. Now I've glanced away from the gates, I'm paranoid I might have missed Bella.

And then I see her.

Tall, willowy, beautiful. Surrounded by three tween girls who seem to bask in her glow. I can't believe I was worrying about not being able to spot her. No one could mistake her. My heart slows and I can barely breathe. That girl is my Holly. I'm sure of it. I'm *convinced* of it. She turns left out of the gates, waves goodbye to two of the girls and links arms with the other, who's small and slender with long blonde hair that reaches right down her back. Both girls' skirts are hitched up way too short – I'm sure they'll unroll them before they get home, because I don't know any parent who'd let their eleven- or twelve-year-old daughter walk around like that.

I follow at a distance, wishing I could see her face again. The yearning for her radiates out from the core of my body through to my fingertips and toes. I never believed my daughter was dead. I always thought she was out there somewhere, waiting for me to come and rescue her. To think that I might have found her is so bittersweet. I've lost all those important years. Years where she's forgotten me. Where she's not even aware of who she really is. That she has a biological family who would love her so much more than this fake, undeserving one. But I can't even tell her about us. Not yet.

The girls are walking in the opposite direction to where I parked my car, so at least I know I didn't end up in the Morrises' road. Unless Bella is going to her friend's house. But as the two of them reach the end of the street, they hug and break off in different directions. I follow Bella, who speeds up now that she's alone. Dusk is falling and she suddenly looks quite vulnerable walking along on her own. The school crowds have thinned and there are only one or two other people around now.

I close the gap between us so we're only a couple of hundred yards apart. I won't get any closer, but the unfairness of my situation hits me again. This child in front of me should be one of the closest people in my life. Instead, she's a stranger. She probably wouldn't even recognise me from last week's brief encounter. Yet I carried her in my belly. Nursed her. Bathed her. Kissed her. Held her. And now… now I mean nothing to her.

This line of thinking isn't getting me anywhere. I can't let myself wallow in self-pity. Proof is what I need. Proof. But how do I get it? I think it must all be tied up with Shaun's prison stay. I need to discover more about that.

Bella turns into another road. It's a housing estate that's never seen better days and probably never will. She hunches her shoulders, keeps her head down and walks even faster now, almost running. I do the same. Despite the drizzle and chilly temperature, I'm sweating beneath my coat.

Bella jogs towards what looks like a low block of flats on the other side of the road. It's built from a brownish brick, with four small windows on the ground floor and four on the first floor. She crosses a narrow path that runs along a scrubby patch of grass and heads into a recessed stairwell illuminated by a security light that flashes on as she approaches. The walls inside the stairwell are covered in multicoloured graffitied tags. She disappears from view but I'm pretty sure she didn't go up the stairs.

Sure enough, one of the downstairs lights in the flat flashes on and I see Bella standing at a kitchen table, talking on her phone. She must be home alone. I have to say, I'm quite surprised that she lives here. The Morrises both gave the impression of having money – I know they said they're renting temporarily but I'd have thought they'd be in a larger property in a nicer area, even for the short-term. Not that someone's postcode bothers me at all, it's just the impression I got from them.

I really should go now. Kate will probably be back soon with Amy and Kieran, and it would never do for her to see me standing here outside their flat. I don't know how I would even begin to explain myself. But I can't seem to tear my gaze away from Bella, her long hair falling forward as she moves around the kitchen, getting a drink of water and snacks from the cupboards. I want to tell her to draw the curtains, that she doesn't know who could be watching her. But I'm glad they're open for now, letting me catch a last look at her before I head home.

I'm absolutely convinced that Bella is my missing daughter. But I need to talk to her, to really connect with her to see if we have that mother–daughter bond. That way, I'll know for certain.

CHAPTER SEVENTEEN

THEN

'Catriona, I don't know what the hell is going on here, but you're really starting to freak me out.' Shadows settle on her boyfriend's face. Dark hollows that Catriona has never seen before. They scare her because she knows that they will only grow deeper and darker. She knows that those shadows are mirrored in her heart. He's running his hands through his hair and his eyes are becoming wild and unfocused. '*Who* is that girl in Gracie's bed? And where the hell is our daughter?'

He's never sworn at her before. It's shocking to hear that word directed in anger at her. 'Darren, I don't know what you're—'

'Don't say you don't know what I'm talking about. Do not say that.'

'But I—'

'Catriona, look at me.'

She senses his eyes boring into her, but she doesn't want to look him in the eye, because then he'll know. He'll see she's lying. And yet the lie isn't even the worst of it.

Darren takes a firm hold of her chin and tilts her face up to his. Stares at her until she succumbs and finally returns his gaze. In his eyes she sees confusion, anger and… yes… *fear*. She doesn't want to tell him the truth. Doesn't want to destroy his life. Why can't he just go along with her? It would be so much better for all of them if he could just accept what she's telling him. Can't he understand that she's only lying to protect them both?

'Where. Is. Grace?'

Catriona angrily jerks her face out of his grasp and tenses her shoulders, ready to trot out her prepared responses with exasperation. But she suddenly finds that she can't keep it up. Her shoulders sag, and slowly she crumples to the ground, covering her head with her arms and letting out a moan that wells up from her core. A guttural inhuman sound that she's never made before. Not even when she was giving birth. This pain is far, far worse.

'Caty, you're scaring me! Caty!' Darren sinks down on the ground and tries to peel her arms away from her head.

'No, no. Don't ask me. Don't talk about it. Please. Please.' She knows that once she says the words out loud, then that will make it real. The lie will disappear and all that will be left is horror and emptiness and the end of everything good. 'Darren, I'm telling you, that little girl in there… it's Grace. It's our daughter. Please believe me.'

'I know something's happened, but I need you to tell me what it is. And I need you to tell me now.'

'I can't.' Salty tears run into her mouth. 'Don't make me.'

'You have to tell me where our daughter is! Tell me!'

'No, no, no.' Her body is so heavy. She sinks lower, wishing she could disappear into the foundations of the building and never surface again.

'Caty!'

A sharp sting on her cheek jolts Catriona from her despair for a blissful shocking instant.

Darren's warm palm returns to caress the skin he slapped only a second ago. 'I'm sorry I had to do that, Caty, but you need to pull yourself together and start talking.' He pauses. 'Or I'm going to have to call the police to report her missing.'

At his mention of the police, Catriona sits a little more upright. Once the authorities become involved, then there will be no hope at all. Perhaps, if she can explain it well enough to Darren now, then he will go along with it. Once she gives him her reasoning. If she can make him *see*. 'Darren,' she murmurs with a gulp, 'something terrible has happened.'

'Where's Grace?'

'Gracie… she… she had an accident.'

Darren jerks to his feet as though electrocuted. 'An accident? What kind of accident? Where is she now? The hospital?'

Catriona flinches and shakes her head.

'She's still in the flat then?'

She stares up at him, trying to process his words.

He glances wildly around. 'Grace! Gracie!' Darren staggers across the hall and into the sitting room. Catriona scrabbles to her feet and follows behind, her mind and body tingling with numbness. He pulls back the curtains and shifts the sofa. Peers in every nook and cranny of the small lounge, even though it's blindingly obvious that their daughter isn't in the room. He does the same in their bedroom. Examining the interior of the wardrobe and sliding partway under the bed, looking behind the curtains. He even yanks the drawers out from their runners, frantically looking, looking, looking. Trashing their room in the process 'Where's our daughter, Caty? What have you done with her? What did you DO?'

CHAPTER EIGHTEEN

NOW

I barely remember making my way home. My head was so full of Bella. Seeing her there alone in her kitchen, thinking she could really be my Holly. I keep flipping between believing that she's mine, to thinking that I'm wrong and I'm fixating on a wish rather than a reality. But each time I've laid eyes on her I've had this knee-jerk physical reaction. A shocking hit of adrenalin that leaves me breathless. When I see her I'm certain, but when I'm away from her there's still a tiny seed of doubt wriggling beneath my skin. Until I get hard evidence one way or the other, I won't be able to rest.

I turn left into our road and see that there are no parking spaces outside our house, so I cruise down the street, finally spotting one right at the end. I turn off the engine and take a moment to compose myself before getting out of the car and trudging up the road towards the house. It seems familiar and different all at once. Bella's house is only a ten-minute drive away from here, yet it feels as though I've been to the ends of the earth and back, mentally as well as physically.

I steel myself at the door, knowing I have to go in and keep up the charade that I was at the dentist. Finally inside, I feel the warmth of our home wrap itself around me. I'm relieved to be back, yet also feeling strangely guilty at my relief. Like I don't deserve to be here. Like I should be doing more to discover Bella's real identity.

'Hello!' I call out.

There's a low murmur of voices from upstairs.

'Hello! Matt?' I peer up the stairs.

A door opens above me. 'Rach? That you?'

'Hi, yes. Everyone okay?' I kick of my shoes and hang my damp coat up on the hook. I'm about to head up there when Matt appears on the stairs. He casts a worried glance over his shoulder and then points down towards the lounge, gesturing for us to go in. Once we're in the room, he closes the door behind us quietly.

'What's wrong?' I'm a little unnerved by his actions. 'Are the kids okay?'

He gives a non-committal waggle of his head. 'It's Jess.'

'What's happened?' I make a move towards the door, wanting to immediately go up and see her, but Matt shakes his head. My skin goes cold. 'What? Tell me what's wrong. Is she hurt?'

Matt puts a finger to his lips with a meaningful look up at the ceiling. 'No, no, nothing like that. She's upstairs, she's fine. Well, not fine exactly.'

'What is it then?' I calm down a little and perch on one of the sofa arms, waiting for him to enlighten me.

'Well, you were right about her mood. I went to pick them up from school and Charlie was his usual crazy, happy self, but Jess barely said two words to me. I tried to tease her out of it but that went down like a lead balloon. She gave me some serious shade, so I thought I'd leave her be until we got home.'

'But did you find out what's wrong?'

'She went straight up to her room, so I brought her up a snack and sat on her bed. Took me a while to prise it out of her, but apparently Kate and Shaun's daughter – I think her name's Amy?'

I nod.

'Yeah, well, this Amy was supposedly her new best friend, and now she won't even talk to her. But Jess said she hasn't done anything wrong and doesn't know why Amy's giving her the cold shoulder.'

My heart drops and I suddenly feel exhausted. 'This is probably my fault.'

'How can it be your fault?'

'Kate probably told her to stay away from Jess.'

Matt frowns. 'Why would she do that?'

'You know – after dinner-gate on Saturday. Me asking about her daughter Bella and the both of them taking offence.'

'Oh.' Matt's expression drops further. 'Yeah, maybe. But more likely it's just kids' stuff. I mean, it's not like Jess has never fallen out with any of her friends before. And it seems a bit of an extreme thing for Kate to do.'

'I know. But it's a bit coincidental that one minute Jess and Amy are the best of friends and then, straight after the weekend, Amy cuts Jess out. Plus, this morning, I saw Kate and she turned her back on me.'

Matt's eyes widen. 'What do you mean?'

I get to my feet and roll my shoulders back and forth, trying to loosen the kinks in my neck. 'She was talking to some of the school mums and I caught her eye. I smiled and waved, but she blanked me. She actually turned away so she couldn't see me any more.'

'That's awful! Are you sure she actually saw you though? Maybe it was just a coincidence that she moved at the same time you saw her.'

'No, she definitely saw me. I caught her eye and her expression changed for a split second.'

'What a cow. Sounds like you and Jess could both do with a hug.'

I step into his arms for a brief moment and then pull away. 'I'll go up and see her. Were you just with her now, before I came back?'

'No. She said she wanted to be on her own, so I was helping Charlie with his maths homework.'

'All right. I'll go up and see how she's doing before making tea.'

'How was the dentist? Sorry, forgot to ask.'

'The what? Oh, yeah. Fine. It was just a check-up.' I hope he doesn't notice the sudden warmth in my cheeks. I've never been a very good liar.

As I climb the stairs, I berate myself for chasing after Bella while Jess has been here feeling so awful. I should have been at home with her, listening and comforting her. But how can I choose between my two daughters? Just because Holly hasn't been in my life for years, doesn't mean she's any less important to me. I really can't shake the feeling that Bella is Holly. And I owe it to myself – and to her – to find out if it's true.

CHAPTER NINETEEN

'Come on, guys, quick, quick, out of the car!' I push my hair from my eyes as the wind whips it around my face, damp strands clinging to my skin like seaweed to a rock.

'Mu-um, why can't we just go home?' Jess is giving me side-eye and being particularly grumpy.

'Close the door and come on! The quicker we go, the quicker we can go back home.'

'Fine.' Jess slams her door with a scowl. I really must have words with her about her increasingly bad attitude, but I'm putting it down to all this nonsense with Amy. We spoke about it last night – admittedly not for long because Jess said it made her too upset to talk about it. Apparently Amy isn't being mean, she's just not being friendly. So I told Jess to give her some space and play with her other friends instead.

'Here's a brolly.' I hand it to Jess and she perks up a little. She likes umbrellas for some reason.

'Can I have a brolly?' Charlie asks.

'You can stand under mine,' I reply.

'Can I hold it?'

'Sorry, Charlie, but you're a bit too short. I'd have to walk on my knees to fit underneath it.'

'I can stand on tiptoes.'

'Aw, Charlie, you are funny sometimes.'

'He can have mine,' Jess says grudgingly.

I smile inwardly. She's a good kid really. Jess hands her umbrella to Charlie and I beckon her closer to shelter with me.

'Why are we here?' Charlie asks.

I take his hand and try to be calm yet cheerful – hard to do, as I'm already soaked through and my heart is going like the clappers. I should have aborted this trip as soon as I saw the storm warning, but I just couldn't bear to wait another day. 'I told you, Charlie. We're going to have a look at St Margaret's Upper School, because Jess might be going there after she leaves middle school.'

'I don't want to go here.' Jess crosses her arms over her chest and stomps along beside me, back to being grumpy again. 'I want to go to Wareham Park Upper School like all my friends.'

'You probably will go there, but it doesn't hurt to take a look at St Margaret's too. It's got an outstanding OFSTED report.'

'What's an Office report?' Charlie asks.

'OFSTED, not office. It means it's a really good school.' I actually have no intention of sending Jess here, but I needed an excuse to come back to see Bella, and I couldn't ask Matt to get off work early again. Plus, with the kids in tow it might be easier to talk to her.

I've parked halfway between school and the Morrises' flat this time. That way, I could offer Bella a lift back home. I push down the voice that's telling me I'm going way too far with this. Because that voice isn't taking into account that I have just as much of an obligation to take care of my eldest daughter as I do my other two children. When I finally prove that Bella is indeed Holly, my dubious actions won't seem dubious any more. They will be the actions of a wronged mother determined to get her daughter back.

'Mind that puddle,' I warn.

'Anyway, Mum' – Jess ignores me, walking straight through the puddle, soaking her shoes and socks – 'we don't have to go to upper school for ages.'

'It doesn't hurt to be prepared. It'll come around soon enough.'

She huffs but doesn't protest about it any more. 'My feet are wet.'

'I told you to mind the puddle. Don't worry, we won't be here for long. You can dry off when we get home.'

As we keep walking, I have to keep telling myself that this is necessary. This is what anyone would do if they were in my situation. I'm not doing anything wrong; I'm simply making sure that my suspicions are correct. Thankfully, I don't feel quite as conspicuous as I did yesterday; not now I have my children with me.

'The upper school's that way.' Jess points to a huge sign pointing down one of the side roads.

'That way's for cars,' I say, thinking on my feet. 'There's a quicker route by foot.'

'Why didn't we drive there?' Jess asks.

'It's too busy round here at the moment. School pick-up time.'

'So why didn't we—'

'Jess, please, can you just be quiet for a few minutes while I work out where we're going?'

'I thought you knew where you were going,' she mutters under her breath.

We carry on battling our way through the wind and the rain, Charlie's umbrella periodically bashing me in the arm. But at least he seems pretty happy, so I don't mind. Eventually, we reach Bella's school building. We're a little late though and there's already a stream of children spilling out through the gates. I curse under my breath and try not to panic. *Please don't let me have missed her.* I debate whether or not to leave the school gates and walk in the direction of her house, in case she's already left, and we can catch her up. But while I'm having that internal conversation, I spot her with the same three friends again.

'Oh look.' I nudge Jess. 'There's Amy's sister.' I point to Bella, who's already halfway down the road.

'Who?' Jess replies.

'You remember Amy's sister, Bella? Come on, let's catch her up.' I keep hold of Charlie's hand and begin jogging down the road, kicking up spray.

'I thought we were supposed to be going to the—'

'Come on! Catch up!' I cry, glancing back to see that Jess has stopped and is staring after me in sullen bewilderment.

Reluctantly, Jess follows. A stab of guilt hits me as I realise my kids must be tired after school, and here I am dragging them around in the rain. But Bella could very well be their older sibling. That's an incredible thought. It's a thought I hold on to as we tear down the road.

At the corner, Bella parts ways from her blonde-haired friend, who isn't wearing a coat and is already absolutely drenched. Bella puts her hood up and continues on her way, not hurrying in the slightest, as though the weather is of no consequence.

Jess, Charlie and I finally reach her, but I wait to catch my breath before saying anything. I haven't planned how to start our conversation because I figured inspiration would hit me when I came to it. We're right behind her now and as we pass by, I tap her on the shoulder.

'Hello. It's Bella isn't it?' I give her a friendly smile.

She stares at me warily. And then transfers her gaze to Jess and Charlie.

'I'm a friend of your mum's. We met briefly last week outside Amy's school. Jess and Amy are in the same class. I'm Rachel.'

'Oh… yeah.' Bella frowns and chews her lip, looking like she's about to walk off at any second. I'll have to try to keep her talking for a minute. I have to get past this superficial chit-chat.

'We were going to have a look at the upper school for Jess, but the weather's so awful I think we'll leave it for another day.'

'So we're not going?' Jess brightens.

'Not today, no.'

'Yes!' Jess gives me her first smile of the day.

'You're starting here?' Bella asks Jess.

'Just thinking about it,' I reply for her.

'Oh, Jess, you'll love it.' Bella's features suddenly come alive and I get goosebumps yet again at how exactly like my Holly she is. To my surprise, she links arms with Jess, and we all start walking along together. My heart swells and lifts as though it's been pumped full of summer sunshine. It's all I can do to restrain myself from throwing my arms around Bella and hugging her tightly.

'Do you like it here then?' Jess asks.

'It's amazing. I've only been here a few days, but I've made so many friends, and the teachers are okay too. It's way better than my last school.' Bella picks up her pace, seemingly relaxed in our company. The two of them have their heads together now, chatting and giggling as though they've known one another all their lives. They're oblivious to me and Charlie, but I don't mind. It's just wonderful to see the two of them getting on. It bodes well for any future changes that might occur…

As we walk, I'm happy Jess and Bella are getting on so well – of course I am – but this isn't really helping me to get to know her. I can't very well interrupt them. They're talking about things so far out of my orbit that if I joined in the conversation she'd think I was just another dorky parent.

We're nearly at the car now and I'm worried about offering her a lift. Is that crossing a line? Or am I just doing the decent thing by giving her some shelter from the storm? I know that's not the main reason I'm offering, but if she's my daughter then why shouldn't I offer her a lift? My thinking is becoming muddled so I have to give myself a shake.

'What are you doing, Mum?' Charlie asks, bringing me back to reality.

'Shaking the rain off.'

'Like a dog?'

'Yes, exactly like that.'

He laughs and starts pretending to be a dog, barking and panting and leaping around like a puppy.

Jess and Bella are so deep in conversation that Jess has walked straight past our car. 'Jess, hang on! We're parked here.'

Jess turns and looks from me to the car with disappointment on her face.

'Let me know if you do end up starting at St Margaret's,' Bella says to Jess. 'You can message me, and I'll look out for you.'

Jess beams, thrilled that this cool older girl likes her enough to keep in contact. 'Can we give Bella a lift home, Mum?'

I could kiss Jess for making this so easy. 'Um, yeah, I suppose so. If she wants.' I turn to Bella with a questioning smile.

'Is that okay?' she asks shyly.

'Of course, no problem. You'll have to direct me.'

She nods.

'Okay, well, let's get in out of this rain.' I unlock the car. 'Bella, if you hop in the front seat I'll put your bag in the boot.'

She does as I say while Charlie and Jess get in the back. Although now Jess is saying that she wants to sit next to Bella.

'It's too wet to start switching places. Just stay where you are for now.' I put Bella's bag in the boot along with my umbrella and slide into the driver's seat. I'm so wet that I actually squelch as I sit down.

'Okay, Bella, which way's home?'

She starts pointing out which roads I should go down and it's hard not to feel like a fraud, having to pretend that I wasn't here only yesterday.

'Are your mum and dad okay?' I ask.

'Fine.' She seems to have gone shy again now it's just her and me in the front. Her easy confidence with Jess hasn't transferred over to me.

I also get the feeling that she'll tell her parents about our encounter today. Kate won't like it one bit. I'm actually really anxious about her finding out, but I can't exactly tell Bella not to mention it. That will sound really suspicious. My worry is that if she tells her mum, Kate might forbid her from talking to me again. Which means that this could be my one and only opportunity to talk to Bella before the truth all comes out about who she really is.

What should I do? I could take a few wrong turns to delay our time together. But that won't work, because she's doing too good a job of directing me.

'It's left here,' Bella says, pointing ahead.

The only other way is to be direct. Thankfully the storm outside is so loud and the windscreen wipers so frantic that Charlie and Jess can barely hear us from the back seat. Before I can talk myself out of it, I open my mouth and start speaking.

'So, do you like your new home?'

'S'okay.'

'I bet it's good to have your dad back though,' I say, feeling like an utter, utter bitch. I snatch a quick glance to see Bella's expression and am rewarded to see her flush deeply. It's a strange feeling, because the last thing I want is to make her uncomfortable, but I also need to know what's going on with Shaun.

'I… I thought no one here knew about that.' Bella starts chewing the skin around her thumbnail.

'Don't worry. I won't say anything to anyone.'

She looks like she might cry. 'It wasn't Dad's fault, you know.'

'Of course it wasn't. Sorry, I shouldn't have brought it up.' I feel like crying myself for making her feel so miserable, but I need to know that Bella is safe. That Shaun isn't violent or anything worse. 'Look, don't mention to your mum and dad that I said anything. I don't want them to feel bad.' She'll probably still tell them, but it's worth a shot.

Luckily, Jess leans forward and starts talking to Bella about school again, which distracts her from my comment about her dad. At least I *hope* it distracts her.

Seeing the state she's now in, there's no way I can ask Bella what her dad was in for, not without upsetting her further, and that's the last thing I want. But it's killing me not to know.

I'll have to find out some other way.

CHAPTER TWENTY

As we turn into Bella's street, I slow the car down, pretending I don't know which one is her house.

'You can drop me here,' she says before we're even halfway down the street.

'It's still pouring,' I reply. 'I'll drop you right outside. Which one's yours?'

Bella gives a cross between a sigh and a huff. 'It's that one.' She points to the squat block of flats at the end.

I cruise down and park as close to the entrance as I can get. I realise I have literally seconds before Bella gets out of the car and leaves, and I don't know when I'll get to see her again. My heart is sick with longing and despair. 'I don't suppose… is there any chance I could quickly use your bathroom?'

Bella inhales. I can't tell if she's annoyed or just breathing. 'Uh, yeah, okay.'

'Thank you so much. I'll literally be two minutes. Shouldn't have had that cup of tea before I left.' I turn to Jess and Charlie in the back seat. 'Wait here, you two. Just nipping in to use the loo. I'll be two ticks.'

'Can I come?' Jess asks.

'No, just wait here. I'm going to lock the car door behind me.'

Bella and I get out of the car. I open the boot and pass her her school bag, then we make a run for the building as the rain pelts us. I follow her into the stairwell, the security light almost blinding me on our way through. As we run in, I can't help imagining that this is our flat and we're running home together out of the storm. That we're going inside to get warm and dry and maybe have a chat about her day and then watch a movie. After years of missing my daughter, this is all I've ever wanted. My heart suddenly feels so full of pain and love that it hurts.

There are two wooden doors ahead of us with security-glass panels. She goes to the one on the left and rummages in the front of her bag for her key. She opens the door and I follow her into the dark hallway. She switches on the light and it's actually really nice inside – white and fresh and stylish, decorated in a minimalist Scandinavian kind of vibe.

Bella puts her key on the hall table and points to a door on the left. 'The bathroom's there.'

'Sorry about this.' I give her an apologetic smile, wishing I could think of something witty or interesting to say, but my mind is coming up blank. I go into the bathroom and lock the door behind me. I lean against it, racking my brains to think of something, anything that will help me to connect with her. To help me find out the truth. But I can't think of anything. And I know I'm playing with fire here. Kate will probably be home at any minute. I clench my fists in frustration and feel like screaming. Instead, I flush the loo, run the tap and unlock the door.

The hallway's empty.

'Thanks, Bella!' I call out. 'I'll shoot off now.'

One of the doors at the end of the hall opens. Bella steps out of what I presume is her bedroom. She's brushing her hair with a green hairbrush. 'Sorry, I was just sorting out my hair. It's a right mess.'

'It's not, it's lovely. But you should definitely get into some dry clothes and dry your hair properly.' I realise how parent-ish I sound.

She gives me a strange look and I can't say I blame her – after all, who the hell am I to tell her how to look after herself? But at least she nods. The thing is, I can't help myself – I don't want her catching a chill. I'm so desperate for Bella to like me that I'm not sure how to act around her – what if she really is my daughter? It kills me that I have to be so restrained and act like I don't care.

'Okay, well, I'll be off.'

'Thanks for the lift,' she says, and I'm touched by her politeness. Not all kids would remember to say thank you.

'Any time.'

I walk back down the hall and turn back to give her one last smile before leaving the flat. But she's gone back into her room and the hallway is empty. I swallow the lump in my throat and leave, closing the door behind me.

Holding the lighted match against the scrunched-up paper, I wait for the flame to catch, watching as a thin line of smoke curls upwards and flattens against the top of the burner.

'How's that hot chocolate?' I smile at the appreciative noises behind me. As soon as the kids and I got home, we stripped off our sodden clothes, took it in turns to have hot showers and then changed into our pyjamas and dressing gowns. I made them an early tea of fish-finger sandwiches, and now we're having hot chocolate with marshmallows and sprinkles while I get the wood burner going.

I'm still worried about what Bella might say to Kate about our encounter today. The flames take hold of the paper and I wait for the kindling to catch before putting a small log into the burner and sitting back on my haunches.

'Do you think Bella will tell Amy that she likes me?' Jess asks, her voice small and hopeful. 'Maybe now she'll want to be my friend again.'

I sigh. 'Maybe. But I think it's better if you do what we said and hang out with some of your other friends for now.' I get to my feet and sit next to her on the sofa.

'But she was going to be my BFF. She promised.'

'I know. Sometimes things don't work out the way we want. Maybe it's for the best.' I hate it when people say that, but I can't think of anything better right now.

Jess puts her hot chocolate down on the side table. 'Why is it for the best? It's *not* the best.'

I put my arm around Jess and pull her in close. She's warm and dry and smells of shampoo and shower gel.

'Mum… you didn't answer my question.'

'Sorry, Jess. I don't know, maybe she wouldn't have ended up being a good friend, so it's better you found out now.'

'Doesn't Amy like you any more?' Charlie asks.

'It's none of your business!' Jess glares at him.

'Hey, hey, calm down. He's only asking.' Jess's body is tense and bristling. I give her another gentle hug, but she shifts away from me with a scowl, planting herself at the far edge of the sofa, her chin in her hand.

The lounge door opens, and Matt pops his head round. Good. Now he's home, hopefully he can distract Jess from her disintegrating mood.

'Daddy!' Charlie zooms across the room and Matt scoops him up, blowing a raspberry on his cheek. 'Urgh, Dad!'

Matt grins and sets him back down. 'What's going on in here? Are you all having a hot-chocolate pyjama party without me?'

'Want me to make you one?' I ask.

'Uh, yeah!'

'You have to get in your pjs first,' Charlie cries.

I can tell that Jess is torn between joining in with the fun and holding onto her bad mood. Thankfully, the former wins and we spend the next hour having a relatively stress-free time.

Once the kids are in bed, Matt and I sit in the lounge, our dinners on our laps, watching *Grand Designs* on catch-up. A couple in Scotland are building a six-bedroom contemporary house by a lake. It's huge – more like a visitor centre than a home.

'Jess seemed a bit happier this evening,' Matt says, muting the volume as the credits roll.

'She's okay. Still a little down, but she'll be fine. How was work?'

'Fine. This week's going really quickly. Can't believe it's Wednesday already.'

'Oh, that reminds me – I've volunteered us both for the Christmas Fayre at school next week. Hope that's okay?' I get to my feet and collect up our empty dinner plates and glasses.

'Should be. What time and what day?'

'A week today, four till seven. We only need to help out for an hour or two.'

'Okay. I should be able to get there by five.'

'Brilliant. Heidi will be chuffed.' As I leave the sitting room with the dirty dishes, I think about how everything I do now is overlaid with thoughts of Bella. She has a bearing on every action and every conversation.

I dump the plates in the sink and return to the lounge. Make myself comfy on the sofa before speaking. Matt is scrolling through the TV menu, trying to find something good to watch.

I clear my throat. 'I found out something this week.'

'Oh yeah?' Matt's only half listening. He's clicking on the trailer for some violent action thriller that I already know I won't want to watch.

'You know Shaun Morris?' I begin.

'Mm.'

'He's just got out of prison.'

Matt puts down the remote and turns to me. 'Really? What was he in for?'

'I'm not sure.'

'That must have been tough on the family.'

'I know.' I wonder how the kids coped with it all. They seem happy enough now, but it must have been a traumatic time.

'How do you know he was inside?' Matt frowns. 'Did Kate tell you?'

'No, she's not speaking to me, remember?'

'Still? So did someone else tell you? Because you know it might not be true…'

I don't want to admit that I've been snooping on Facebook and I certainly don't want to tell Matt I mentioned it to Bella. I'm only glad that Jess didn't say anything this evening. Matt already thinks I'm mistaken about Bella. 'I saw something about it on one of Kate's Facebook posts. It popped up on my feed.'

'What? She put it on Facebook? That's a bit weird. You'd think they'd want to keep something like that quiet.'

'*She* didn't put it on there. Someone commented that he was "getting out".'

'Maybe you misread it?'

I pick up my phone and open up Facebook. 'I'll show you.' I go onto Kate's page but for some reason I can't see any of her posts. 'There's something wrong with this. Hang on a sec.' I spend a couple of minutes logging out and then logging back in, but I still can't see any of Kate's posts. I click on another friend's profile page and find that I can see all *her* posts fine. So why can't I…? Then it hits me – Kate must have unfriended me, which is why her posts are now hidden. *Shit.*

Now I'm worried that Bella must have told Kate about our conversation. And as a consequence, Kate has unfriended me. It's too much of a coincidence to be anything other than that. I wonder if Kate will confront me about it. I need to come up with an answer that won't make me sound like some crazy stalker. Should I be the one to confront her? Speak to Kate about Bella? No. Not yet. I need more proof and I don't want to scare the Morrises away. They might leave the area and then I'd lose Holly all over again.

'Have you found it?' Matt leans across to look at the screen.

'I think she's unfriended me.'

'Wow, that's a bit harsh.' Matt's expression darkens. 'All because of what happened on Saturday night? I didn't think what you said was *that* bad. Maybe a little intense, but not actively rude or anything.'

'I think it's because she knows I'm on to her. She knows I suspect about Bella.'

Matt doesn't reply.

'What do you think?' I press.

'Rach, don't take this the wrong way, but I really don't think Kate took your daughter. Can't you see how much of a crazy coincidence that would be?'

'Doesn't make it impossible though.'

'No. No, you're right. Not impossible. But I'm worried that you're not seeing things straight. That you might be fixating on it too much. Don't get me wrong, I totally understand why you'd think it. Honestly, I'm a bit worried about you.'

'What would you do if it were Charlie who went missing?' I know I've asked him this before, but sometimes I think people don't realise what it's like. How you would do anything. How you would grasp on to even the tiniest shred of hope.

'I know. I'm sorry.' Matt scratches the stubble on his chin. 'Have you booked another appointment with Robin?'

His question annoys me. The fact he believes I can be cured of my suspicions by talking things through with an 'expert'. 'I'm seeing him again next Monday.'

'Okay. Well that's good.' He relaxes back into the sofa.

But speaking to Robin won't change the fact that Bella is the spitting image of Holly. That Kate is acting really suspiciously. And that Shaun has spent time in prison, for goodness sake. There's something not right with the Morrises. And I'm sure it's got something to do with me and my daughter.

CHAPTER TWENTY-ONE

THEN

Catriona and Darren stand beneath the white paper lampshade in their bedroom, the only thing still intact after the mess he's just created while searching for their daughter. Darren's hands grip her shoulders, his ragged breath hot on her face. His own face is white with fear and anger. It's a side of him she's never seen before. It's a side of him that should scare her. But it doesn't. She understands it. She feels it herself.

'If you don't tell me where our daughter is, I swear... I'll...' He exhales, shakes his head and releases her shoulders. 'Don't make me do something I shouldn't.' His voice breaks.

'It was an accident, Darren. A terrible accident.' Her voice is devoid of emotion now, as though she's reading from a script.

'Tell me.' He sits heavily on the edge of their double bed, as though his legs can't hold him upright any more, and stares down into his lap.

Catriona walks away from him towards the wall, where she splays her hands against the grubby cream paintwork for a moment before dropping them to her sides and turning back around.

'Gracie... she got a bit mucky after her lunch – she had tomato sauce all over her face, in her hair. Such a messy eater.' Catriona risks a glance at Darren, but his head is still bowed so she carries on. 'I decided to give her an early bath with all her toys to play with – the stacking cups and all her little play characters. Of course, you know what she's like – screamed blue murder about getting in, and then once she was in there having a lovely time with her toys, she didn't want to get out. So I thought I'd drain most of the water and leave her to play for a bit longer while I did the washing up.'

Darren raises his head slowly. 'You left her in the bath? By herself?'

'The water wasn't deep. Only a few inches. Honestly, it only just covered her legs. And she was so happy in there pretending to be the Little Mermaid. I… I didn't realise she was in any danger. I didn't *know*!'

Darren gets to his feet and runs both hands through his hair. 'What happened?'

'I… I finished washing up – it only took me a few minutes – and I went back in to check that she wasn't getting too cold. And…' Catrina's mouth stays open. She can't finish the sentence. All she can see in her mind is her daughter's pale body face down in the water. Unmoving. 'I don't know how it could have happened! *I don't know!*

'How *what* happened? *What?*' Darren cries. 'Was she injured? Not breathing? Did you check her pulse? Call an ambulance? WHAT HAPPENED? I need you to spell it out for me, Catriona. Where is our daughter?'

'Don't shout at me! Please! I can't think straight. I can't… I can't…'

Darren clenches his fists and for a moment, Catriona thinks he's going to hit her. Not that this worries her. She deserves it. It's all her fault. She didn't keep their daughter safe.

But Darren relaxes his hands and steps away from her. Sits back down on the bed and starts to cry, which is far worse than his anger. 'Please,' he whispers, shaking. 'Tell me exactly what happened.'

'She drowned.' Catriona's voice is flat.

'No,' Darren sobs.

'She's gone, Darren. Our baby is gone.' Catriona stands there helplessly.

'The paramedics… couldn't they save her? Did they try? Did *you* try?'

'I did. I tried. But she was already… she was gone.' Saying the words out loud doesn't make it seem any more real. She has to get him to see that she has a solution.

'How do you *know* she was gone?' he spits. 'You're not trained. Maybe you just needed to do CPR on her, and she would've been fine. Oh God, it's too late. Is she at the hospital? Did they take her away? Do we need to go there now? I can't believe this is happening. Our beautiful girl. *Why?* You should have called me. Why didn't you call me?'

'I'm so sorry, Darren,' she cries. 'I'm so, so sorry.' She kneels before him and lays her head on his lap, hugging his legs. He stiffens at first, and then folds himself down on top of her and they sob together. Racking, terrifying, out-of-control sobs that do nothing to lessen the pain.

After a while, when her eyes are raw and her skin dried out from the tears, she slides away from him and sits back on her haunches. 'Darren,' she says in a small voice.

He raises his head a fraction.

'You have to listen to me.'

He gives the tiniest shrug, so she continues.

'The old Gracie, she's gone. She drowned.' Catriona says the words while trying to hide the meaning from herself. They're just words that mean nothing. She tells herself they're not true. The truth she wants to believe is that Grace is asleep in her bed. She needs Darren to believe this truth too. He has to. 'Everything will be fine, Darren. It can go back to how it was before. Because… because I found another Gracie. She'll be ours. It won't be any different, I promise.'

Darren's eyes widen and his mouth drops open as he starts to understand what Catriona's telling him. As he starts to realise the implications of the other girl in their daughter's room. 'That child in Gracie's bed… who is she? Where… where did you get her?'

'I told you. That little girl is *Grace*. She can be Grace. All you have to do is agree with me, and then it will all be okay.' Catriona realises that Darren won't accept this solution immediately. It will take time for him to process it. To realise that Catriona's right. That she has their best interests at heart. That other woman in the shopping centre, she didn't deserve to have her child, not after she left her unsupervised in a public place. Catriona pushes out the little voice accusing her of doing something similar – leaving your child alone in a bath isn't exactly the action of a responsible mother either. But it was an accident. She's only human. *And so is that other mother*, the voice replies.

'That is not Grace,' Darren replies, his eyes hardening.

'It is.' Catriona nods emphatically. 'It is Grace. Don't you tell me otherwise. Don't you tell me that!'

'Caty…' Darren's voices is trembling now. 'Caty, I think you're in shock. I think you might have done something terrible. And we have to put it right.'

Catriona's ears twitch as she hears a soft crying from the back bedroom. She stands and turns away from Darren. 'Gracie's crying. Maybe she's thirsty. I better go and see if—'

Darren leaps to his feet, grabs her arms and pulls her back. Turns her around to face him. 'You never told me where she is. Where's our daughter?' Catriona turns to the window, staring out into the black night. There's nothing to be seen but darkness, but the implication is clear. In case it isn't, she manages to utter two words:

'The churchyard.'

It was stupidly easy to find a small patch of soft ground hidden from view behind the old Elizabethan church. The weather was so vile out there that the grounds were deserted. At least she knows her child is buried in consecrated ground.

Darren stares in horror at her muddy clothes, not wanting to understand their significance. 'Oh sweet Jesus. You… you…' He points to her. 'And Gracie is…' He turns towards the dark pane of glass and convulses. Catriona thinks he's going to vomit. But he swallows and coughs, pulling his phone out of his pocket. 'I'm calling the police.'

CHAPTER TWENTY-TWO

NOW

I'm helping out in the café kitchen today, making waffles for a table of office workers who've come in for an earlyish Christmas brunch. Work is both a blessing and a curse at the moment. It helps take my mind off all the stuff with the Morrises, but it also means I don't have any time to devote to finding out about Bella. I'm here at the café, when I could be spending time working out what to do. Planning how to get that hard evidence I'm looking for. I have a few vague ideas of how to go about it, but they all seem a bit extreme. And I'm still too wary of going to the police.

If only Matt were more on board. I could really do with talking to him about this. Getting his opinion on the best way to go about things. Although really I already know his opinion – don't do anything, apart from talk to Robin.

I plate up the waffles and start bringing them out to the office workers, who are already quite raucous despite the absence of alcohol. Dee and I had to push three tables together next to the window to accommodate them all, and Dee decorated their table with tinsel and crackers. We don't normally have party bookings, and this has got her mind working overtime about how we can get more.

'Mmm, this looks great,' an older lady in an orange party hat says as I put her plate in front of her.

'Hope you enjoy!'

'I'm sure we will.'

The bell above the door rings and I glance around, checking to see if there are any spare tables. There's one left, by the counter. I look up with a smile, ready to direct whoever it is to the table.

It's Kate. She doesn't look happy.

I clasp one hand in the other and try to stay calm, but there's a lump in my throat and I'm suddenly really hot.

Kate looks chic in a Barbour and jeans, her hair in a ponytail. She has an oversized navy umbrella in her hand that's dripping all over the café floor. I wonder how she manages to always look so smartly and expensively dressed, given that they live in a tiny ex-council flat.

'Hi, Kate.' I go for breezy and friendly, wondering if I can brazen this out. 'How are you? Are you here for brunch? You're in luck – there's one table left.'

Her facial expression hasn't changed from stony. 'I need to talk to you.'

'Oh. Yes, sure. Thing is, I've already had my break and my shift doesn't finish until two thirty. You're welcome to pop over with the kids after school, if you like?'

'Rachel!' Dee's calling. She's pointing to a table near the back where a couple want to pay their bill.

I nod and hold my fingers up to indicate I'll just be a couple of seconds.

'I need to speak to you now. It's urgent.' Kate's voice is clipped, monotone. It makes me feel slightly queasy and also a little hysterical, like I could laugh out loud. The feeling reminds me of an incident back when I was at school, sitting an English exam. The invigilator was this really strict teacher who everyone was afraid of. My friend Karen and I couldn't stop laughing, even though we were terrified of getting in trouble. In the end, we were sent out and both given detentions.

I glance around the café, but it's so busy there's no way Dee will stand for me nipping off to talk to a friend. We're short-staffed as it is – Chrissie called in sick today, so Dee's already a bit tense. 'I'm sorry, Kate, I can't get away right now. As you can see, we're rushed off our feet.'

She presses her lips together. 'Fine. Two thirty, down by the river.'

I raise an eyebrow, as though surprised by her attitude. Even though I'm not surprised at all. 'Okay,' I reply with a small bemused smile. 'See you later.'

She doesn't reply. Just turns and leaves. The bell jangles loudly as the door crashes shut behind her. I realise I'm shaking.

'Rachel.' Dee has come over to where I'm standing by the door. She looks almost as pissed off as Kate did. 'What was that about?'

'Sorry. Just one of the school mums wanting to chat.'

'Look,' she says crossly under her breath, 'I'm trying to run a business here. It's fine to talk to friends when we're quiet, but not when it's busy like this. I need you to get back to the customers.'

'I'm so sorry, Dee. I did send her away.'

Dee nods and gets back to work. But she's not happy and I don't blame her. I haven't been fully focused on work for days. She must really be regretting giving me those extra hours for after Christmas. I hurry over to the couple waiting to pay, with several backward glances at the door, hoping Kate doesn't come back in.

The next few hours go by too quickly. Everyone seems to be in a festive mood, wishing us a Happy Christmas and leaving generous tips. As the time ticks closer to two thirty, I realise I'm dreading meeting Kate. She's obviously going to have a go at me, but I'm not sure exactly what she's going to say. Maybe she'll simply warn me away from Bella. But what if she threatens me? I'm starting to feel a little scared by her. If she's capable of stealing someone's child, what else is she capable of?

Once my shift ends, I find myself dawdling – cleaning a few more tables and tidying the area by the cash register. It's quieter in the café now and I know I should go and meet Kate, but I'm putting it off.

Dee checks her watch. 'Isn't it time for you to pick up Jess and Charlie?'

I realise that if I don't want to be late to school, I really better go and meet Kate. I take off my apron. 'You're right. Okay, I'm off. See you tomorrow. Sorry about earlier with that friend coming in.'

'Don't worry about it. I'm sorry I got a bit snippy. You can't help it if people you know drop by.'

'You had every right, Dee. We were busy.'

'Will you sit down for a minute?' She gestures to one of the empty tables.

'I really should get going…'

'Just for a minute, Rach.'

Anything to delay talking to Kate. I take a seat opposite my friend and wonder what she wants to talk to me about.

'I hope you don't mind me saying something, but… how are you doing?'

'How am I doing?' I'm not sure what she's referring to. 'I'm okay.' I shrug.

She gives a nervous smile. 'Don't get mad with me, or Matt, but, well, he told me what's been going on.'

My heart starts thumping against my ribcage. 'Told you? Told you *what*, exactly?'

Dee's cheeks turn scarlet as she realises I'm not happy. 'Uh…'

'Told you *what*?'

'That he was worried about you. He just wanted me to keep an eye on you at work.'

'You haven't answered my question, Dee.' I realise my tone is harsh. I know it's not Dee's fault my blabbermouth boyfriend couldn't keep a secret, but I hope this isn't what I think it is.

'He told me about your eldest daughter going missing.'

I grit my teeth and clench my fists.

'I'm so, so, sorry, Rach. You know I won't talk about it, or mention it, or tell anyone. You know I won't. I just want you to know that I'm here for you, if you ever need to talk about it.'

I inhale deeply, trying to calm my breathing. 'Thanks, Dee. But Matt should never have said anything to you. What happened in my past is private.' I scrape my chair back and get to my feet unsteadily, tears pricking behind my eyes. This is how it starts – you tell one person, then they tell another, and they tell another. And pretty soon the whole damn town is talking about you behind your back, pointing and whispering. 'I've got to go.'

'Rachel, wait. I'm sorry. I…'

I wave her apology away. I don't have time for this. I know it's not her fault that she knows, but I'm so annoyed with Matt, I can't pretend to be nice to Dee right now. I march away from her, collect my things and leave the café without looking back.

CHAPTER TWENTY-THREE

Outside, the light is dull, but the town is bustling with people. I wish I were one of them – laughing with friends and family, shopping, socialising, eating, drinking. I wend my way through the crowds, nodding without smiling to a few familiar faces, until I reach the end of the street. I can't believe Matt told Dee about Holly. I know he'll say it's because he was worried about me, but it wasn't his secret to tell. I shake my head. I have to put Matt and Dee out of my mind. I have to try to focus on Kate instead. Because she's not happy at all, and this isn't going to be a very pleasant encounter.

Up ahead, I'm shocked by how much the river has swollen since I last saw it a few days ago. It's spilling over its banks and into the car park and has even started lapping over the causeway. A car drives across too fast, spraying two huge arcs of water, like liquid wings. The driver and passenger are a young couple, and through the windscreen I can see they're laughing their heads off. I'm letting other things distract me, I need to press on.

I glance around, looking for Kate, but I don't see her. She didn't specify exactly where to meet, but I'm sure she can't be too far away. I have the sudden, terrifying thought that she might have brought Shaun with her. What will I do if it's both of them together? I don't think I'm feeling brave enough to face the two of them on my own.

Then I spot Kate's Fiat parked at the furthest edge of the car park, away from the river. I exhale in relief – it looks like the passenger side is empty. There are several wooden benches dotted about by the river, but they're all damp. Anyway, this doesn't feel like a sitting down and chatting occasion.

Crossing the car park, I try to breathe normally as I skirt around several huge puddles and weave through the parked cars. As I approach, Kate's car door opens. She steps out and heads my way without giving me any eye contact whatsoever until we're almost face to face. And then she looks at me with an expression somewhere between distaste and anger. It's a look that makes me physically recoil.

I should probably say hello, but I can't seem to find my voice. So we stand facing each other for a moment that feels like forever. Eventually she breaks the silence.

'Rachel, I'll make this quick because it's school pick-up soon. I need you to tell me why you met my eldest daughter after school.'

'Why I… Sorry, what?' This isn't good. Bella must have spoken to her. Of course, I knew she would. She thinks Kate is her mum.

'Yesterday,' Kate says carefully. 'You met Bella after school. Why exactly did you do that?' Her brown eyes bore into mine.

'I didn't *meet* her. We bumped into her and she got talking to Jess.'

'And you gave her a lift home?'

'Yes. It was pouring. A proper storm. We were all soaked through.' I'm trying to make my voice sound light, but I know I'm coming across as defensive. 'Jess suggested we give Bella a lift home. I'm sure you'd have done the same for one of my children if you saw them walking home in the pouring rain. I didn't realise that was the wrong thing to do. If it was, I apologise.'

Another silence hangs between us for a moment. Cars drive past us, still coming and going. It's started raining again, cold drops stinging my cheeks.

'Let's say I believe you,' Kate says with a faint sneer. 'Let's say I can just about manage to swallow that it was pure coincidence you happened to be outside Bella's school, after asking strange questions about her the other night.'

'Strange que—?'

'Because it's the next part that has me puzzled.'

'The next part?' I frown as though confused, even though I know just what she's going to say.

'Yes. The part where you mentioned her dad. My husband Shaun. The part where you mention to Bella that you knew about her dad coming home?'

'I…'

'You?'

I don't know how to answer. So I go for a version of the truth – the same half-truth I told Matt. 'A post popped up on my Facebook page.'

Kate's shaking her head now and I know she's not going to buy it. 'What's that got to do with anything?'

I continue on regardless. 'I can't remember what the post was about, but someone commented about Shaun getting out, so I just assumed. I didn't mention anything about prison to Bella. I just said that it must be nice to have her dad home. That's all. Nothing untoward.'

'Bullshit.'

'I'm sorry?' I'm taken aback by her sudden fury.

'I said, *bullshit*. That post didn't magically pop up. You went looking for it. There's something very wrong with you, Rachel. You've been creeping around my family ever since we met. I have no idea why, and I'd be grateful if you didn't talk to my daughter again. In fact, I'd rather you stayed away from *all* my children.'

I knew Kate wouldn't be happy about me talking to Bella, but all these vile things she's saying about me are making me bristle with anger. Now would be the perfect time for me to come back with my suspicions about her. She's acting all holier than thou, like I'm the one in the wrong when she's the wrong-doer. The *evil-*

doer. Actually, I wouldn't have expected anything else from her. When a person knows they're in the wrong, or they're cornered, they often act as the aggressor. Trying to deflect the blame. To make out that they're the injured party. I won't let her pressure me into showing my hand too soon. I won't let her rile me up so I say something I may regret. I need to remain calm. To get proof before Kate has a chance to up sticks and disappear with Bella for good. So I need to act fast. At least Kate didn't mention anything about me going into their flat to use the bathroom. Maybe Bella forgot to mention that part.

'Please don't repeat what you know about Shaun to anyone else.' To my surprise, Kate's anger is suddenly dissipating. She almost sounds like she might cry. 'We've had to leave everything behind to get away from the stigma, and I don't want it all raked up again. Once people know about things like that, they gossip, and it's just not fair on the children. Shaun has paid for what he's done… we all have.'

'I won't say anything,' I reply, feeling almost sorry for her now. 'I promise.'

'Thank you.' She's back to being icy once again.

I wish I had the balls to ask her what is was that Shaun actually did that got him arrested. But I can't bring myself to say anything. Anyway, there's no way she'd answer me so it would be a waste of time. 'I'm sorry we got off on the wrong foot,' I say instead.

Kate looks as though she's going to say something, but then she changes her mind, gives me a last contemptuous stare and strides off, back to her car.

I watch her go, unsure about what to do for the best. Should I go after her? Try to patch things up? My gut tells me it would be pointless. Besides, I really don't want to talk to the woman. The thing is, it's now going to be ten times more uncomfortable at school for us, and also for our kids. And now that I can't see Bella legitimately, it's going to be absolute torture. I'm glad I had the willpower to keep my suspicions about Bella's identity to myself. It's not something that can be blurted out in anger. I need to work this all out more carefully before confronting the Morrises.

My phone pings, and I glance at it to see it's an apologetic text from Dee. I don't have time to think about it or compose a reply right now. I better get going or I'm going to be late for school pick-up. I only hope I'm able to steer clear of Kate when I get there.

CHAPTER TWENTY-FOUR

'Can I have one of your reindeer ones?' Charlie asks Jess. They're sitting at the breakfast bar writing out their Christmas cards to take into school tomorrow while I cook their tea.

'No, you chose Santa ones. The reindeer cards are mine.'

'Maybe you could swap a couple?' I suggest as I fill a saucepan with water.

'My teacher likes animals,' Charlie says. 'I want to give her one with the reindeers.'

'Mrs Barker?' Jess asks.

Charlie nods.

'I like Mrs Barker.' Jess sighs. 'Okay, here you go.'

I glance across and give Jess a wink. She smiles back at me, basking in the pleasure of having done something nice.

Charlie beams from ear to ear as he takes the card from her. 'Thanks, Jess. You're the best. Do you want one of my Santa ones?'

'No, that's okay, I had one left over anyway.'

'I thought we bought exactly the right amount?' I query. Maybe she doesn't want one of Charlie's cards because she thinks they're too babyish. 'I've probably got one or two spares with Christmas trees on, if you like?'

'No, it's okay.' Jess shakes her head and gets back to writing her cards. From the set of her shoulders, I can tell her fleeting good mood has evaporated.

'Everything okay?'

She shrugs.

'Jess?'

'I'm not going to give Amy a card.'

'You're not?'

'No. Because I don't think she's going to give one to me.'

'You two still not talking?'

'No. She's best friends with Shayla now.' She still hasn't turned around to face me. Instead, she's hunched over her cards.

'Well, that's okay. At least you've got lots of other friends. And they're going to love your reindeer cards.' I reach up into one of the cupboards for a jar of pasta sauce, wishing I could make things right between her and Amy. But it's impossible.

The front door slams. Matt's home. The kids slide off their stools and go into the hall to greet him. I suppose I could have a flaming row with him about how he went behind my back and spoke to Dee about Holly. I was furious with him earlier, but I don't want an argument. In my heart of hearts I know Matt thought he was doing the right thing. I know he thought he was looking out for me.

I also wish I could tell him about mine and Kate's encounter in the car park today. But then I'd have to explain about meeting Bella yesterday, and he wouldn't understand. So instead, I'll pretend everything's perfectly okay and normal. This state of affairs would never normally happen. Usually Matt and I would tell one another about any strange happenings in our day. It feels so wrong to keep this from him. Uncomfortable. Like there's a stone in my shoe that I'm not allowed to take out.

'Hey, Rach.' Matt comes into the kitchen with both children talking at him at the same time. Two entirely different conversations that he's managing to follow perfectly.

'Hi, Matt. Good day?'

'Not bad.'

We kiss, and I'm struggling with all my conflicting emotions – anger, love, irritation, frustration – but most of all, I'm simply aching to hold onto him longer than our usual quick hug. I want him to embrace me and make everything all right. I have this overwhelming urge to tell him every single detail about the past few days. To throw myself on his mercy and ask him to help me sort it all out. Instead, I keep it all inside, smile and start grating some cheese into a bowl.

The children hop back up onto their stools and show Matt their cards. He makes suitably appreciative sounds before turning to me with a smile. 'Hey, guess what?'

'What?'

'Mum said she'd babysit tonight so we can go out for a drink.'

'*Tonight?*' Normally, I'd jump at the chance for a night out with my lovely man, but I have things I really need to do.

'Yeah, thought I'd be a bit spontaneous for a change. It's almost Christmas and it would be fun to have some time for just the two of us.'

'Why can't we come?' Jess asks.

'Because it's a school night,' Matt replies, bopping her on the nose with his forefinger.

'So?'

'So you'd be tired tomorrow. And children aren't allowed in bars.'

'Are you going to get drunk?' Charlie asks.

'Charlie!' I turn to look at Matt, who grins at me. 'How do you know about getting drunk?'

'Bethany Marshall said her mum got drunk at the weekend and fell asleep on the sofa.'

'Well, Mummy and Daddy won't be doing *that*,' I assure our son, giving him my sternest face.

'So?' Matt asks me. 'What do you think? Thought we could get a taxi to the Hungry Horse. Then if it stops raining we can walk home afterwards.'

'It sounds good, but would you mind if we didn't go tonight? It's just, I'm pretty tired and I'm starting to get a throbbing head.'

I tip the pasta shells into a pan of boiling water, which bubbles up too quickly and starts frothing over the hob.

'Really?' Matt's eyebrow quirks up. 'A headache? But we hardly ever go out.' He reaches up to get some pasta bowls out of the cupboard.

I didn't realise he'd be so disappointed. He clearly doesn't believe my headache excuse. To be fair, I thought it sounded lame when I said it. I consider changing my mind and agreeing to go. Our relationship has been suffering lately, which is totally my fault. But I need some down time to make my next move with the Morrises. I can't give that as an excuse, because Matt wouldn't understand. 'Sorry, Matt. Can we save it till the weekend, or one day next week?'

His shoulders droop. 'I suppose we'll have to. I was really in the mood to go out though.'

'So, why don't you? You should text some mates and go out with them.'

He turns up his nose. 'I suppose I could. But I really wanted to go with my gorgeous girlfriend.' He twinkles at me in the hope of getting me to change my mind. But I'm too wound up to go out and relax in some wine bar with all Matt's attention focused on me. To pretend that everything's okay, when my brain is racing with things I can't speak to him about.

'Sorry. I'm just not up to it tonight.'

'Okay. Maybe I'll call Stu and Mike.'

'Good idea.'

'I'll have to cancel Mum. She was excited about coming over.'

'Is Gran coming round?' Charlie asks.

'Not tonight,' I reply.

He huffs and pulls a disappointed face.

'Can she come round anyway?' Jess asks. 'Even though you're not going out.'

'Not tonight. Let's ask her over at the weekend.' I drain the pasta and blink as the steam rises into my face.

Matt's mum, Stella, is a lovely woman. She adores her family – myself included, even though Matt and I aren't married. She and Matt are really close, and I guess you could say that Matt is a bit of a mummy's boy. But that's uncharitable of me; her husband Doug died a couple of years ago, so Matt's just looking out for her. She keeps herself busy though, and has an active social life – dance classes, art club, the WI – Stella does it all. Everyone knows her and everyone loves her. Her family – she's one of four sisters, all with children – have lived in Wareham for several generations so she's a real part of the community. I'm lucky to have been accepted into such a warm environment. And it's great for the kids, who love their gran.

We take our bowls of pasta through to the dining room and eat all together for a change. Matt sits and eats, interrupted periodically by texts from his friends as he arranges their evening out. Normally, we wouldn't have phones at the dinner table, but because I turned down Matt's invitation, I don't say anything. The kids point out the unfairness of it and Matt finally puts his phone down, but his attention isn't on us any more. He bolts his food and then goes up to get ready while I sort out the children's bedtime.

Finally, they're both tucked up, and Matt is out of the house. Now I can settle down and make the phone call I've been itching to make ever since I came up with the idea. I take a cup of herbal tea into the lounge and sit with my feet tucked under me. The wood burner is roaring, and the room feels cosy and warm. I shouldn't be nervous ringing up one of my friends, but I am. It's not the actual phone conversation that has my heart racing and my palms sweating – it's the thought of what it will lead to.

I call the number, hoping she'll pick up.

'Hi, Rachel.'

'Hi, Heidi. I'm not disturbing you, am I?'

'As long as you're not calling to say you can't help out at the fayre next week!'

'As if I'd do that to you. I know how much work you've been putting in. Matt said he can get there by five.'

'Brilliant.'

I twirl a lock of hair around my fingers and hope I can make my next sentence sound casual. 'I just thought I'd mention that a new mum, Kate Morris, said she and her husband Shaun wanted to help out at the fayre. Shall I give you her number so you can work it out?'

'Oh, yes, Amy's mum. Don't worry, I've already spoken to her and both she and her husband are manning the bottle stall. It's the most popular stand, so I thought it would be a good way for them to meet everyone.'

'Great idea.' This is perfect. Even though Heidi can't see me, I'm smiling anyway.

'Kate seems really nice, and Ella says Amy's great.'

'Yeah, lovely family,' I say, shaking my head and rolling my eyes, hoping that didn't sound too sarcastic.

'How's things with you and the kids? Once the holidays are over we'll have to meet up for a coffee.'

'Definitely. We'll get something in the diary.'

We make a little more small talk, but my mind isn't here on the phone with Heidi, it's racing ahead to next Wednesday when I'm going to have to let Heidi down. Because while all the Morrises will be helping out at the school fayre, their flat will be unoccupied.

CHAPTER TWENTY-FIVE

THEN

'What do you mean, you're calling the police?' Catriona cries, a bolt of panic crashing through her. 'You can't do that. Darren. Please!' She's aware that the sound of crying is still coming from the back bedroom. She needs to go in there. To check that the little girl is okay. But she can't leave Darren alone with his phone. She can't risk him calling the authorities.

'I have to call them, Caty. There's no other choice.'

'There's always a choice. We *have* a choice. Please! It was an accident!'

'You're in shock, Catriona. A deep, dark, horrible shock. We both are. I can't get my head round any of it. I can't even believe it's real.' He's panting now, gasping. 'I need to call them so we can sort this all out. We can't do this on our own. We have to tell them what's happened. God help you, I know it was an accident, but…' He tails off for a moment and stares at the wall as though searching for answers. 'That girl out there in Gracie's bed' – his voice breaks – 'that was just you trying to make things right. But it's no good. You can't do that to another family. You can't take someone else's child to replace your own. No one can replace our beautiful Gracie. No one!'

'But—'

'No! No buts. We're doing this.' Darren unlocks his phone.

Catriona's head swims and she realises that if her boyfriend makes the call, he will be ruining any chance she'll ever have at happiness. They'll take Grace away and her room will lie empty forever. Catriona will have to face things that no mother should ever have to face. 'Don't do it, Darren,' she pleads. 'If you love me, don't do it.'

'Sorry. You know I love you, but I have to.'

Catriona can't let that happen. She lunges at him, trying to snatch the phone. 'Give me it!' Instead of grasping the phone, she ends up knocking it from his grip and it slides across the laminate floor with a clatter and a scrape. Darren drops down to retrieve it, but before he can get hold of it, Catriona lifts her foot and stamps on the thing with the heel of her boot, feeling the crunch of glass and metal.

'No! What did you do that for?' Darren picks it up and turns it over in his hands. The screen is now a maze of cracks. He presses a few buttons and swears. 'Great. It's broken.'

'I couldn't let you ring them, Darren.' The crying from the other room has turned from sobs into wails. 'Just come with me now and see our little girl. Once you see her, you'll know I'm right. You'll feel better about everything, I *promise*. Come on.' She tries to take his hand, but Darren recoils from her. Catriona can't believe it.

'*Feel better about everything?*' He shakes his head. 'You're crazy! How can we ever feel better about any of this?' Darren darts around her and slips out of the room. Perhaps he's changed his mind. Maybe he's going to see Grace for himself before making a decision. But following him into the hall, Catriona realises she's mistaken. Darren is reaching for his coat on the peg by the front door.

Her pulse spikes. 'Where are you going? Don't leave!'

He doesn't respond, just tugs his coat on and zips it up.

'Darren! We need to decide what we're going to do.'

He turns back for a moment, despair in his eyes. 'There's nothing to decide. If I can't call the police, I'll drive to the station instead.'

Catriona's mind races forward to what will happen if the police get involved. Why can't Darren understand? She has to stop him. He pulls the front door open, letting in the howl of the wind and the lash of rain, the roar of traffic, and the hiss of wet tyres on tarmac.

He's halfway out the door already.

'Darren, wait!'

He stops for a millisecond and she thinks he's going to relent and come back inside. But their white UPVC front door closes behind him with a hollow click.

'No, no,' she moans, crossing the hall and pulling the door open again, spatters of cold rain flying into her face. She can't leave Gracie on her own. She needs to go to her. To comfort her. But she also can't let Darren speak to the police. She's wracked with indecision. Darren is a little way down the path now, a dark blur beneath the wavery street lights. She can see his van parked on the opposite side of the street. He dashes into the road. There's a blaring car horn and a whine of brakes. A sickening thud.

Catriona's stomach drops. She stands stock still for a moment. Then, without thinking, she pulls the front door closed behind her and races towards the road, a dull pounding in her gut. The traffic is backed up now and there's a bright glow of intersecting headlamps. People are staring, pointing. Hands cover mouths, mobile phones are pulled out of raincoat pockets.

Above the dented bonnet of a dark-coloured car is a cracked, blood-smeared windscreen, and on the ground lies a twisted-up body.

Darren.

CHAPTER TWENTY-SIX

NOW

I take a sip of water and realise we're already halfway through my counselling session. It only feels like I've been here five minutes. To be honest, we haven't really covered any new ground, I've simply been exploring my feelings about Holly.

'So why now?' Robin gives me a quizzical look. 'Why did you decide to tell Matt about Holly after all these years?'

An image of Bella flashes up in my mind. 'I'm not really sure.'

'Did something happen to make you want to confide in him?'

'I…' I break off, not sure what to say. Part of me wants to tell Robin about Bella. Part of me is *desperate* to share the news with him. But only if he isn't going to be cynical. And how can I possibly know that in advance? I gaze at an artfully placed fern in a wicker plant pot, wondering if it was Robin who designed this room or if he had help. I wonder if he's married or has a partner, a family. There are no photos in here. Nothing personal. I'll have to ask Matt.

'Look, Rachel, you don't have to tell me anything you don't want to. But remember that everything you say here is treated in the strictest confidence.'

I shift on the sofa and glance across at Robin, who's giving me a gentle smile. It must take years of practise to perfect that particular smile, which contains just the right combination of encouragement and detachment. It's like he's conveying this aura of not being bothered either way, so that I'll trust him. If he was too pushy, I'd run a mile. I imagine this is some kind of body-language, animal-instinct thing, like not looking directly at a bear. Maybe therapists learn it at counselling college. I decide to trust him.

'Something did happen, actually.'

Robin waits for me to continue. To give him credit, he keeps his face blank and doesn't appear remotely smug that I've started to open up.

'A couple of weeks ago, a new family started at my daughter's school.' My heart starts beating in my ears as I'm transported back to the day I first met the Morrises. I can't believe it was only two weeks ago. It feels as if this has been weighing on me for months. 'I got talking to the mum, Kate Morris. She seemed really nice. But then when I saw her daughter…' I take a breath and pick up my glass for another sip of water. Rain spatters against the window intermittently. The ceiling light flickers. 'Her daughter is the spitting image of Holly. I don't mean she bears a passing resemblance – I mean she looks identical.'

Robin nods thoughtfully. 'So this girl brought back memories for you?'

'More than just memories. It was like a punch in the stomach. The pain…' My voice breaks and I have to take a few steadying breaths. I'm not sure I can go on.

'And this is what prompted you to speak to Matt?'

I nod.

'Remind me, how old was your daughter when she was taken?'

'Two years and eight months.' I can barely get the words out.

'So this child you saw the other week was a similar age?'

Robin hasn't grasped what I'm telling him. He thinks the girl I saw is a toddler. Maybe I should let him continue thinking that. 'No. Kate's daughter, Bella, is exactly the same age my Holly would be now.'

'So she looks how you would imagine your daughter to look now?'

'Yes.'

Robin nods and writes in his notepad.

'The thing is,' I go on, feeling more in control of myself now, 'she doesn't just look like her, it's more than that – her eyes are the same shade of green, her face is the same heart shape, she has the same nose, the same freckles, same hair colouring, everything. And her family have just moved here from the same area of London where Holly was taken.'

Robin's soft concern falters for a moment as he begins to grasp what I'm telling him. 'So, what are you saying exactly?'

'I'm saying that there's a possibility that Bella…' I already know that this was a mistake. Robin's features have rearranged into a sympathetic expression that screams doubt and cynicism. Not that I'm expecting him to say anything remotely unsupportive, but he'll assume I'm some poor deluded cow who's clutching at straws. 'Never mind.' I lean back into the sofa and wish I'd never let Matt persuade me to come here.

'Please, go on.' Robin's soft concern is back.

'It's fine. I know what I'm saying sounds implausible.'

'That doesn't matter. You're here to tell me how you're feeling. Not to tell me what you think I want to hear.'

'Fine.' I sit up straighter. 'I believe Bella might be my missing child.' Saying it out loud like that is really quite something. My body feels strangely light, but I feel the air in the room grow heavier.

Robin's nodding goes on for quite a while this time. I can see he's gathering his thoughts. Deciding how to play this. 'Have you told anyone else your thoughts about Bella?'

'I told Matt.'

'What does he think?'

'Probably the same as you – that I'm mistaken. That it's just a coincidence.'

'I don't *think* anything, Rachel. I'm just here to listen, and for guidance if you need it.'

'Okay, sorry.'

'It's okay, don't apologise. Have you mentioned your thoughts to anyone else?'

'No. I can't. Not without evidence.'

'Have you ever mistaken anyone else for your daughter over the years?'

'Never. The feeling I got when I saw Bella, it was so powerful. I felt as though I'd jumped into another life. The life I was supposed to have with my first daughter. But I'll never have that, will I? It's too late. Even if it turns out that Bella really is Holly, she doesn't know me as her mother. I'm just some random stranger. She'll never be able to call me "Mum", will she?' My voice has grown thick and unstable. I'm no longer choosing my words carefully. They're rushing out in a torrent of emotion.

'I mean, if Kate abducted my daughter when she was two, then Kate is her mum!' I spit out my words. 'This *criminal* has had the joy of raising my baby.' I realise I may have gone a bit too far. I might be coming across as a bit unhinged. And I'm *not*; I'm just a mother trying to be reunited with her child. I attempt to slow my breathing. 'I mean, I know there's a slim chance I'm mistaken, which is why I can't say anything to anyone yet.'

'I can see how meeting Bella has triggered all these old feelings,' Robin says carefully. 'You saw someone with the same looks as your child, who's the same age, from the same area. All these factors together have set off a series of emotions in you.'

'Don't you think it's possible that she's my daughter?' I'm annoyed with myself for asking the question. It makes me sound desperate and needy, and I don't want Robin's pity.

'I don't know,' Robin replies. 'Looking at the odds, it would be quite a coincidence.'

'Unless Kate has sought me out on purpose. Whoever took my child can't be a mentally stable person, can they? What if she's moved here to mess with me in some way? To taunt me.'

'Is it just Kate and this daughter? Or does she have other children?'

'She has a husband and two other children. And that's another thing! She and her husband Shaun have blonde hair, the same as their two younger children. But Bella has dark wavy hair and green eyes. Nothing like them at all, but exactly like my Holly.'

Robin purses his lips. 'Not all family members look alike. I have dark hair, but my brother's hair is light brown.'

'I know. I know all this. It's just when you add everything together…'

'Look, our time's up for today, but would you like to have another appointment this week? It seems like there's a lot we haven't covered. I have a slot at six on Wednesday, if that's any good.'

I can't believe our time's up already. 'I can't do Wednesday.' That's the evening of the Christmas Fayre. I wonder what Robin would say if I told him what I was planning to do. Call the police, probably.

'That's a shame. I really think we could benefit from talking this through sooner rather than later.'

'How about now? Maybe another half hour?' I feel wrung out, but there's still a lot more I want to talk about.

'Unfortunately I've got another client coming in fifteen minutes. If you can't do Wednesday, we'll have to leave it until next week. But I'll call if I get a cancellation, okay?'

'Oh, okay.'

We both get to our feet at the same time.

'At least I didn't need any tissues this week.' I give Robin a half-hearted smile, which he tries to return, but his jaw is tight and there are lines etched across his forehead.

I put my coat on and wind my scarf around my neck, worrying that perhaps I went too far. I know you're supposed to open up in a counselling session and talk about everything on your mind, but what if I've said too much? Also, I probably shouldn't have mentioned Bella and Kate's names. Well, it's too late now.

'Are you parked close by?' Robin asks. 'Do you need me to walk you to your car? It's not very nice out there.'

'Thanks, I'll be fine.'

'Okay, Rachel. Take care.'

'Bye, Robin. Thank you.' I leave the cosy warmth of his room and walk down the stairs and out onto the dark, glistening pavement. I try to look at things from Robin's point of view. Try to see me as he sees me. But I can't seem to do it. I can only see the reality of my situation. And whatever Robin sees it isn't the real truth, rather it's his narrow perception of my life. It's helpful to talk to him, but I don't think he gets my situation the way he thinks he does.

I speed up, anxious to get back to my car and out of the cold. Once I get home, I'm going to have a hot shower and then climb into bed with a book. Escape from it all for a while if I can.

CHAPTER TWENTY-SEVEN

I park two streets away from the Morrises' flat and sit in the car for a few moments, contemplating all the different ways that this could go wrong. But if I don't at least try, then what does that say about the type of mother I am? If Bella is my daughter, I need to know. I need to do everything I can to discover the truth.

I've already called Heidi to let her know I'm ill with a migraine and that I can't make the school fayre. I've assured her that Matt will be along to help out. Heidi was sympathetic, but I could hear the stress in her voice, and I feel terrible for letting her down. My friend Lou-Anne has said she'll look after Jess and Charlie with her kids until Matt gets to school. So that means I've got over three hours until the fayre ends and everyone starts making their way home. Hopefully, this 'errand' will only take me half an hour at most.

I get out of the car and find that my legs are soft and shaky. I hope, now that I've gone to all this trouble, that I'm strong enough to actually go through with it. The air is damp and cold, but at least the rain is holding off for now. The smell of salt and vinegar wafts across the road from a nearby fish and chip shop, mingling with diesel fumes and wet tarmac. I lock the car and start walking, my eyes darting everywhere, checking there are no familiar faces. The last thing I need is for someone I know to spot me in this area – I have no cover story, and my mind is so frazzled right now that I can't even think of anything remotely plausible to explain why I'm here. So I keep my head down and hope that my hood and the fast-falling darkness will shield me.

I reach the Morrises' street quickly and do a quick scan of the area. The only people I can see are a woman going into her house at the other end of the road, and a couple of teenage girls, their faces caked in severe make-up, walking towards me, but paying me no attention. They're laughing and looking down at their phones. I pass them without any eye contact.

I was banking on most people not being home from work yet and luckily it seems I was right. There are very few cars parked, and most of the houses are in darkness. The houses and flats that do have their lights on have their curtains drawn and their blinds pulled down. Everyone is either out or already hunkered down for the evening.

A dog barks as I walk past one of the houses, making me jump. It sets off a chain of other dogs barking around the neighbourhood. Someone yells at their pet to shut up. I hope there aren't any dogs in Bella's building. I don't remember any barking last time I was here, but I obviously don't want any undue attention drawn to me.

Kate's Fiat isn't parked out front. I don't know what car Shaun drives, but Heidi assured me they were both helping out at the fayre, so I reckon I'm ninety-nine per cent safe. In any case, all their lights are off – at least the ones I can see.

I walk purposefully over to the entrance of the block and go into the same stairwell I walked in with Bella last week. I stand before the same two heavy-duty wooden doors with their safety-glass panels. I'm really regretting not swiping Bella's key when I had the chance last week. It was right there on the hall table when I went in to use the bathroom. It would have been so easy to slip it into my pocket. Too late now. I'll just have to improvise. It's a rough neighbourhood so it's not out of the question for them to have a break-in. But it would have been less traumatic all round if I could have let myself in and out without arousing any suspicion.

There's no obvious way to get in here – no windows or anything, so I walk out of the stairwell and back down the path. The windows at the front are too exposed – I can't see anyone else in the road, but that doesn't mean there isn't someone looking this way. I can't take the risk. Instead, I follow the narrow path and slip around the side of the building that's hidden from view by a row of scrubby bushes.

I can hardly believe it when I see one of the small top-light windows on the ground floor is open. It's part of a larger opaque glass window that I'm guessing is the Morrises' bathroom. I walk up to the dark glass, take my torch out of my pocket and stand up on my tiptoes. Shining the torch through the small open window, I'm faced with the very same bathroom that I went into last week. I allow myself a small smile of relief. The open part of the window is far too small for me to crawl through, but at least I know that the window I'm about to break will lead into the Morrises' flat, and not some neighbour's who might be at home.

I pull on my gloves and take a fragment of ceramic spark plug out of my pocket. It's something I researched on YouTube – how to break a window quickly and safely. The video is supposedly to give people a way to get out of their car if they ever get trapped – but apparently it works just as well on any window. Anyway, I'm about to find out.

I stand back and throw the shard of ceramic at the window, gasping as, with a crunching sound, the whole pane breaks into hundreds of spiderweb cracks. I pull a folded bedsheet out of my bag and drape it down through the open top light, dropping the material as best I can so it lies on the floor in the bathroom beneath the window. Then, I wrap my torch in a small towel and use it to gently push the cracked glass out of its frame and onto the sheet below. The majority of it comes out easily, in random sized chunks, luckily not making too much noise as it lands on the sheet.

I have to admit, I wasn't at all sure this was going to work. I had no opportunity to test out the method beforehand so I'm both relieved and nervous that I've actually managed to do it. Before attempting to climb through, I nip back along the building to glance out onto the road and check that the sound of breaking glass hasn't brought any of the neighbours running.

All is quiet and still. Just the sound of distant traffic from the main road beyond.

When all the pieces of glass are out of the lower frame, I unwrap my torch and lay the towel on the sill before hoisting myself up and through the window, landing on top of the glass fragments below with a noisy crunch. I freeze and cock my ear, listening. There's no sound from within. I exhale and tiptoe across the bathroom floor towards the door. The hall beyond lies in darkness. I switch on my torch, walk through and take a moment to get my bearings. The front door is to my right and Bella's bedroom is all the way along the hall at the end, to my left. That's where I'm headed.

My heart is thudding double-time now. I've actually done it. I've broken in, and I've also broken the law – something I've never done before. Something I never thought I'd ever do. My biggest regret is that when the children get home and discover the broken window, they might be scared by the fact that someone's been in their house. They might have sleepless nights worrying about the break-in. Unfortunately, I can't avoid that happening, as there's no way for me to reassure them.

Bella's door is firmly closed. I grip the handle and push open the door. I shine the torch around the small space and see that there are two beds in here. Amy and Bella must share a room. I hope that's not going to be a problem for me.

My torch beam rests on a pretty white dressing table littered with hair products, make-up and jewellery. Then I spot Bella's green hairbrush. That's what I've come for. I move carefully across the floor, stepping over discarded clothes, empty plates and tumblers. Directing the torchlight down onto the brush, I heave a sigh of relief when I see that its bristles are thick with Bella's dark hair

– exactly what I need. Amy must have her own brush, because I can't see any of her blonde hairs in this one, thank goodness.

I fumble in my pocket for the Ziploc bag and open it up with my gloved fingers. Then I take Bella's hairbrush, pull out several clumps of the hair and shove them into the bag.

Okay, I need to get out of here now. I creep back across her bedroom, deciding to try going out through the front door. I don't fancy climbing out over all that broken glass. I must already have some of it embedded in my shoes and coat, but it's too dark to check myself. I'll be so relieved when I'm out of here and back in my car. Hopefully, now I have some of Bella's hair, I'll finally be able to determine without a doubt whether or not she's my daughter.

The bedroom door has swung shut behind me, so I pull it open again and step into the hall, my torch in hand.

'Kate?' A gruff, croaky voice in front of me makes my blood turn to ice and my legs turn to jelly.

It must be Shaun.

With a shaking hand, I shove the Ziploc bag into my coat pocket and shine my torch straight ahead. Shaun is shielding his eyes from the beam and fumbling for the light switch on the wall.

What should I do? What should I do?

I can't overpower him. I should run before the light comes on, but my body is frozen in place. He's blocking my route to the front door and to the bathroom – the only two means of escape, unless I risk running into another room and hoping I can open another window. If I don't move now, I'll be trapped in here with a criminal. Possibly a dangerous one. I don't even want to think about what he might do.

The overhead light blinds me for a second until I refocus and see a dishevelled Shaun standing before me, dressed in a T-shirt and crumpled pyjama bottoms. I'm thrown for a moment – he looks ill. His eyes are bloodshot, his chin is a mass of patchy stubble, and there's a glaze of sweat across his pallid face.

'*You…*' he says drowsily.

'I'm-I'm sorry!'

He blinks. 'What are you doing here? Is Kate back? Are you here with Kate and the kids?' He looks around wildly.

'Are you okay?' I ask, sidestepping his questions. He really doesn't look well. I'm trying to work out whether I could manage to duck beneath his arm and make it to the front door. But what if he grabs me? What if he really is dangerous? And even if I'm able to get away, he could still call the police, have me arrested.

'God, I feel like shit.' He blinks and cringes against the light. 'I've got flu. Don't feel good at all. Why are you here?'

'You look terrible. You should go back to bed.' This is weird. He's so out of it that I could probably leave and he'd think he'd hallucinated me.

'*You!* What are you doing here?' Shaun barks at me this time, suddenly more alert than a second ago. He wipes the back of his hand across his clammy forehead. 'Stop shining that thing in my face!'

'I'm sorry.' I turn off the torch and take a small step back. 'I… I left my wallet here when I dropped Bella off the other day.' It's a crap excuse, but it's all I can come up with.

'How did you get in?'

'I knocked but no one replied. So I saw an open window…'

'You broke in through a *window*? Kate was right about you.' He staggers a little and puts his hand against the wall to steady himself.

'I'm sorry. Look, I've got my wallet now. I'll go.'

'You can't just come into our property like that. It's breaking and entering.'

'I know, I know. I'm sorry.' And now I'm stressing about the broken window. About how I'm not going to be able to bluff my way out of it. He'll see it after I've gone and know I'm responsible. What the hell am I going to do? 'Look, Shaun, I did something I shouldn't have.'

'You need to go. I don't feel well. It's really hot in here. Are you hot?'

'I'll go, I'll go in a sec, but please just listen.'

Shaun coughs, sinks down onto the hall floor and leans back against the wall.

'Shaun, I'm sorry, but I broke a window to get in.'

'What?' He's suddenly alert again. His eyes widening and then closing as though he's in pain.

'The bathroom window, it's broken. I'll pay for it. I'll sort it out. But please don't tell Kate I was here. She really doesn't like me.'

Shaun nods and gives a short laugh. 'I know.'

'What did she say to you about me?' I ask.

'Did you say you broke a window? This wall is so nice and cool.' He presses his cheek against the paintwork.

'Don't tell Kate I was here.' I reach into my pocket and pull out my purse, taking out a ten and a twenty – that's all that's in there apart from a couple of ten-pence pieces. 'Here.' I thrust the notes into his hand. 'That's all I've got on me but let me know if I owe you any more for the damage.'

'I don't want your money,' he snarls, trying to throw the notes back at me. They flutter down onto his legs. 'I don't want your charity!'

'It's not charity. I'm trying to pay for—'

'I don't want your money! Take it back.'

'But the window's broken.'

'I can fix a window. I'm not useless.'

'Okay. Look, Shaun, I'm going to go now, okay. Do you need any help getting up?'

'Get out, Rachel. Don't come here again.'

'I won't. Please don't tell Kate I was here.' I sidle past, stepping over his outstretched legs, wondering whether he'll even remember this encounter. Wondering if I'll get a visit from the police or a call from Kate. I open the front door and leave the Morrises' flat.

The cold night air jolts me back to reality and I'm shivering from the shock of it all. The chances are that Shaun will tell Kate what happened and then she'll know for sure that I'm on to her. What if they move away and take Bella with them? What if I lose my daughter for a second time? I can't let that happen. I just can't.

CHAPTER TWENTY-EIGHT

THEN

Catriona takes refuge in the glitzy hotel bathroom for a few minutes. She avoids looking at herself in the mirror. Instead, she goes straight into a cubicle and locks the door, sits on the loo seat and exhales. How did she end up here? At the funeral of the man she loved?

Darren's parents paid for it all – the casket, the hotel, the catering. *Everything.* They live up north, in Middlesbrough, and it's been almost a year since she's seen them. Darren had a falling out with one of his sisters when she accused him of not doing enough after their dad had a heart attack last year. His mum and dad took the sister's side over Darren's, and Catriona had been angry on Darren's behalf. She had counselled him against making up with them. Said they were out of order. That it was impossible for him to be there all the time while he had work commitments and a young family to look after. But now she feels bad about that. At least it meant they hadn't seen Grace for ages, since she was little more than a baby.

Darren's family felt terribly guilty about the rift, so they saw to all of the funeral arrangements. *Insisted* upon it. They drove down to London after they heard the news. Then drove Catriona and Grace back up with them a week later. And they've been taking care of Catriona like she's one of the family. It suited Catriona to have the funeral away from London, and they're doting on Grace. Darren was their only son. His parents and two sisters are beside themselves with grief and guilt. So now Grace is *everything* to them. Their only tangible link to their son and brother.

She knows it's wrong, but Catriona didn't invite any of their London friends to come to the funeral. She couldn't risk them seeing Grace and asking questions. Consequently, Darren's family are the only people here today whom she actually knows. Catriona realises she can't hide away in the loos all afternoon, but the funeral at the crematorium earlier was brutal. Watching Darren's casket slide beyond the curtain. Knowing where it was heading – to be incinerated. She has the fleeting thought that he's with Grace in heaven. But she can't think that, because if she does then she'll have to think about the other Grace. Her mind blurs. She shakes away the image, blinks and stands. Tells herself she only has to endure an hour or two more before this is over.

She attempts to smooth the wrinkles from her black dress, but they refuse to fall out. Instead, they remain stubbornly creased in thick black folds across her thighs and belly. The material is cheap, shiny. She'll probably get rid of the outfit after today.

Back in the vast reception lounge, Catriona feels lost for a moment until she spies Grace who, upon seeing her, detaches herself from Darren's dad, runs across the patterned carpet and throws herself at Catriona, wrapping her arms around her legs.

'Hello, baby. Have you been looking after Nanny and Grandad?' Catriona crouches down and kisses her daughter's cheek.

Grace nods.

Catriona is amazed and thankful that her little girl only had a couple of days of tears after Darren's accident. The worst of her fears have been at night, when she sobs for her mummy. But once Grace is awake and being cuddled by Catriona, she's perfectly happy again. If perhaps a little subdued. She also seems to fully accept that Catriona is now her mother. She answers to the name

Grace easily. It almost scares Catriona how smoothly the child has adapted. But whatever the reason, Catriona is grateful.

After that day, she only allowed herself to watch the local news once. Grace's face flashed up on the TV screen, making Catriona feel physically sick; only she went by a different name. A name that Catriona doesn't want to think about. They filmed her white-faced parents putting out an appeal. There was also a grainy piece of security footage showing a figure wearing a hoodie, leading Grace away from the play area. But it was impossible to tell whether the person was a woman or a man.

Catriona worried that the story was going to take hold nationally – that it would capture the nation's hearts and she would be discovered. But a recent terrorist attack eclipsed all other stories and dominated the media. The local story of the missing girl soon faded, never even making it onto the national news. Catriona was amazed by the lack of coverage, but after some research she discovered that thousands of children go missing in the UK every year – one every three minutes according to police figures – and hardly any make the national headlines.

Catriona was surprised that her car wasn't traced. That it wasn't picked up on a security camera. That the police didn't come knocking on her door. She wasn't careful at all. She was reckless. None of it was planned. That whole day was a nightmarish blur. Even though she's had to speak to the police and hospital staff about Darren's accident, no one has mentioned a single thing to do with Gracie. Catriona has kept her indoors, and the trip up north has helped remove them from the situation. No one suspects anything out of the ordinary.

'Catriona, love, how are you holding up?' Darren's mum comes and puts an arm around her and squeezes tightly, enveloping Catriona and Grace in a soft, squishy cuddle.

Catriona sniffs. 'I still can't believe it. Darren was the love of my life, you know.'

'He worshipped you and Gracie. If only we hadn't fallen out. We should have come down to visit you all sooner. It's just, with Geoff being poorly and our silly argument with…'

'You can't beat yourself up about it, Pat. You had to take care of Geoff after the heart attack. At least Darren managed to make it up to see you at the end of the summer.'

Pat lets out a long breath. 'Thank goodness. But we were going to ask you to come and stay this Christmas. It was going to be…' She breaks off and starts rooting around in the pocket of her jacket. 'Need another tissue. Shoulda brought a box of them with me.'

Catriona passes her a packet from her bag.

'Thanks, love.' Pat fishes out a clean tissue and blows her nose. 'It was going to be our way of making it up to you. All the family together, with the cousins all playing, having a laugh. What am I going to do without my boy? I can't believe he's gone.' She holds the tissue to her mouth for a moment, trying to stem her emotion. 'Will you still come… for Christmas? Say you will. We need you here. With us.'

'That sounds good,' Catriona replies hesitantly, unwilling to commit.

'Better still, you should stay. What's the point in you going back? Thank goodness we have this little angel.' Pat swings Grace up into her arms. 'She's a beauty, isn't she? Growing up so fast. And she's starting to look so much like her daddy. It's the eyes.'

Catriona nods, swallowing, thankful that it's been such a long time since Grace's grandparents last saw her.

'Seriously though, Catriona, I wish you'd take us up on our offer to move up to Middlesbrough permanently. We'll find you a pretty flat near the house. We'll all look after you. You wouldn't want for anything. Gracie would have all her family around her. It would be so good for both of you. You like it up here, don't you?'

Tempting though it sounds, Catriona knows that it's too risky. What if Grace starts talking about the things she remembers? A quick visit with her grandparents every few months is one thing, but seeing them day in, day out – that's just asking for trouble. 'It's lovely of you to offer, Pat, but I'm a London girl. All my friends are there, you know?'

'I just thought with your mum and dad gone… wouldn't you like us to look after you both? I know you two weren't married, but I still feel like I'm your mother-in-law. You can treat me like a second mum. I know I can never replace your own mother – God rest her soul – but…' She breaks off, tears trailing down her cheeks.

Catriona takes her hand and gives it a squeeze. 'Come and sit down, Pat.' She leads her over to an empty table and they sit next to one another on the red faux-velvet chairs, Grace snuggling into Pat's sizeable lap. If only life could be as simple as her and Grace staying here with Pat and Geoff – letting the kindly couple look after them both. But it's an impossible fantasy.

In fact, she and Grace won't be able to stay in their flat either. She can't keep any ties to her current life. There are too many people who knew Grace before – neighbours, pre-school, the doctor's surgery, friends. At least they won't think it strange – her moving away – not after what's happened with Darren. It'll be understandable, really. No one will blame her. She regrets that their disappearance will break Pat's heart but she'll let Darren's parents know she's leaving London – of course she will.

All the memories in their little flat had been crowding in on top of her. She can hardly stand to be in there now. Thinking about the churchyard beyond the garden makes her shiver uncontrollably. She wonders if one of the neighbours might have seen her going out there on that nightmarish day. But they're usually all at work, and nobody mentioned anything. She's dreading going back to that dark shell of a flat once more. She's desperate to escape it for good.

Catriona stares around at all the people eating and drinking and talking about her boyfriend. Pitying poor Grace, who will now be growing up without a father. She didn't really realise what a popular person he was. There must be over 200 people here – school friends, family, old work colleagues. There would have been even more if his London friends had been invited. But then, Darren was always so friendly. So kind and chatty. Not like her. Catriona's a bit of an introvert, really. That's why their relationship worked so well – they balanced one another out. They were perfect together. How has it come to this?

'Hey, love, it's okay.' Pat rubs Catriona's shoulder.

'What?'

'Mummy's crying,' Grace says, leaning over and stroking her cheek.

Catriona realises that tears are dripping down her face. She hadn't even noticed. Pat returns the packet of tissues; Catriona pulls one out and wipes her face, feeling self-conscious. She knows that crying is expected at funerals. There have been many tears throughout the day, but she still doesn't like to show her emotions in front of so many strangers. 'It's okay, Gracie,' she says to her sweet daughter. 'Mummy's okay.'

'Let it all out, love,' Pat says. 'No good keeping those emotions bottled up.'

Catriona nods and sniffs. But she can't allow herself the luxury of being emotional. She's going to have to toughen up if she wants to survive. If she wants to make a good life for her little family of two. Her priority has to be Grace now. Nothing can be allowed to get in the way of them being together. Even if the thought of starting over terrifies the life out of her.

CHAPTER TWENTY-NINE

NOW

I rush back to my car, head bowed against the gusting wind, wondering if I should have tried to talk to Shaun some more. Begged him to promise that he wouldn't say anything to Kate. But he was in no state to listen and even if he promised me a thousand times, how could I trust he'd even keep his word? Kate's his wife, after all. I'm shaking and panting now, my legs so wobbly that I'm not sure I'll even make it back to the car. What was I thinking, breaking into their property? Am I losing the plot?

I need to work out what I'm going to say if the police come knocking. I also need to have a story lined up for Kate if she calls me up. I suppose I could simply deny it. If I race home now and get into bed before Matt and the kids get back, I can still use my migraine excuse as a kind-of alibi. My family already think I'm unwell, but lying doesn't come easily and I'm sure everyone will see right through me. None of this feels right.

The only thing that could possibly make all of this okay is if I could prove without a shadow of a doubt that Bella is my daughter. Surely if that happens, then breaking into their flat will be seen as a necessary crime. At least I now have the DNA sample I need. I put my gloved hand to my coat pocket, where Bella's hair lies secure in its plastic bag. Right now, this bag's contents could well be my most valuable possession. As long as some of Bella's hairs contain root follicles, then they should be okay for testing. I'm almost scared to send them off to the lab. What will I do after all this if Bella isn't my daughter? What will I do if she *is*?

My heart lifts slightly as I reach my car and slide inside. I'm desperate to get away from this area. To be safely back home with the door closed and locked behind me. I also need to get rid of my shoes, and possibly even my coat. They'll have glass fragments in them. Plus, I'm sure I read something somewhere about the police being able to match shoe treads to marks made at the scene of the crime. I should wash my hair too. I rest my forehead on the steering wheel for a moment. This is all too much. I don't think I thought this through properly. *No, it'll be fine.* I'll just bin all my clothes from tonight, vacuum out my car, have a shower and get into bed. I still have around two hours until the fayre ends.

I drive home slowly, carefully, paranoid that I'm going to crash the car and ruin my cover story. The traffic is slow and heavy – a combination of rush hour and Christmas shoppers. At last, I turn into my road and allow my shoulders to relax. There's a parking space opposite the house. I pull into it and then check the street is clear before darting across the road and in through my front door. Like a rabbit bolting into its burrow.

My heart pounds, but I can't relax yet. I empty my coat pockets, slip off my trainers and my coat, and pad into the kitchen, where I retrieve a bin liner from under the sink. Back out in the hall, I put the old trainers in the bin bag, along with my spare coat and the rest of my clothes, relieved that I least didn't wear my thick parka for fear of being recognised. Maybe I'm going overboard – after all, I only broke a window. I didn't steal anything of value. I didn't *kill* anyone – but I've watched enough crime dramas to know that disposing of clothes is the very minimum precaution I should take. Next, I run upstairs and shove the bag containing Bella's hair into a suitcase that's under our bed. Then I throw on some fresh jeans, a jumper and some boots, thunder back down the stairs, grab the bin bag and open the front door.

Our road is deserted, so I make a dash for it and dump the bin bag on the back seat before getting into the car and driving away a little too fast. I travel a couple of miles – away from the direction of Kate and Shaun's place – to an out-of-town car park that has several large recycling bins. I drive over to the clothing bank and park right next to it. There's no one else in this part of the car park apart from an older woman standing in front of one of the bins. Getting out of my car, I see she has a boot full of cardboard boxes stacked with bottles. As she feeds each one into the bottle bank, the smash of glass reminds me with a shiver of where I was earlier. Of what I did.

'Work Christmas party,' the woman says as I pull down the door to the clothing bank. 'In case you thought all this lot was mine!'

I give a brief smile and nod before turning away and depositing the refuse bag full of clothes into the bin.

'I think you're supposed to take the stuff out of the bin liner,' she says as another of her bottles smashes into the bottle bank.

'Oh, okay, thanks.' Sometimes, I really wish people would mind their own business. I upend the bin bag and shake out its contents.

'You must be chilly,' she adds.

I realise I'm not wearing a coat, but although I'm shivering, I can barely feel the cold. 'I'm fine. This is just a quick stop – heater's on full blast in the car.'

'I'm wearing about five layers and I'm still freezing.'

She obviously wants to chat, but I don't have the time or energy. 'Have a good Christmas,' I say, dumping the refuse bag into the regular bin, along with my gloves.

'Thanks. You too.'

I slip back into my car and drive off, glad to be away from the woman, uneasy knowing she's seen me dumping my clothes. I head home once again, hoping I get there before everyone else.

I can't see Matt's van in the street, so it looks like my luck is still holding. I park in the same spot I vacated earlier and turn off the engine. I should probably vacuum out the car, but I'm across the road from the house; I'll draw too much attention to myself. And quite honestly, I just don't have the energy. I'm wrung out. Exhausted. At this rate, the migraine excuse will become a self-fulfilling prophecy.

I heave myself out of the car and back into the house, telling myself that whatever else happens, at least I have Bella's hair. That's what tonight was about, and in that regard it was a success. Even if I feel grubby and terrible about what I had to do to get it.

Suddenly, I realise I really am absolutely freezing. Going out without a coat was a daft idea. I'll have a shower, wash my hair and crawl into bed with my phone. Because as well as filling out the form for sending off the DNA sample, I also, finally, want to get some deeper online research done. I need to find out why Shaun went to prison. To find out if he committed a violent crime. And, more importantly, if his children are in danger.

Half an hour later, I'm sitting up in bed with my phone. My heart rate has slowed a little now that I'm home and safe. Although how long that will last is anyone's guess. I'm still on high alert for sudden phone calls and knocks on the front door. I can't believe it's only six thirty. It feels like at least ten o'clock. Matt and the kids will be home within the hour, so I don't have much time.

When Shaun and Kate were round here the other week, I remember him saying he owned a building company. Perhaps it's listed online somewhere under his name. I'm not sure how that will help me, but if I could at least find out where it's registered, that might give me somewhere to start.

I do a Google search for 'Companies House Shaun Morris', and it comes up with the name 'Shaun Richard Morris'. I click on it. The listing shows the correspondence address as The Ridings, 48 Goldfinch Lane, Crouch End, London, and shows his company name as 'Build Morr'. The fact that this Shaun Morris is the director of a building firm based in the right area of London convinces me that this must be the right Shaun Morris. The address sounds residential, so he probably registered the company at his home address. The company status shows as 'dissolved', and it says that Shaun Morris resigned as company director just under two and a half years ago.

I tap the company name and there's a heading that says 'People'. Once again it shows Shaun Richard Morris as a director, but underneath his name it lists a second person – Catherine Margaret Morris. Catherine must be Kate, surely. There's little doubt that this was Kate and Shaun's company. Maybe now I'll be able to find out some more about them.

I tap the address into Google Maps and zoom in. I love how the map system shows you what the actual road looks like and that you can scroll past each house taking a look over walls and fences, as though you're actually walking past. Sure enough, The Ridings is situated in a residential road. And not just any residential road – it's wide and leafy and doesn't even look like it belongs in the centre of London. The properties on this road must be worth a fortune. It takes me a while to locate number 48, but when I finally do, I raise my eyebrows. It's a large, semi-detached, double-fronted Victorian villa with a huge paved driveway. It must have been a real wrench to leave that beauty and move into their tiny flat on the outskirts of Wareham.

As I save the address, I get a fluttering of nerves in my belly about what I'm going to have to do. But before that, I need to go onto the DNA-testing website and activate the kit they sent me. I check the time – it's already past seven o'clock. I don't think I'm going to have time to sort out the form and DNA samples before Matt and the kids get home.

My brain feels like chewing gum. I close my eyes and sink back into my pillows, trying to slow my breathing and stop the panicky sensation getting any worse. I'm okay when I'm doing something, but as soon as I stop, waves of anxiety start to attack.

I'm saved from thinking too hard by the sound of the front door opening. I lean over to turn off my bedside light, but I change my mind at the last second – I don't want to be in the dark. It'll be fine to leave it on. I'll say I've been resting.

'Can I put my new decoration on the tree?' Charlie's voice floats up the stairs, loud and excited. It makes me smile and want to rush downstairs to give him a hug.

'Shh,' Matt says, trying to be quiet. 'Mum might be asleep.'

'Can we show her what we got from the fayre?' Jess asks.

'Maybe tomorrow.' The stairs creak and the landing light comes on. As the bedroom door opens and Matt walks in, I'm hit with a mixture of dread and relief. 'Hey, you,' he says gently. 'Didn't think you'd be awake.' His cheeks are pink, and his hair is mussed up from the wind. It hurts how much I love him.

'Hello.' I sit up and force out a sleepy smile. I'm terrified he'll be able to see straight through me. Know that I've lied.

'How've you been?'

'I'm so sorry I couldn't be there this evening.'

'That's okay. You can't help being ill. Are you feeling any better? Want a cup of tea or something to eat?'

I shake my head. 'No, I'm fine. Maybe just some water?'

'Yeah, sure.'

His thoughtfulness makes me feel even more guilty. 'How was the fayre? Not too hectic I hope?'

'It was pretty good actually.' Matt grins. 'Charlie had a great time helping me on the decorations stand, and I barely saw Jess – she was off around the hall with her friends. Far too cool to hang around with her boring old dad.'

'That's good. I'm gutted I couldn't go. I think it's the first one I've missed since Jess started in Kindergarten.' I want to ask if he saw Kate there, but I bite back the question. It's not a good idea to mention anything to do with the Morrises after what I did this evening.

'Never mind. There'll be plenty more school fayres to go to.'

'Heidi wasn't annoyed, was she?'

'Course not. She told me to send you her love and to tell you to get well soon.'

'That's sweet of her.' Now I feel even more guilty.

'I'll go and get your water. Back in a sec. Try to get some more sleep.'

I listen to the heavy tread of his footsteps going back down the stairs. How will I ever fall asleep knowing that Kate is probably back home by now too? What will she make of the broken window? I don't even know if Shaun will remember what happened. But if he does, at least he was semi-delirious, so he's not exactly a reliable witness. I should try to relax. Try to do what Matt suggested and get some sleep. There's nothing I can do about the Morrises right now anyway. If they call the police, they call the police. I'll simply deny everything.

I turn onto my side and close my eyes. But my heart is still racing, my stomach still churning. Sleep won't come for me tonight. I'm sure of it. Especially as I've already decided what I'm going to do tomorrow.

CHAPTER THIRTY

The road into London has been surprisingly quiet. I'm only a few miles from my destination and I thought it would have taken me a lot longer to get here. In the end, I decided to drive, as the train fare was ridiculously expensive, and the coach was going to be too slow to get me home in time for school pick-up. Plus I couldn't risk either service being cancelled and leaving me stranded. Luckily I know the route well, but I hadn't banked on the strange and unsettling emotions it's stirring up to be back this way again. I haven't visited London since I moved away, and I keep being thrown off guard by odd fragments of memories as I draw closer to the area where I used to live.

No one knows I'm here – not Matt, not Dee. It's my day off today and I was supposed to be doing some last-minute Christmas shopping, but that will have to wait until the weekend. I still have no idea what I'm going to buy anyone, and it will all have to go on the credit card as I have nothing left after the expense of the DNA test and today's petrol. That thirty quid I gave Shaun towards the window was the last of my cash.

After breaking into the Morrises' house last night, I was fully expecting Kate to call or text, or maybe even send the police over. But I've heard nothing. I guess that means either Shaun thought he hallucinated me, or Kate thought he was too delirious for his story to be reliable. Either that, or she's worried that I'm on to her. The thought of the Morrises leaving the area with Bella is far scarier to me than a visit from the police.

I got up at three this morning and crept into the bathroom to sort out mine and Bella's DNA samples, placing each one carefully in the vials the DNA-testing company sent me. It took me a while to find a company who would actually test hair. Most of them only use cheek swabs. This particular firm asked for five strands of hair each with the root follicle attached. I managed to extricate three from the clump of Bella's hair that looked like they had the follicles, but I couldn't find any others. I'll just have to hope that three are enough. Maybe I should have taken the hairbrush away with me to give me more of a chance to find intact follicles, but I didn't want Bella to notice that it was missing and then mention it to Kate, who might then put two and two together.

I stopped off at the post office after dropping Jess and Charlie at school. I doubt I'll get the results before Christmas, but at least they'll be in the process of being tested. I've waited so many years that a few more days won't hurt too much.

I've come to a complicated roundabout, and I panic about which lane I'm supposed to be in. My thoughts and worries about Bella are put on the back-burner for the moment as I try to negotiate tricky new routes and one-way systems. I could have put the address into my phone and used the satnav to guide me there, but I'm worried about my phone battery dying.

Finally, I get onto the North Circular, and even though the buildings and landmarks around have changed somewhat, the road itself is reassuringly familiar. I drive over the Brent Cross Flyover and turn off onto Falloden Way. Past Highgate Woods and then onto Shepherd's Hill. I recognise a couple of restaurants and cafés that have stood the test of time, as well as a park I remember visiting with my firstborn…

I exhale and give myself a shake. Now is not the time to get emotional. I need to detach myself from these memories in case they swallow me whole. Stay focused and concentrate on the route. The traffic is heavier now, the roads crowded with Christmas shoppers. As it starts to drizzle, the Christmas lights and car headlamps blur through my rain-smeared windscreen.

I follow the directions I scribbled down earlier, and within only a few minutes find myself driving along Goldfinch Lane. Set a few streets back from the main road, it has the feel of a wide country avenue – aside from the parking-restriction signs everywhere. I'm not sure what I'll do about those. I guess I'll have to chance it and hope no traffic wardens come along while I'm parked here.

The lane is lined with trees, their branches bare for now, but come the spring I bet it feels like a leafy little haven. I drive slowly, trying to spot house numbers to give me a clue as to whether I'm heading in the right direction, but the houses all seem to have name-plaques on their walls instead of street numbers – The Maltings, Courtenay House, Meadow View (not sure that one's strictly accurate, unless they have a really large garden), Orchard Villa, The Willows. And then I reach it – The Ridings.

I cruise past slowly, taking in the wide expanse of driveway and the smart brick facade. I can just picture the Morrises living there. The Ridings suits them much more than their current flat, but I guess Shaun's stint in prison must be responsible for them losing all their money. I have a clear vision of Bella growing up here in privileged luxury. Spending time in her beautifully decorated bedroom. Cosying up with rest of the family at Christmas around a traditional open fire. Running around on the lawn in summer wearing a succession of expensive, pretty summer dresses. I only hope that amidst all that privilege and wealth, she's been loved and cared for. That's the only thing I care about.

I pull up just beyond the property, in front of their neighbour's hedge so my car is screened from view. I take a swig of water and then check my face in the rear-view mirror. My eyes are bruised with dark circles, my skin mottled and blotchy. At least I washed my hair last night, so it looks nice and shiny. I also dressed relatively smartly today in my black jeans, blue polo neck and wool coat. It doesn't guarantee I won't get the door slammed in my face, but hopefully at least *one* of the neighbours will speak to me.

There's no point sitting here trying to work up the nerve. I don't have the luxury of time anyway. Not if I'm going to get home before anyone notices I'm missing. I may as well just get this over with. I take my umbrella out of the pocket in the car door, grab my handbag and step out onto the pavement. I'll try knocking on the door of the house I've parked outside. Walking around to the wrought-iron entrance gate, I see that this property is attached to The Ridings, so I'm hoping whoever lives here will know Kate and her family quite well.

I crunch my way across the gravel driveway, ring the doorbell and wait. No one comes immediately, so I ring again and use the door knocker for good measure. Finally, I'm rewarded by the sound of footsteps from inside growing louder. Through the opaque glass beside the wooden door, I see an inner door opening. There's a rattling sound, and then the front door opens. A woman roughly my age, wearing sweatpants with her hair pulled up in a messy bun, peers through a gap in the door – she has the chain pulled across.

'Hello?' she says sharply, with no pretence at friendliness.

'Hi, I'm so sorry to disturb you,' I say in what my mum would have described as a 'telephone voice'. 'I wonder if you can help?'

She doesn't reply. Just stares at me impatiently.

I'm not sure I'm going to get anything useful out of her, but I plough on anyway. 'It's a bit awkward, but I've got these new neighbours – Shaun and Kate Morris – and I understand they used to live next door to you.' I nod in the direction of The Ridings.

The woman's expression grows darker and I'm nervous that she's about to slam the door in my face. 'The thing is,' I continue, 'I heard that Shaun Morris just got out of prison and I wondered if you were able to tell me if I should be at all worried about him. It's just, I have young children and—'

'Sorry, I can't help you,' she says tersely, and closes the door.

I stand there for a moment as the rain patters against my umbrella, wondering if she can't help me because she's friendly with them, or because she's scared of them. Or maybe it's because she kept to herself and didn't know them at all. Reluctantly, I walk away and decide to try the neighbours on the other side of The Ridings. As I reach the pavement and start walking, I notice an older lady opposite pulling her wheelie bin back inside her driveway. I catch her eye and give a little smile, which she returns.

'You'll get clamped if you park there,' she says in a not-too-unfriendly tone.

'Thanks for the warning. I won't be here long.'

'The wardens are quick off the mark around here.'

'Oh no, really?' I glance up and down the road, but I can't spot anyone. I absolutely can't risk getting clamped. 'I don't suppose… do you mind if I have a quick word?'

'A word? Sounds ominous.' She peers at me from under the hood of her navy raincoat.

'Not really.' I cross over the road. Since I've been here, not one vehicle has driven down the street. 'It's peaceful down here, isn't it?'

'It is. We've lived here for thirty-four years,' she replies with a satisfied smile. 'Wouldn't want to live anywhere else. My son keeps telling us to sell up and get somewhere smaller and more manageable, but I love this road. And it's so handy for the shops.'

'I don't blame you. I wouldn't want to move either if I lived on this street.'

'Are you local?' Her eyes narrow and she looks me up and down.

'Used to be. I'm in Dorset now.'

'Now that's a lovely county – used to go there as a child on holiday. What brings you back to London? Visiting friends?'

'Well, it's a bit awkward.'

'Oh yes?' Her eyes widen in anticipation of what I'm about to say. I notice her coral lipstick has bled into the little corrugated-cardboard lines around her mouth.

Taking advantage of her eagerness, I ask, 'It's about the family who used to live opposite – the Morrises. Did you know them?'

'Kate and Shaun? Yes. Terrible business, all that.'

It sounds like I might have hit the jackpot with this older lady. Her eyes are bright and alert now, like she's itching to indulge in a bit of gossip.

'Well…' I lower my voice for dramatic effect. 'They've moved to Dorset and now they live next door to me.'

'Do they now? I wondered where they'd gone. Didn't leave a forwarding address. I suppose they didn't want any disgruntled contractors and clients following them. One day they were here, the next they were gone. Did you know their house was repossessed? The new owners got a bit of a bargain, I hear.'

'I didn't know that.'

She nods sagely, crossing her arms as though settling in for a good, long chat, the insistent drizzle not putting her off one bit. 'Yes. I always thought Kate was a bit stuck-up. Seemed all right to begin with – the two of them came and introduced themselves when they moved in, must be seven or eight years ago now – but they never really took the time to stop and be friendly. I mean, good manners cost nothing. We're a little community round here, but she never wanted to be part of it. We were lucky if we got so much as a nod from her. Shaun was a bit more approachable, but then we all know where *he* ended up. Melanie in number fifty, she's another snooty one. You were just round there a minute ago, weren't you?'

'Uh, yes.' I need to steer her back to the Morrises. 'But I was actually hoping to find out about Shaun.'

'Oh?' She folds her arms across her chest and purses her lips. 'Find out *what* exactly? I don't really like to talk about other people's business, you know.'

'Of course not, it's just…' I pause.

'Just *what?*'

'Oh, never mind. It's probably not fair to ask you. I'd better go and move the car before I get clamped.'

'You'll be fine. The warden walked down here about two minutes before you arrived. It'll be at least another hour before she comes back. Probably more like two.'

I stifle an eye-roll. A minute ago she was telling me I'd get clamped, when she knew the whole time that I'd be safe for ages. 'That's great. But still, I should go. You don't need me here, keeping you out in the rain.'

'I don't mind. So, what was it you wanted to ask me?' She leans forward. 'I can't promise I'll be able to help you, but I'll try my best.'

'That's so kind of you, but…' I pause as if weighing up what to do for the best. 'Well, if you're sure…'

'I am. Ask away.'

'Like I said, the Morris family have moved in next door to us. The thing is, I heard recently about his stint in prison.'

'Terrible business,' she says again.

'Well, we have two young children and so naturally we were a little worried—'

'Of course you were. Who wouldn't be?'

'So I wondered if you knew what it was that he was convicted of, and whether you could tell me if you think he's dangerous, or violent.'

She shakes her head and repeats her favourite line: 'Terrible, terrible business. But I can put your mind at rest on that score; you've no need to worry about Shaun.'

'I haven't?'

'No, dear. He's not violent as far as I'm aware. He went to prison for tax evasion.'

'Really?' That news has really surprised me. I was convinced she was going to tell me he was guilty of GBH or assault, or some kind of domestic violence. But tax evasion… I mean, it's bad, of course it is, but it's not exactly dangerous. 'Are you absolutely sure that's what he was in for? It's not just a rumour? Because I know how these things can spread.'

'One hundred per cent sure.' She gives me a self-satisfied smile. 'Bit of a scandal, actually. He was working on a few local building projects and he had to abandon them halfway through – he'd already been paid deposits for the work which, I might add, his clients lost. Thousands of pounds apparently. He didn't pay his tradesmen either. My nephew owns a roofing firm and told me all about it. There was quite an outcry at the time. I think one of his clients went to the papers, but I believe only the local one picked it up.'

That's why I couldn't find anything online – I didn't dig deep enough. I make suitable tutting noises. 'So there's nothing I need to be wary of from the Morrises?'

'Not really. Other than not employing them for any building work, obviously.' She gives a little laugh.

'Of course.' I wonder if there are any other little nuggets of information I can winkle out of her. I need to be subtle, though. I drop my shoulders and look sad. 'It must have been awful for their children.'

'I know, poor mites. I hardly ever saw them when they lived here – probably in their rooms on their devices all day. Not like when we were young – climbing trees and playing out in the fresh air. I can't understand the fascination with those screens. It's like some kind of brainwashing.'

'Mmm.' I don't want to get drawn into a whinge about how things were better in her day, and I don't think she has any further information. 'Well, it's been very nice chatting with you. Thanks for letting me know about Shaun, and sorry again for keeping you out in the rain.'

'Not at all. Always happy to help. Glad I could put your mind at rest.'

I cross back over the road and get back into the car. She gives me a little wave, and it's clear she's not going back inside until she's seen me drive off. I wanted to sit here for a moment more and digest what she's just told me, but it looks like I'm going to have to move on, because I don't fancy sitting here while the woman waits for me to leave. I need to get some more petrol anyway, and I'd better pick up a sandwich and some more water for my journey home.

I start up the car and drive slowly away. I can still see the neighbour standing on the pavement in the rain, watching my car, until I indicate left and turn out of Goldfinch Lane.

I feel strangely deflated now. And so tired. Now the adrenalin has worn off, my lack of sleep last night is finally catching up with me. Of course I'm glad that Shaun doesn't appear to be dangerous. That it was white-collar crime, nothing to do with anger, or violence. But surely the fact that Shaun was in prison at all shows that he doesn't play by the rules. That he's capable of breaking the law to get what he wants. So there's every likelihood that he's broken the rules before and taken something else that didn't belong to him – like a child.

CHAPTER THIRTY-ONE

THEN

All the furniture belongs to the landlord, so there's a surprisingly small amount of stuff to pack up. Just clothes, toiletries and some crockery, cutlery and ornaments. While Catriona gets on with wrapping plates and mugs in sheets of old newspaper, Grace is in the hall playing with a couple of large cardboard boxes. Catriona has propped the door open so she can keep an eye on her while she works. She smiles as she listens to her sweet conversation. At the moment, Grace is pretending to be a cat. One of the boxes is her house, and the other box is her cat-sister's house.

Hearing Grace talk about a sister – albeit a 'cat' sister – induces a mild panic in Catriona. The image of a woman with a pram flashes into her mind – the woman from the shopping centre. The child in the pram was obviously a sibling. Catriona needs to make herself think about something else. To block out all these unhelpful memories. But it's hard when Grace keeps triggering them with her make-believe chatter. Catriona tells herself that's all it is – *make-believe*. It's nothing more sinister than that. If by some chance it *is* a real memory, well, she's young enough for it to fade.

Catriona tries to think back to when she was a child and she's pretty sure the earliest memory she has is of an incident at nursery, when one of the helpers told her off for getting paint on the floor. She must have been about four at the time. Grace isn't even three.

A sharp pain flashes across Catriona's index finger. She glances down and twists her hand to see a thin red line along the side of her forefinger – a paper cut. She sucks the skin and goes over to the cupboard where she keeps the first-aid kit. She rinses her finger under the tap, pats it dry, then sticks a plaster on it. How can such a small cut be so painful? She sighs and returns to her task.

She finally left Darren's family last week, after they made her promise to come back and spend Christmas with them. Catriona could tell they would rather have kept her and Grace in Middles-brough. They really didn't want to let them go. But Catriona said she had too much to organise. That she would see them in a few weeks' time. She hates lying to Geoff and Pat, as they're such lovely, warm people. She knows she's lucky to have their support, but Grace comes first. She can no more keep Darren's family in her life than she can go to the police station and confess everything. No. She and Grace must start afresh. A single mum and her daughter moving to a new place.

To make a cleaner break, Catriona will tell Darren's parents that she and Grace are moving abroad to be with relatives. Maybe Australia or somewhere like that. She hasn't worked out the details yet. She'll say that reminders of Darren are too painful. At least that part will be the truth.

Catriona has never been the bravest person – Darren did all the organising for both of them, paying the bills and sorting out their finances, and she preferred it that way. That will have to change now. She'll have to put herself out there. Get a job. Look into what benefits she might be entitled to in the meantime. All this feels so overwhelming. For the past four years, she's been a stay-at-home mother. Darren didn't mind the fact she wanted to give up work to be with Grace. She only earnt minimum wage anyway, as a cashier in the local supermarket. He was supportive of her wanting to be a full-time mum. Catriona stops what she's doing for a second, angrily wiping away a stray tear. *She couldn't even do that properly.* But there's no room for self-pity. She has to learn to toughen up.

She's already put a deposit down on a tiny one-bed flat. She hasn't even seen the place in real life, but it looked okay online. One thing has come to light – she didn't realise that Darren had a small life-insurance premium. She's now due a small lump sum that will help her get started. No amount of money could ever replace Darren, but at least it will go some way to getting them settled in a new area.

'Hey, Gracie. Shall we have a snack?'

'Yes pwease.' Her daughter's voice is muffled inside the box.

'Chocolate rice cakes?' Catriona asks.

'Yay! Chocowate!'

Catriona tapes up the box she's been filling with cleaning products and Tupperware and wipes her hands down the sides of her jeans. 'Come on then, let's wash our hands.' She opens Grace's box, swings her up into her arms and kisses her soft cheeks, making her daughter giggle and squirm. She's all hot and crumpled from being inside the box, but this only makes her ten times more adorable. Catriona is determined to become the best mother in the world. She will take perfect care of her daughter – cherishing her, nurturing her, making sure she has everything she needs. Grace will be her number-one priority, not just in thoughts, but in actions. Always.

'Mummy, I have juice?'

'Let's have a nice glass of water instead.'

Grace wrinkles her pretty nose.

'Better to have water, sweetie. You don't want all your teeth to fall out.'

Grace's eyes widen, and she puts her fingers up to her mouth, touching her baby teeth. Catriona smiles reassuringly at her and then sets her down on the kitchen floor. She feels so protective it almost hurts. She realises she needs to make a good life for the two of them. She needs a good job, new friends, maybe she even needs to meet someone new – find a father for Grace. It's disloyal to even be thinking this, but she's only twenty-eight. She can't let the past destroy her life. She has to think about their future.

Through the window, Catriona's eyes are drawn upwards to the church steeple, dark against the ice-white sky. The thought flickers into her head that she should maybe have planted a tree or a shrub in the church grounds. Marked the spot with something beautiful. But that would have drawn too much attention. And perhaps there should be no reminder as, after all, she does still have her Gracie. She wonders if the spot will ever be discovered. But she can't think like that. And in any case, she can't do anything about it now.

Soon, once she's out of this flat, she won't have to think about any of this again. It will be a clean slate. Time will heal everything.

CHAPTER THIRTY-TWO

NOW

The traffic is heavier on the drive back from London, three-lane tailbacks seeming to materialise out of nowhere. I still have three hours before I need to be at school, but at the rate I'm crawling along, it will take at least four.

My phone buzzes and I glance over at the passenger seat where my mobile sits on top of my handbag. It's a text from Matt. I wait until the traffic comes to another standstill before quickly glancing at his message:

> *Mum's picking the kids up after school. They're going to help decorate her tree this evening.*

My shoulders suddenly feel less tense. Thank goodness for Stella! I quickly tap out a reply:

> *That's great. See you later.*

I wait for Matt's response, but he doesn't text back. Must be busy at work. At least I don't have to stress all the way home about missing school pick-up.

In the end, it takes me over three and a half further hours to get back, so I would definitely have been late.

Turning into our road, I'm surprised to see Matt's van parked outside the house. He's home early. Although the house is in darkness, which is weird. My stomach lurches at the thought of going in and lying to him about where I've been all day, making up some story about Christmas shopping. I realise I just can't do it. I think I'm going to have to come clean. Not about all of it – not about breaking into the Morrises' flat – but just about where I was today.

Now that I'm closer to getting the DNA results, I feel like the whole truth is going to come out soon anyway, so I may as well start being more honest. The thought of not holding onto the lies any longer lifts my spirits. I'm a little anxious about how Matt will react, but I'm sure he'll understand how important it was that I made sure Bella wasn't in any danger from Shaun.

The streetlamps are already on and rain spatters my face as I exit the car and stretch out my limbs. I'm not used to driving for such a long period of time. I could do with a walk around the block, but it's not really the weather for it and now that I've decided to be more honest, I don't want to put off telling Matt where I've been.

I open the front door, happy to be home. I also realise that I'm hugely relieved to have found out Shaun isn't necessarily dangerous. His prison stay had been really weighing on my mind, my brain conjuring all these awful scenarios, and I'd been fearing for the Morrises' children's safety. Knowing they're not being abused has diffused some of my desperation to get Bella away from him.

'Matt?' The hallway is dark, as is the rest of the house. But no, I'm wrong, there's a light on behind the kitchen door. I switch on the hall light and open the kitchen door with a smile on my face. But the kitchen is empty. I shiver, realising the heating isn't on, so I open the boiler cupboard and override the timer, feeling a flicker of satisfaction at the sound of the system firing up. That will soon get the place toasty.

But where's Matt? He must be upstairs getting changed after work.

I leave the kitchen and peer into the lounge, just in case he's in here – 'Matt?' – but it's dark, so I turn to go upstairs.

'Hello, Rachel.'

I jump at the sound of Matt's voice coming from inside the unlit lounge. 'Matt, what are doing in here?' I turn back around and see a dark shape on the sofa. 'Why are you sitting in the dark?' I switch on the light and stare at him in confusion. He's hunched on the sofa, swigging lager from a can. There are several empties scattered around him, some on the sofa, some on the floor, as though he's just dropped them there without a thought. He doesn't even look up at me. 'Matt? What's wrong? Are the kids okay?' My limbs start to tingle, and my chest tightens.

'They're fine. They're at Mum's.' His voice is toneless. It makes me nervous.

'What time are they getting back?' I really don't want them walking in and seeing Matt in this state. I start collecting up the beer cans from the floor.

'They're staying over at Mum's tonight.'

'What? Why? It's a school night. They haven't got—'

'They'll be fine. Mum's taking them to school in the morning.' He sounds annoyed, impatient.

'What about all their stuff? Toothbrushes and pyjamas… Jess has got her guitar lesson tomorrow.'

'I said they'll be fine.' His voice has hardened even more. He belches and drops his empty beer can onto the floor. 'I need another drink.'

'Matt! What's going on? Why are you drinking in the dark? Why are you talking to me like this?'

He doesn't reply, just lumbers to his feet and leaves the room.

'Where are you going?' My heart pounds uncomfortably as I follow him into the hall and through to the kitchen, where he opens the fridge and pulls out another six pack of beer. I drop the empty cans I'm clutching into the recycling bin and put a hand on his arm. 'Matt, you're scaring me. Why are you being like this?'

He shrugs my hand off and I flinch. I don't understand what's going on. Did he find out about me breaking into the Morris's place? Is that it? My skin goes cold. Maybe if I start explaining. But I don't know where to start and I don't even know if that's the reason he's acting like this.

'Matt! Talk to me.'

He breaks a can out of its plastic ring and pulls off the tab, pouring an indecent amount of the liquid down his throat in one go.

'Matt, please!'

He looks at me for the first time since I got home, but his eyes are glazed and distant.

'Can we sit down and talk?' I beg.

'We should have talked ages ago. *You* should have talked.' Matt gives a bitter laugh and lurches past me back into the living room. He flops back down on the sofa.

I perch on the arm of the other sofa, uncomfortable and fearful about what he's discovered. I take a breath and exhale out through my mouth. 'I went to London today to speak to Kate and Shaun's old neighbours.'

'What did you do that for, Rachel?'

His cutting tone is like a knife to my stomach. 'Why are you speaking to me so horribly? Matt, this isn't like you.'

He gives me a look that chills my heart. 'While you were snooping around in London, I went to see Kate and Shaun today.'

'You went to see Kate and Shaun? *Why?* Whatever they told you, it's probably all lies.'

'Lies? So you didn't break into their house last night?'

Shit.

'You didn't smash a window and go into Bella's bedroom? That's a lie, is it?'

'I…'

He shakes his head and takes another slug of beer.

'You followed her home from school, Rachel. She's a child. Someone else's child!'

'She's *my* child.'

'She's not your child. She's nothing to do with you. Look, I was patient and sympathetic because of what you told me about Holly. But you've gone too far. You need help.'

I get to my feet and start twisting my fingers. 'What did Kate say to you? Did you find anything out about Bella?'

'I know you think Bella is your child, Rachel, but you have to accept that she's not. You have to stop all this.'

'How do you know she's not mine? *You* don't know.'

The look Matt gives me is one you might give a stranger – a pitying look filled with disdain. It makes my insides quiver with fear. Doesn't he love me any more? Has his patience run out after so short a time of knowing my secret? Is this the end of us? My world is tilting and shifting. I feel as though I'm sliding off the edge and I can't hold on.

Matt bows his head and rests his forehead on his arms. Like it's all too much for him. Well maybe it is, but what about *me*? He doesn't know what it's like to lose a child. I really thought he'd be more understanding. I'm gutted at his lack of sympathy.

'She's mine,' I insist, even though I know this line of conversation will only push him further away. But I can't spare his feelings, because I can't deny my daughter. I can't do it. Not even to appease Matt. 'If you could just wait for the results of the DNA test, I'll be able to prove it to you.'

He glances up at this, confusion on his face.

'Please, Matt, don't look at me like I'm crazy. You know me, you know I'm a rational person. But I know in my bones that Bella is Holly. She's mine.'

'What DNA test? How the hell did you get Bella's DNA? Christ, is that what you were doing breaking into Shaun's place?' He sighs heavily and puts his beer can on the coffee table. 'I can't even get drunk properly.'

'What else did the Morrises say?' I sit back down on the edge of the sofa, chewing the skin around my fingernails.

'I spent the afternoon with them at their place. Sounds like they've had a hell of a time recently.'

'*They've* had a hell of a time?' I shake my head in disbelief at the thought of them all chatting away together. At the thought of Matt going behind my back. Talking about me.

'You've really got it wrong about them, Rachel. They were nice. Understanding. I told them what you'd been through and they were shocked.'

'You told them! About Holly?'

'I had to. It was the only way I could explain your actions. People don't just break into other people's houses for no reason. When I told them your story, they were lovely. Kate even cried. She said she felt terrible for giving you a hard time.'

I bite back a retort. I don't believe her act for a moment. Of course she'd pretend to be sympathetic. What else would she do after Matt told them my suspicions? They're hardly going to admit to it.

Matt flexes his fingers. 'There's another reason why Kate and Shaun were so cagey when you started talking about Bella at dinner that night…'

'Oh?' I wait to hear what other lies they've fed Matt.

'Bella isn't their biological daughter. She's adopted.'

For a second, I'm not sure I've heard right. 'Adopted?' I almost laugh. That proves my theory even more.

'It's not common knowledge,' Matt continues, 'and Bella doesn't know yet, which is why they were understandably upset when you started asking questions about her at dinner.'

'They *would* say that though, wouldn't they? They're not going to admit that they took my daughter! The fact that they're now saying she's not even their biological daughter makes me even more sure they're guilty. They're just saying she's adopted to wriggle out of a DNA test.'

'They showed me proof, Rachel. Her adoption papers, baby photos, they even have a baby book with everything documented. I was embarrassed that they felt the need to prove it to me. I told them I didn't need proof. Poor people. So you see, Rachel, they wouldn't have all those things if they'd taken her when she was a toddler, would they?'

'Photos? Documents?' I sneer. 'Those things are *easy* to fake. Anyone can put together a few pictures and a baby book. It's not like Photoshop doesn't exist!'

'They also said they were willing for you to have a DNA test to prove she's not your daughter.'

I daren't tell him that I've already sent off the samples. My shoulders slump. I'm suddenly exhausted. Defeated. Tears begin to roll down my cheeks – more because of Matt's attitude than anything else. He doesn't want to comfort me. He isn't affected by my tears. Instead he's shifting in his seat, looking at the door like he wants to escape. I can't believe he would believe the Morrises over his own family. 'Matt—'

I'm interrupted by the doorbell. Matt jumps to his feet.

'Is that your mum with the kids? They can't come in now. I'm a mess. You're drunk.'

'I'm not drunk. And it's not my mum.'

'It's not the Morrises, is it?' A wave of horror washes over me at the thought of having to have this conversation with them here and now while I'm so upset, while Matt so clearly isn't on my side. 'Don't answer it. Please.'

But he already has his hand on the lounge door…

CHAPTER THIRTY-THREE

I debate whether to slip out the back door and drive away. Or go and hide upstairs in our room. If it's the Morrises come over to have it out with me, I can't face them. I really can't.

Matt leaves the room, presumably to answer the door, but then he comes back in for a moment. He gives me an indecipherable look – somewhere between pity and… fear. 'I'm sorry. Please believe me. I didn't want to do this, but you've gone too far.'

My chest constricts at his words. 'Do *what*? Matt, what are you talking about?' The doorbell rings once again, accompanied by a sharp rap on the knocker. A chill descends on me as Matt actually starts to cry. *What the hell?* 'Matt, what's the matter? Who's at the door? Matt, talk to me.'

He doesn't reply. Instead, he takes a deep breath, wipes away his tears with his fingertips, squares his shoulders and strides down the hall. I follow him, my heart drumming, terrified that I'm on the verge of having an almighty argument with Kate and Shaun. An argument I simply don't have the energy for right now.

'Matthew Bernshaw?' A woman's voice. Not Kate's. She's wearing a long raincoat.

Over Matt's shoulder, I also catch sight of the high-vis jacket and black hat of a police uniform.

My stomach lurches. 'Is it the children? Are they okay?' All thoughts of Kate and Shaun are put aside at the idea that something might have happened to Jess or Charlie. I try to hear what they're saying, but Matt is talking to them in a really low voice and the male uniformed officer catches my eye before looking back at Matt. Finally, Matt steps aside, and everything seems to slow down as I wait for the police to tell me why they're here.

The plain-clothes policewoman – at least I assume she's police – steps into the hall and looks me in the eye. I'm beginning to feel uneasy. The way she's looking at me isn't good – not at all. I take a single step backwards to put some space between us. My cheeks are hot and my legs suddenly feel weak.

'Rachel Farnborough, I'm arresting you on suspicion of—'

I stiffen. 'You're *arresting* me? Matt, what's going on?' The woman is still speaking, listing out these things she thinks I've done and telling me about my right not to say anything. I can't make out what she means, it all sounds muffled and strange, as though I'm under water. Surreal, like I'm in some hideous nightmare.

'Matt!' I look at him for an explanation, but his head is angled away from me. He won't catch my eye.

The policeman takes hold of my forearms and places my wrists together in front of me. I'm too dazed to realise what he's doing and so I keep my hands where he's positioned them. But now he's putting cold, metal handcuffs on my wrists. This has to be a joke, surely?

Suddenly everything speeds back up and my hearing returns as though my ears have just popped. Maybe they think I tried to take Bella. 'What are you doing? Look, there's been a mistake. I didn't try to take Bella Morris. I was only following her to see if she was my daughter. My own daughter was abducted nine years ago.' I turn to Matt. 'Matt, tell them. Tell them I didn't hurt Bella. Tell them about the DNA test. *That* will prove everything.'

But Matt isn't saying anything. He's really crying now. Tears streaming down his face. His eyes red, his face pale. He doesn't look like my Matt at all. 'Matt, tell them!' *Why won't anyone listen to me?*

Then it dawns on me. 'It's *Kate*, isn't it? Kate must have reported me.' I glower at the policewoman. 'Did Kate Morris call you?

Whatever she told you, it's all lies. She's covering everything up because she has my daughter. She stole her from me. She's the one you want.'

But the policewoman doesn't appear to be listening. 'Let's talk about it when we get to the station. Right now, I need you to calm down and come with us.' She's trying to make me go with her out of the house. I don't want to leave. I can't go. What about the kids? It's Christmas next week and I haven't even bought their presents yet.

'It's the other way around!' I cry. 'You're arresting the wrong person! It's Kate and Shaun! They're the ones who stole my daughter! They're the guilty ones; not me!' I grab hold of the stair railings with my cuffed hands. If I hold on long enough, they'll have to listen to me. I'll make them understand that I'm innocent.

'Can you let go of the bannister, Rachel?'

'Her name is Holly, not Bella! I'm sorry I broke into their house, but I had to get proof!' I grip on even tighter. I'm not going to budge.

'Rachel,' she says, 'you need to let go and come with us.'

'I'm not going anywhere. You have to listen to me.'

'We'll listen to you at the station.'

'No, please. Matt, tell them.'

'If you don't let go,' the policewoman says, 'we're going to have to remove you by force.'

I shake my head. She can't touch me, surely. Something like that must be against procedure. I strengthen my grip as the policeman takes a small black rod from his belt. He gives me a look that says don't be stupid, but I've chosen a course of action now and I won't back down. This whole thing is outrageous. 'You can't make me— Ow!' I let out a string of expletives. I'm not one to normally swear but that hurt so bad.

'Come on, Rachel. Let's go.'

The pain in my fingers is intense. But it fades into irrelevance as I realise I'm no longer gripping the stair railings. His rap on the knuckles worked. The two police officers are leading me out of my house and into the street; into their car. I don't know what's happening, but I don't feel well at all. I don't feel at all like myself. Why isn't Matt coming with me? He hasn't even stepped out of the house.

And then I realise…

Before he answered the door Matt *apologised* to me. He said he was sorry and that he didn't want to do this. And now it's so blindingly obvious what has happened – it wasn't Kate Morris at all; it was Matt who called the police.

It was Matt who betrayed me.

CHAPTER THIRTY-FOUR

THEN

Catriona turns the key and opens the door to her new flat. To her new *life*. She's just driven down from London and was hoping to get here in the light, but she was late leaving, and then Grace had a little accident, so she had to change all her clothes, by which time Catriona was so stressed that she needed to sit in the car and try to calm herself down for half an hour. Now she's finally here, but it's dark, and everything looks really different to how she imagined it would be. She's not sure she can do this.

Online, the flat looked so bright and airy, so welcoming and fresh. But right now, it all feels strange and wrong, the overhead lights casting a too-bright yellow glow edged with deep shadows. It smells of paint and the air inside feels damp. She mustn't cry. It will all seem better after a night's sleep – isn't that what everyone always says?

She hadn't realised how awkward it was going to be to manage a young child on her own while trying to move into a new place. Luckily, the flat is fully furnished, but even so, she still has to negotiate the stairs with Grace while bringing up all her stuff. She works out the best way to do it is to balance Grace on one hip while carrying a bag or case with her free hand and wedging another one under her arm. At least the weather isn't too bad for December – dull but not raining and not too cold either. It could have been a lot worse going from the car to the flat, laden down with her possessions in the pouring rain. She should try to count her blessings.

Grace is snoozy after the car journey, so she's resting her head on Catriona's shoulders, her thumb firmly planted in her mouth. After several tricky trips up and down the stairs, carting up the essentials like bedding and food, Catriona decides to call it a day. She'll bring the rest of her gear up tomorrow. It should all be okay left overnight in the boot. There's nothing of worth in there anyway. Just some clothes and knick-knacks.

Once Grace is ensconced on the grey sofa with a bag of apple rice cakes and a beaker of water, Catriona goes into their bedroom. She could only afford a one-bedroom flat, so Grace will be sleeping in with her, but that's okay. She prefers it that way. At least the beds look decent – two singles with brand new mattresses, still in their plastic. After manoeuvring the mattresses out of their packaging, she makes up both beds with her own duvets and pillows.

Hot and tired after her exertions, Catriona surveys the room. It's actually starting to look a little better in here now the beds are made up. Tomorrow she can really get to work on the rest of the flat – open some windows, let the air in, check out the neighbourhood. She might even treat herself to some fresh flowers.

She pops back into the lounge to check on Grace. She's fallen asleep on the sofa, the empty packet of rice cakes rising and falling on her chest as she breathes. Poor lamb is tired out. Catriona moves the packet aside and carries Grace into the bedroom. She gently lays her on her bed, changes her into her pyjamas and covers her over with the duvet.

Now that Grace is asleep, Catriona is tempted to do what she always does in the evenings now – go on her phone and see if there are any updated news stories about the missing girl and her parents. It's become a bit of an obsession – finding out everything she can about them. The parents' names are Rachel and Andrew and the daughter's name is Holly.

Back in London, the mother was on the local news several times putting out appeals for the return of her daughter. She was very vocal and very visibly upset. The father was quieter. Less emotional. The couple didn't seem close at all. Their body language was stiff. Almost hostile. Or maybe Catriona imagined that part.

Apparently, the father was in Spain working at the time of the abduction. The local media hinted that he might have been behind the whole thing – especially as he just flew back there this week. But he hasn't been arrested or named as a suspect. They also said that he's got another woman over there. That he abandoned Rachel to be with this Spanish woman. Of course, it's all speculation.

Other news stories have implied that it could have been the mother, Rachel, who arranged the whole abduction. People can be so cruel. So vicious. So uncaring. The truth is, the public don't have a clue what really happened – they just go by what the papers tell them, titillating stories made up to cause outrage or pity. Catriona can't help wondering what it must be like for Rachel. How she's coping. She has a baby daughter called Jessica, so that must keep her going. Catriona doesn't know what she would do if anything happened to Grace. It doesn't bear thinking about. She pushes away the image of the bathwater… of the churchyard back in London with its freshly turned earth. She swallows down bile.

'Mummy?' Grace has opened her eyes and is staring around in panic at her unfamiliar surroundings.

'It's okay, Grace. Close your eyes. It's sleepy time now.' Catriona strokes her daughter's hair until she falls asleep once more. Then she chides herself – all this time she's still been thinking of herself as *Catriona* and her daughter as *Grace*. But she can't afford to make those kinds of slip ups. She shakes her head and mutters, 'I'm not Catriona. She's not Grace.'

Catriona has already changed both their names by deed poll to give them a fresh start. She signed her new name on the rental agreement too. It means they can both live without fear of being tracked down by friends and family from their former lives. It means they'll be almost impossible to trace. But in order for that to hold true, she has to get used to thinking of herself and her daughter by their new names. Catriona and Grace are gone. No more. She mustn't even *think* the names. She decides the only way to truly get used to their new names is to keep saying them aloud. Maybe a bit of role playing will help them sink into her brain.

Catriona goes back out into the lounge, stands to face an imaginary person and pretends to shake their hand. She feels faintly ridiculous, but this is too important for her to make any mistakes. She also decides to try to soften her London accent. That way, hopefully, she won't stand out as much in this unfamiliar Dorset town.

'Hello,' she says. 'Nice to meet you. Yes, this is my daughter. Her name's Jess. And I'm Rachel. Rachel Farnborough.'

CHAPTER THIRTY-FIVE

NOW

There are 136 tile squares in the ceiling of my room. I've counted them all. As I lie on my bed, I'm looking up at them, trying to work out some kind of game I could play in my head using them as a board. Like sudoku or something. Anything to stop the rush of jumbled thoughts cascading through my mind.

Everything has finally come out into the open. What I did. *Who I really am.* I know it's probably hard for other people to believe, but the truth shocked *me* more than anyone. I honestly didn't know who I was or what I'd done. I couldn't believe I had somehow blocked out my past and become this whole other person. But through all the shock and trauma, that's exactly what I'd done.

When the police arrested me five months ago, I went into a kind of shut-down mode. I entered a semi-catatonic state and had to be admitted to a psychiatric hospital – which is where I am now. Which is where I'll probably be for the foreseeable future. It's taken the doctors weeks to get me to accept who I really am. To make me understand that I never actually had a child who was abducted. That my name isn't even Rachel Farnborough.

It's Catriona Devon.

I still get muddled from time to time. Flipping between Rachel and Catriona. They say I may have dissociative identity disorder

– the medical term for a split personality – but my doctor hasn't formally diagnosed me. He still says it's too early to say for certain.

I sit up in bed and start counting the tiles again. I'm pretty sure there are 136 of them. I can't remember if that's right, or if I imagined it. I'd better count them again; just to make doubly sure.

Once I've finished counting, I stand and walk around the small room to stretch my legs. It's almost time for my morning walk outside in the grounds. I feel edgy in anticipation of it. I can't sit still. Whenever my brain is unoccupied it returns to all the memories. It's like a lucky dip – sometimes they're good memories of me and Darren and Grace, or perhaps of Matt, Jess and Charlie. But more often than not they're bad memories… of scented water and dark earth and blank expressions that make me want to scratch my brain cells out.

My pacing becomes more frantic. I don't have a watch or a clock in here so I can't tell if the nurse is late today. What if they forget to come? Or if they've decided I can't go out for some reason? I don't *have* to stay in this room – it's not like they've locked me in or anything. But it makes me nervous, going into the common areas by myself with all the other patients and staff and visitors. I feel as though I'm on display. So I like to wait until I can walk out with a member of staff. It makes me feel more secure.

If they do forget me, I might just have to be brave, because I really do need to get out of this room. I miss going out, walking down by the river. I miss working with Dee, and the school run. I miss London and its big, anonymous parks.

I remember now, how my little Gracie used to love going to the park. She used to be fascinated with the squirrels and the birds. We'd feed the ducks and go to the play park, sometimes taking a picnic and making a day of it. It was lovely when Darren would come with us too. I was so proud of our lovely little family. That's all I ever wanted… a little family of my own. It wasn't too much to ask for, was it? Or maybe it was. Every time I think of her, I get this whooshing in my ears and a pressure on my chest. I spoke to Dr Medway about it, and he told me those sensations are all part of my grief. I never really mourned Grace when she died. So getting my memories back has been painful. It's as though I've lost my daughter all over again.

That's why, when I saw Bella with her distinctive colouring, I had such a physical reaction – she reminded me of my Grace. The real Grace.

But, at that time, I was so entrenched in my Rachel persona, the person I'd convinced myself I was for years, that I couldn't make the connection to my daughter Grace. Instead I believed she was Holly, the missing daughter I'd invented. *Rachel's* missing daughter, who never really existed. And Jess… well, I believed she really was my daughter.

I know the truth now. Seven years ago, my daughter Grace died. She drowned in the bath. It was an accident. I'm starting to understand that. But it doesn't stop me feeling like I was to blame. Like I was an unfit mother.

I carry on pacing in my room, my anxiety levels rising. I really do need to get out of here. I can't even settle to counting the tiles again.

Those false memories I had of Holly were in fact real memories of my dead daughter Grace. Because it was Grace who had the same heart-shaped face and freckled snub nose as Bella. The same dark hair and green eyes. That's why it hit me so hard when I saw Bella. It was as though Bella was my poor little Gracie returned from the dead. Living the life she was supposed to live, instead of drowning in a few inches of water and lying forgotten in a London churchyard. The truth was trying to surface in my mind.

I put my fist into my mouth to stop the tears. Although Dr Medway says it's good to cry. It's healthy. But if I break down again then I might not get my morning walk outside. And I really do need that walk. I should try to think about something else.

Something less upsetting. My mind scrolls through for something else to latch onto. Something other than Grace…

It lands on Kate and Shaun – two innocent bystanders who got drawn into my dark and complicated web. Poor Kate had already been through so much with her husband's spell in prison, their bankruptcy and then having to move away from all their friends. She must have thought she'd landed in crazy town after she met me.

A knock on the door heralds the arrival of one of the nurses. *Thank goodness*. They've come just in time to save me from my dark anxieties. The nurses are generally nice, but I can't help feeling self-conscious around them. After all, they know exactly what I did. They know my whole sordid story. I wonder if they gossip about us – *us* being the inmates, or patients, or whatever we're called. They must. They must have their opinions. Or maybe they're bound by patient–clinician confidentiality. Some of the nurses are quite friendly. Others are more detached, efficient, *brisk*. I squirm at the thought of other people looking at me, judging me, pitying, fearing, loathing. Or maybe that's all in my head, and they don't have an opinion one way or the other.

'Morning, Catriona.'

Oh good; it's Jenny, one of the friendlier psychiatric nurses. Though she can be quite intimidating to look at, with her broad shoulders, meaty arms and ruddy face, I think she's quite a gentle soul.

She smiles. 'It's lovely out there today. You ready to come out for your walk?' Her voice is soft and kind, her smile genuine and sweet. In another life I might have thought she was patronising in the way she talks to me like I'm a child. But in this life, here and now, her warm tone calms me. 'Are you okay?' She frowns. 'Have you been crying?'

'I'm fine.' I try to keep my voice as neutral as possible, although that's not too difficult – the medication they've given me has taken the sharp edge off my emotions. Even though I can still feel them, they've become cushioned and soft.

'All right,' Jenny says brightly. 'Come on then.' We walk out of my room together and along the pale-blue corridor that leads out to the garden. I do get bored of being inside for so many hours at a time, but it doesn't stop me feeling light-headed when I leave the building. Being outside reminds me of a life beyond these walls. It's a life that I yearn for. It's also a life that terrifies me.

'You're quiet today, Catriona.'

I nod, unable to make small talk. 'Lots on my mind.' The air is fragrant with the scent of sunshine and cut grass. I inhale and enjoy a brief two-second beat of pleasure.

'Want to talk about it?' Jenny asks.

'Maybe.'

'I know it's hard to bring up the past,' Jenny says, 'but it's better to get it all out in the open than have it swimming around in your head all day. Shall we walk down by the tennis courts?'

'Okay.'

It sounds posh – a hospital with tennis courts, but the truth is, they're a couple of tatty concrete courts with ripped nets and faded white lines. The hospital building used to be a hotel, so there are remnants of it, like the swimming pool and the balconies – which they've had to box in for obvious reasons. We walk side by side, slowly, as though I'm an invalid.

'I've been thinking about the Morrises and about Holly,' I begin.

'Oh yes?'

I can detect some apprehension in Jenny's voice. She's waiting to see if I know who Holly is. Whether I think she's my daughter or whether I remember the truth. Although the fact I answered to 'Catriona' must have given her a heads up that I'm not 'Rachel' today.

'Holly Faisal,' I clarify. 'The child I took from the shopping mall.'

She nods and smiles, realising that this is probably going to be a good session. A session where I understand who I am and what I've done. 'You've been thinking about her?'

'Yes.' I exhale. 'I actually can't get her out of my mind. I can't stop thinking about the day of Grace's accident. After... after it happened, I visited that shopping centre and I took that little girl home with me. Someone else's child. I took her!' Some days – like today – it astounds me that I could have done such a thing.

'I watched the news afterwards and I found out who she was. They said her name was Holly Faisal, and I saw her parents – Rachel and Andrew Faisal. They put out an appeal on TV. The mother, Rachel, she was crying. It was *terrible*. But I didn't do anything about it. I didn't call the police and own up to what I'd done. On some level I knew who she was, and I knew that what I'd done was wrong, but I ignored it. I kept on going with my fantasy that Holly was Grace. How could I have done that? How *could* I?' I clasp my hands in front of me to stop the trembling that's started up.

Jenny doesn't reply. We keep on walking, past the buddleia bushes, which have blossomed pink and purple since I last came down this way. Like shooting fireworks.

'Darren was so upset when he got home that night and realised what I'd done. He was devastated. He tried to get me to see sense, but I just wouldn't listen to him... It's my fault he's dead. I as good as killed him.' My voice is wavering now too. Perhaps I should have stayed in my room. Coming out here and talking about it all feels almost as bad as keeping it in my head. Makes it feel more real.

'You were in shock.' Jenny pats my arm. 'Your daughter had just died. Neither you nor Darren were thinking straight.'

'I still can't understand why I did it! Why I took Holly. It was like I was on autopilot. Like I had no control over myself. I know that sounds like a pathetic excuse... And then after Darren's accident, I completely lost it.' As hot tears start to fall down my cheeks, I stop walking for a moment, transported back to that nightmarish evening. Darren's death pushed me over the edge of reason. That's when I began to descend past the point of sanity into a perfectly created delusion.

Online, I became obsessed with Holly's family – empathising with their plight and feeling distraught on their behalf. I was distancing myself from any blame. Absolving myself of any responsibility. I was beginning to believe that *their* pain was *my* pain. And somewhere along the way, I somehow managed to start thinking of myself as Rachel. I imagined that it was I who had been abandoned by my husband Andrew and left alone with our baby daughter Jessica, who in reality was the stolen child Holly.

Jenny passes me a tissue and I use it to dab my tears and blow my nose. We continue walking, our soft-soled shoes barely making a sound on the concrete path.

'Do you feel at all like Rachel today?' Jenny asks. 'Because you sound like you have the real situation quite clear in your mind. You sound like you know who you are.'

'I do feel clearer today. I know I'm not Rachel. I miss her, but I know I'm *not* her. If that even makes sense.'

'Why do you think you feel so clear about your identity today? Is there something you can pinpoint? A reason why?'

One of the groundsmen emerges from a large wooden shed with a selection of tools. 'Hey, Jenny.'

'Hello, Fred,' she replies. I notice her cheeks are a little flushed.

After we pass him, I give her a nudge. 'Are you and he…?'

'What? *No.*'

'But you'd like to?'

Her face and neck flood with colour.

'You would! You should ask him out.'

'Don't be daft. Anyway, we're not here to talk about me.'

'No, but it's nice for a few minutes to think about something else other than my wreck of a life.' My voice catches and I bite my lip.

'Look, Catriona. You can heal from this. I've seen people go on to lead productive lives after extreme trauma, but you have to let us in to allow us to help you. You're doing really well today. Just keep it up.'

Her words comfort me, but they also make me realise that a 'productive life' is probably code for making the best of things. The reality is that my life has gone to shit. 'It's nice of you to say that, Jenny, but I committed a terrible crime. I'll be in here for years. I'm not sure how "productive" my life can be in prison, or in hospital. Not that I deserve anything else.'

'It's early days, Catriona. Just take it one day at a time. You're already able to remember your real identity. That's a huge step.'

'Even if it's not all the time.'

'Like I said, it's early days. You had a trauma and you invented a situation that would help you to deal with that trauma.'

'I know. It was weird. In my head, Holly Faisal somehow became mixed up with the memory of my daughter Grace. Thinking that she'd been abducted was easier to handle than the truth that she'd drowned. Because that way, it felt like it wasn't my fault, and there was always the chance that one day' – my throat constricts and it takes me a moment to continue – 'that one day she'd come back.' Talking about Grace like this makes my heart hurt. The pain in my chest is crushing, and I have to stop walking again. Take another moment to catch my breath.

'There's a bench up ahead,' Jenny says. 'Do you want to sit?'

I nod and we veer across the short, springy grass to sit on the bench, which faces a neat flower bed. I feel like an elderly person, resting here like this.

'Do you have any other thoughts about why you used Rachel's name, and why you used the name Jess for her daughter Holly?' Jenny asks.

'I'm not sure.' I twist my fingers in my lap. 'I don't think it was a conscious thing. I found stuff online about Holly's family and discovered that Rachel's husband Andrew moved to Spain to be with another woman. He left her alone with her youngest daughter, Jessica. I guess, in a weird way, I empathised with her because I was also alone with a young daughter.

'Before I left London and moved to Wareham, it felt like a logical step to change our names for a fresh start. I can't remember making the decision for me to become Rachel, and for Grace, sorry *Holly*, to become Jessica. On some level I must have realised their surname was too distinctive, that it might have been recognised. So I altered it slightly from Faisal to Farnborough. From the moment we moved into our new flat, we became Rachel and Jess Farnborough. Just a single mum and her daughter making a new start alone. It felt natural.

'Once I made the change, it was easier to slip into the role I'd cast for myself than to dwell on my real past. It felt less stressful somehow. As Rachel, I was the victim rather than the perpetrator, which was easier to live with. People tend to feel sorry for the victims.'

'You didn't tell anyone about being a victim until you confided in Matt last year,' Jenny observes.

'I know. I couldn't bring myself to speak about it. I only met Matt a couple of weeks after moving to Wareham, and I didn't want to talk about my past – not the real version or the imagined version. So I skirted over it all.' My fingertips trace over the rough grain of the bench. It could do with sanding down.

'How are things with Matt now?'

An image of Matt inserts itself into my brain and I want to sob for the loss of him. For how much I've hurt him. 'He won't bring Jess or Charlie to see me. He won't tell me what's happened to her. I don't even know if she's been told her true identity, or whether she's been reunited with her birth parents. I feel so bad for him – having to deal with all that by himself.'

'He'll have help – social services and the like.'

'But still. It must be hellish. Jess is *his* daughter too. Maybe not biologically, but where it matters...' I'm crying again. How can one person cry so many tears? I lost my Grace, and now I've lost Jess and Charlie too. Three of my babies that I'll never be able to care for again. Okay, I know Jess was never truly mine, but she still *feels* like mine. I cuddled her, kissed her, bathed her, laughed with her. I *know* her. And whatever happens from now on, I believe I was a good mother to her. We had a beautiful relationship.

In my more lucid moments, like today, I feel such deep shame for how I must have messed up Jess's life. I wonder how she'll ever manage to recover from the truth. She doesn't know Rachel and Andrew Faisal. She has no idea who they are, what they're like. They're her parents and yet they're strangers to her. And how will Matt explain everything to my little Charlie? Will my children ever want to see me again? I wouldn't blame them if they didn't. Then I realise I'm *still* thinking of Jess as mine. But she isn't. She's Holly Faisal. And I am not her mother.

My tissue is thin and soggy now; I do my best to mop up my tears again. 'I don't blame him, you know.'

'Matt?'

'Yes. I don't blame him. He did the right thing, telling the police about me. He's a good man. The best.' I picture his distraught expression when the police came to the house and arrested me. He was crying so hard. I'd never seen him lose it like that before. Other than when Charlie was born, but that was just a few emotional, happy tears. This time it was different. These were tears for a broken heart. A broken life.

I didn't understand what was going on. I thought the police were arresting me for breaking into the Morrises' flat, or perhaps for following Bella home. I still believed the Morrises had stolen my daughter. I thought the police had got it all wrong. But it wasn't that at all.

Matt discovered the truth about me when Robin contacted him after our last session. Robin was worried about client confidentiality, but he feared for Bella's safety. And because Matt was his friend, he thought he should make him aware of the possible danger that I might pose to Bella. Robin didn't believe I was mentally stable. It turns out he was right.

Then the Morrises' old neighbour Melanie rang Kate after I'd knocked on her door asking questions. Kate had grown fearful that I was going to expose the fact that Bella was adopted, and that Shaun had been in prison, so she called Matt to ask what was going on. To ask him to make me stop digging into their lives. After he explained my (fake) history to them – that I'd had a child who was abducted – the Morrises were more understanding. But my recent behaviour had set off further alarm bells in Matt's head.

He was really shaken up by it all. After Kate and Shaun left, Matt began searching online for stories relating to a missing child named Holly Farnborough. He wanted to verify my story. All he found was a story almost identical to the one I'd told him, apart from a few vital differences – the year didn't match, and the surname didn't match, but more crucially, the photograph and footage of Rachel was not of me. And the child who went missing did not have green eyes. She did, however, bear an uncanny resemblance to Jess.

Matt put the pieces together and was horrified to realise there was a possibility that Jess was indeed the abducted child. Of course, he was still hoping it wasn't true. He said he was praying for the evidence to be circumstantial. But he knew he had no choice but to tell the police what he thought he might have discovered. Once they confirmed that it was all indeed true, Matt was devastated. He told me he had loved me but couldn't forgive what I'd done. He said he loved Jess like she was his own, but in the end, he knew that Jess's real parents deserved to know what had happened to their daughter. They deserved to be reunited. To have some happiness back in their lives.

Although it cuts me up to lose Jess, who I truly believed was my daughter, I do agree with Matt. If Rachel Faisal can experience the joy of holding her child in her arms, then I should be happy for her. After all, I've been living my life as Rachel for the past seven years, going through her anguish. Living with the devastation of a missing child. So who knows more about how she must feel than *me*?

I lurch to my feet with an overwhelming desire to be back inside my small room.

'You ready to go back in?' Jenny asks with a concerned smile.

I nod and start walking, faster this time, suddenly yearning to lie on my bed and count my ceiling tiles again. When I've finished counting them, I'll probably have to count them once more, just to make sure the number's right.

There's another reason why I'm so desperate to get back to my room. Because something else has started up in my mind. A new thought. The germ of a possibility…

Maybe one day in the future – when I've served my time and the doctors believe I'm well enough to rejoin society – I'll eventually get out of here. And when I do, perhaps I'll get one last shot at happiness. All I'll have to do is to persuade Matt that Charlie needs his mum. That my son is better *with* me than without me.

It won't be easy to win Matt around – not after everything that's happened – but at least I'll have time to work on him. To make him see that I *know* what I did was wrong. That I've been ill but I'm getting better. The loss of Jess is brutal, and not something we could ever completely get over. But a new start for the three of us could be the best thing for our ultimate happiness. The perfect way to heal. Because I know that deep down Matt still loves me. So it would make perfect sense for us to be a family once more.

That's all I've ever wanted. And after everything I've been through, I'm determined to get my happily ever after. Whatever it takes…

EPILOGUE

Dear Diary,

My name is Rachel Danes. I was once Rachel Faisal, but I've been divorced for six years so I reverted to my maiden name. The woman from social services – Kerry – told me that writing a diary might help me to make sense of what's happened. I don't know if that's true or not, but at this point in time, I'm willing to try.

My life this past seven years has gone from being a nightmare to being non-existent. An echo of a life. Like no one can hear me properly and I can't connect with reality. I get up in the morning to take my daughter Jess to school, I go to work as an admin assistant at the big insurance firm down the road. I come home, make dinner, try to keep the place tidy, but my heart isn't in it. My heart isn't in anything.

If it weren't for Jess, I would be dead. Sounds brutal, but it's the truth.

And then, last week, a miracle happened. It didn't start off as a miracle – I had a visit from the police and from social services. Just the sight of them in their uniforms and suits with their air of officialness brought it all rushing back. The horror of losing my baby. The pointed fingers. The blame. The collapse of my marriage. Here they were again. To cause more chaos and upset.

And then I thought maybe they'd come to tell me they'd found Holly's body. That I would finally be able to lay her to rest and have some closure. A kind of peace, if you like. But that wasn't it at all.

It was something else. Something I never believed could ever happen. They asked if they could come in, and of course I had to say yes. So they came in and sat on the sofa in my sad little flat and I sat opposite them on one of the dining-room chairs. And they told me the thing they'd come to tell me:

Holly is alive.

They had to repeat themselves several times because I couldn't accept what they were saying. I thought I was in bed, asleep. Dreaming. Because what they were saying was the thing that I never thought I would ever hear. I'd fantasised about it, of course I had. But that was all in my mind; not in real life.

<u>Holly is alive!</u>

Even writing the words fills me with joy and gives me proper goosebumps. Not only is she alive. But she's happy and healthy and has never been harmed physically or emotionally – so they say. She's a well-adjusted ten-year-old girl who goes to school and has friends and a family. <u>A family</u>.

Only they're not her family, are they…

Kerry, the woman from social services, told me that I'd fainted after they told me she was alive, but one of the officers rushed over and caught me before I slid off the chair and hit the floor. When I came around, we were still in my lounge and they'd sat me on the sofa and made me a cup of sweet tea. I said I didn't want tea, I wanted to see my daughter. I stood up, but I was all woozy, so I had to sit back down again.

All those years of imagining the worst. Each day going to hell and back. Wanting to end it all. But somehow keeping a tiny spark of hope burning. Hope that mocked and denied me every day. Until now.

But even now, after the best news imaginable, Kerry told me that the situation is not straightforward. That Holly doesn't know who she really is. She thinks her name is Jess! How weird is that? They named her Jess – same as my youngest.

Holly believes her parents are this other couple called Matthew and Rachel. Rachel, same as me! Only Kerry explained that the woman who took her was mentally disturbed and Rachel is not her real name. Kerry reassured me that Jess hadn't been harmed and wasn't in any danger, only that this woman 'Rachel' thought she was me! I don't quite get it, to be honest. All I know is that I want to see my daughter. I <u>have</u> to see her.

Surprise, surprise, bloody Andy doesn't want to know. He went quiet on the phone when I told him his eldest daughter was alive. I know he was choked up. I could tell by his silence. But then he cleared his throat and said that it was probably best if he didn't get involved. That his family needed him in Spain. 'Probably best!' What an absolute bastard. Well, at least I know where he stands. Which is abso-bloody-lutely nowhere, as usual.

Anyway, enough about my loser ex-husband. I kicked up a huge fuss after the authorities said I couldn't see Holly straight away. I mean, who do they think they are? They can't just tell me she's alive and then say, 'Oh and by the way, you can't see her.' She's my daughter!

After I had a chance for it all to sink in, I got on the phone to social services and went down to their offices, and then to the police station. I threatened to sue and to go to the papers. I haven't felt so alive in years. It's like someone's lit a fire under me. I feel like I could do anything.

Finally, after an emergency court hearing yesterday, the authorities have agreed that I <u>can</u> see her. I can actually see my daughter! The only thing is, I can't tell her who I am. Not yet. I have to pretend I'm a relation – an aunt. I'm not sure how I'll be able to stop myself from crying all over her. From hugging my baby and kissing her and swinging her around in my arms.

How will I manage to keep myself together? I can barely do it now. I'm crying all over my diary. Smudging the ink.

But after having another long chat with Kerry, I do understand that this is what's best for Holly, not what's best for me. I have to hide my anger about what happened. I have to be calm and laid-back about it all. And I have to call her Jess, because apparently that's her name now. She's been through a rough time, thinking her fake mum has had a breakdown. Kerry told me the woman – her fake mum, the woman who stole her from me – has been arrested and sectioned. Good job, because if she wasn't locked up I'd probably have killed her.

My poor Holly. It tears me up inside thinking what she must be going through. They haven't explained to her yet that this woman isn't her real mother. They have to take things slowly. Which is why I have to start off being her aunt.

But whatever she calls me – aunt, friend, mum – I'm here for her now. I may not be able to tell her who I am straight away. I may have to be patient. It could take weeks, or months, maybe even years to reconnect with her properly. But it doesn't matter. Because my baby is alive.

She's alive.

And now… so am I.

A LETTER FROM SHALINI

Thank you for reading *The Other Daughter*. This was one of those rare books whose plot arrived into my head fully formed. I do hope you enjoyed reading it as much as I enjoyed writing it. If you did enjoy it, and want to keep up to date with all my latest releases, just sign up at the following link. Your email address will never be shared and you can unsubscribe at any time.

www.bookouture.com/shalini-boland

I love getting feedback on my books, so if you have a few moments, I'd be really grateful if you'd be kind enough to post a review online or tell your friends about it. A good review absolutely makes my day!

When I'm not writing or spending time with my family, I adore chatting to readers, so please feel free to get in touch via my Facebook page, through Twitter, Goodreads or my website.

Thanks so much,
Shalini Boland x

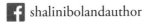 shalinibolandauthor

@shaliniboland

 4727364.shalini_boland

shaliniboland.co.uk

ACKNOWLEDGEMENTS

Thank you to my incredible publisher, Natasha Harding. I thank my lucky stars every day that I have such a wonderful editor to work with. You absolutely 'get' my stories and always know just the right changes and enhancements to suggest! I love our brainstorming chats and meetings. I really do believe you've changed my life!

Thanks also to everyone at Bookouture, especially Oliver Rhodes, Peta Nightingale, Kim Nash, Noelle Holten, Alexandra Holmes, Hannah Bond, Natalie Butlin, Alex Crow and Jules Macadam. I don't think a more wonderful team exists.

Thanks to my copyeditor Fraser Crichton for your fab suggestions, and also for some of those dry comments, many of which make me laugh out loud.

Thanks to my fabulous proofreader Lauren Finger who always does such an incredible job, and is the 'continuity queen'.

Thank you once again to Sammy H.K. Smith for advising on the police-procedural aspects of my book. As always, any mistakes and embellishments in procedure are my own.

I feel very lucky to have such loyal and thorough beta readers. Thank you Terry Harden, Julie Carey, Deanna Finn and Amara Gillo. I always value your feedback and opinions.

Thanks to all my lovely readers who take the time to read, review or recommend my books. It means more than you can know.

Huge love to my daughter Billie Boland who inspires me every day.

Finally, I want to thank Pete Boland who is the most supportive husband ever.

Made in the USA
San Bernardino, CA
20 April 2020